MURDER
AT
OCHRE COURT

Books by Alyssa Maxwell

Gilded Newport Mysteries
MURDER AT THE BREAKERS
MURDER AT MARBLE HOUSE
MURDER AT BEECHWOOD
MURDER AT ROUGH POINT
MURDER AT CHATEAU SUR MER
MURDER AT OCHRE COURT

Lady and Lady's Maid Mysteries
MURDER MOST MALICIOUS
A PINCH OF POISON
A DEVIOUS DEATH

Published by Kensington Publishing Corporation

MURDER
AT
OCHRE COURT

ALYSSA MAXWELL

KENSINGTON BOOKS
www.kensingtonbooks.com

KENSINGTON BOOKS are published by

Kensington Publishing Corp.
119 West 40th Street
New York, NY 10018

All Kensington titles, imprints, and distributed lines are available at special quantity discounts for bulk purchases for sales promotion, premiums, fund-raising, educational, or institutional use. Special book excerpts or customized printings can also be created to fit specific needs. For details, write or phone the office of the Kensington Special Sales Manager: Attn. Special Sales Department. Kensington Publishing Corp., 119 West 40th Street, New York, NY 10018. Phone: 1-800-221-2647.

Library of Congress Card Catalogue Number: 2018932843

ISBN-13: 978-1-4967-0336-1
ISBN-10: 1-4967-0336-7
First Kensington Hardcover Edition: August 2018

eISBN-13: 978-1-4967-0337-8
eISBN-10: 1-4967-0337-5
First Kensington Electronic Edition: August 2018

10 9 8 7 6 5 4 3 2 1

Printed in the United States of America

To Dad. You and Mom instilled in me a love and appreciation of beautiful, old things, along with their history. And for that I'm grateful.

Acknowledgments

Many thanks to Jeannie Mathews for a wonderful tour of Ochre Court and for graciously providing me with fascinating details about the house. Any errors are mine and not hers.

Much appreciation goes to Tyler Hughes who maintains The Gilded Age Era and Doses of History blogs. These have provided some invaluable information on the Newport cottages, especially period pictures and floor plans. https://dosesofhistory.blogspot.com/

MURDER
AT
OCHRE COURT

Chapter 1

Newport, Rhode Island
July 1898

"Take my advice, Miss Cross, and marry a rich man. Then you may do whatever you like."

The train from New York City to North Kingstown, Rhode Island, jostled me from side to side on the velvet seat while trees and shrubs and the occasional house streaked past the window to my right. The car was about half-full, and soft murmurs and light snores provided accompaniment to the rumble of the tracks. I had faced forward as I usually do, not at all liking the sensation of being propelled backward through space at unnatural speeds. The woman in the seat opposite me, however, seemed to have no such qualms. She sat upright—not rigidly, but proudly, one might say, the kind of bearing that spoke of an unwillingness to bend to the persuasion of others.

"But," I said and paused, still baffled by her last bit of counsel, "you achieved so much *before* you were married, ma'am."

"True enough. But I was lucky, and I was willing to do whatever it took. Are you so willing, Miss Cross?"

Why, yes, I believed I was, but before answering, I studied her, taking in the square chin, the blunt though not unpleasing features which, like her posture, projected an air of uncompromising confidence. I sighed. I'd spent the past year in Manhattan reporting for the New York *Herald* and pursuing my fondest dream—only to find myself enveloped by the same frustrations that had thwarted my career in my hometown of Newport. What was I doing wrong?

Elizabeth Cochrane Seaman, better known to the world as journalist Nellie Bly, smiled slightly at my hesitation. "There is only one sure path to personal freedom, Miss Cross. Money. And for a woman who has none, there is only one sure way of obtaining any. Marriage."

"But—"

"Ah, you're going to argue that marrying for money is wrong, that such a woman is destined for unhappiness and will find herself subject to her husband's whims."

I nodded.

Her smile grew. "I didn't say to marry just any man. Do you imagine I'd be willing to exist in anyone's shadow, husband or otherwise?"

A face with patrician features and dark eyes formed in my mind's eye, but I dismissed it, or at least the notion of marrying a certain man for his money. That opportunity had come and gone and I had never regretted, for a moment, standing on my convictions. No, that wasn't quite true. I would never marry for money, but there were times I wondered what my life would be now had I given in to temptation. . . .

A jolt brought me back to the present. "Your living in someone's shadow is hard to fathom, Mrs. Seaman, with everything

I've read about you. But your husband is—" I broke off, appalled at the impertinence of what I'd been about to utter.

"Forty years older than me, yes, that is correct." Unfazed, she darted a glance out the window, blinking against the rapid flicker of sun and shadow against the moving foliage. "Still, we are compatible. I am quite fond of my husband, Miss Cross, and we are happy together. I have compromised nothing, yet I have achieved my goals and am living the life I desire. That is precisely because I have always known what it is I want, and I have never veered from the course that would take me exactly where I wished to be."

The train jerked as it switched tracks, tipping us a bit to one side. I caught myself with the flat of my palm against the seat. Mrs. Seaman merely swayed as a willow in a breeze, then steeled her spine. The train slowed as the trees yielded to the wooden platform and green-painted depot darkened by soot. The sign read NORTH KINGSTOWN. I unsteadily got to my feet and reached to retrieve my valise from the overhead rack. Even though I stood on tiptoe, the bag, having slid from its original placement, eluded my grasp. A gentleman from across the aisle intervened, easily sliding out the thickly brocaded piece and swinging it down into my arms.

I thanked him before turning back to the individual I'd idolized for more than a decade, who now left me confused and not a little uncertain whether my admiration had been warranted or not. Everything I'd believed about this remarkable woman, this brilliant journalist, tumbled about my mind in chaos. Was she no different from my Vanderbilt aunts and all the other society matrons whose lives seemed to me as empty and artificial as paper flowers?

She winked at me. "You see, Miss Cross, men are not the enemy. Find one you can trust, one who makes you laugh, and most importantly, one with enough money to make your dearest desires come true."

*   *   *

Nellie Bly's parting words echoed in my ears long after we parted. Once again, a dark-haired, dark-eyed promise rose up inside me, and a whispered echo breathed across my heart. *Marry me, Emma.* But I couldn't have, at least not then. Which was not to say I would never be married, or never marry Derrick Andrews, who had once proposed to me in a rash passion formed of danger and a narrow escape with our lives. Under those circumstances, it would have been wrong of me to accept his suit, wrong to mistake an ardor of the moment for something more permanent.

Then, too, there was Jesse Whyte, a man I had known all my life, a good, honest soul whose lifestyle fit well with my own, and who had also made his intentions clear. It seemed the only intentions that remained *un*clear were my own. What did I want? My independence, my career . . . Beyond that, I didn't quite know.

For now, I had other matters to think about, an assignment to complete, and a different sort of decision to make.

It took two coaches and two ferries to bring me to my destination, and by the second ferry ride, which conveyed me across Narragansett Bay from Jamestown to Newport, those other matters occupied the better part of my attention.

Silas Griggson needed to duck when passing through the doorway into the interior of the ferry. Thin and wiry, he nonetheless occupied his tailored suit as though every inch of it had been designed to fit him perfectly, which it had. He certainly didn't buy his clothing off department store racks, but visited New York City's finest tailors. A real estate developer and self-made man, Griggson certainly fit one part of Nellie's description of the man I should marry. But trust? Laughter? What I had learned in past weeks and what I suspected about Silas Griggson turned my blood to ice, albeit not enough to persuade me to maintain a safe distance from him.

No, I'd had my eye, figuratively if not literally, on Mr. Griggson for some weeks now, and what I had learned alternately piqued my curiosity and made me queasy. As the ferry rocked its way across the tossing harbor, my mind's eye conjured rubble and dust, arms and legs askew, sightless eyes, and blood. . . . A building erected by Silas Griggson's construction company had collapsed, yet the inquiries had held him blameless.

He spoke to no one but his accompanying manservant during our passage across the bay, but then, I hadn't expected him to be sociable. No, if business concerns had brought him to Newport, he'd wait until the appropriate society functions to approach any potential collaborators about his plans. I inwardly fumed about what those plans might entail. I knew only that Silas Griggson had never visited Newport before, and I longed to see him make an about-face without having set foot on my island.

Again, as in the past, I wondered where he initially came from. My exploration of his past had revealed suspiciously little—a modest upbringing, a typical boy's schooling with no mention of university, working his way up through the building trade, and investments that had increased his fortunes. Where had the funds for those investments originated? There the waters clouded. The trail ended. A working man one day, a construction mogul the next. . .

Did he notice me taking his measure from across the crowded way? Did he see me as I scrutinized his clothing, his bearing, mentally taking notes on every particular from his slicked-back hair to the glossy tips of his shoes? I doubt it. After only a year in New York City, I wasn't well-known enough there to have become conspicuous, not like I was in

Newport where everyone knew me. That suited me fine. When Silas Griggson finally made my acquaintance, the fact that this green young chit from the local Newport populace had exposed his secrets would shake him to his very core.

Or so I hoped.

When the ferry arrived at Long Wharf in town, a hand clasped my elbow as I stepped down onto the gangway. The touch startled me and I nearly lost my footing. The fingers tightened, and a male voice spoke brightly in my ear.

"Steady there, Miss Cross. It *is* Miss Cross, isn't it?"

I craned my neck to look up at, not Silas Griggson as I'd initially feared, but a much more youthful countenance. The features were only vaguely familiar, and I searched my memory for a name.

"It's Sam Caldwell, Miss Cross. Don't you remember me? We met at the Vanderbilt dinner party back in November. The Neily and Grace Vanderbilts, that is." He fell into step beside me and tipped his military pattern cap, the sun glinting on the gold eagle emblem. Behind him traipsed his servant, a callow youth who struggled beneath the weight of two rather heavy-looking portmanteaus. "May my man relieve you of that bag, Miss Cross?"

"No, thank you." I tightened my hold on my valise and nodded to the livery-clad footman. Then I took in Sam Caldwell's uniform with its gold braid and officer's insignia. "Captain Caldwell, yes, of course. Forgive me for not remembering right away."

"It was several months ago, and a lot has happened in the interim." The captain hunched lower as he spoke to enable me to hear him over the commotion of people exiting the ferry. Broad shouldered and trim waisted in his army uniform, the captain struck an impressive figure with his high cheekbones and the slightest of dimples in his chin. We stepped onto the dock together, whereupon he released my elbow and offered his arm to guide me to the end of the quay. His servant trailed close behind us, his gait faltering beneath his burden. "I've been away fighting in the war, Miss Cross."

"Yes, I believe Neily mentioned that. I am most relieved to see you have suffered no serious injuries, sir. The war goes well for our side, I understand." I had heard the latest off the telegraph wires in the *Herald*'s newsroom before I left New York. When the war with Spain began, I'd indulged in the briefest fantasy that James Bennett, the *Herald*'s owner, might send me to Cuba or perhaps even the faraway Philippines along with the other reporters to cover the fighting, or, at least, to observe the effects of the war on the local people. I very nearly laughed out loud, there beside Captain Caldwell, at such a naïve hope on my part.

"It should all be over shortly, Miss Cross, with the Spaniards sailing home with their tails between their legs. Their forces are depleted and suffering from yellow fever."

Despite the oddity of his mixed metaphor, I emitted a sound of both approval and admiration. "I'm sure it will be a great relief to your family, to all the soldiers' families."

"Indeed. Tell me, are you here to report on Miss Cooper-Smith's coming-out?"

I couldn't help smiling at his eager tone. True enough, the *Herald* had sent me north to cover what promised to be the social event of the summer Season. And while Mr. Bennett hoped for an article rife with as many scandals as fashion details, I had pounced on the opportunity for other reasons entirely. Miss Cooper-Smith's father, an architect, often collaborated with Silas Griggson on building projects. Was he culpable in Mr. Griggson's chicanery? I intended to find out.

Evasively, I replied, "That, among other things. Are you among Miss Cooper-Smith's hopeful suitors?"

He blushed at my blunt attempt to play the gossip columnist, but shook his head. "Not I, Miss Cross. But I am invited to the festivities." We strolled a few paces in silence, and then he said, "It's awfully swell of Mrs. Goelet to hold this shindig at Ochre Court, what with Miss Cooper-Smith's own mother having passed on. Do you know what Mrs. Goelet has planned for the event?"

I stared up at his handsome face, thinking how much of a boy he appeared at that moment, not at all the fearless soldier capable of leading men into battle. Yet I couldn't decide if he was flirting with me, or insulting me, by using such slang as *shindig*. Surely he would not have done so with Miss Cooper-Smith, or any young woman of the Four Hundred with whom he had limited acquaintance.

I decided either way, he meant no harm. "I do not, Captain, but even if I did, you know I couldn't discuss the details. Though you'll be able to read a thorough description afterward in my column in the *Herald*." The sight of a carriage up ahead prompted me to slide my arm from his. "There is my brother, Captain. It was a pleasure to see you again, and thank you for walking with me." Once again, I nodded to the servant. It irked me, always, that such individuals were often treated as if they did not exist.

The captain tipped his hat. "I'll see you at Ochre Court, then, if not sooner, Miss Cross. Good day."

Thanks to Brady's new brougham and matching pair of Cleveland Bays, the ride home passed much more swiftly than if he'd come in my shabby gig pulled by my aging roan hack, Barney.

"You didn't have this the last time I saw you in New York. It's a lovely vehicle," I told him as he made the turn off Thames Street onto Wellington Avenue. He was taking the long way around Ocean Avenue to Gull Manor, and I was glad. It had been months since I'd glimpsed the glorious hills, cliffs, and wide open sea. "And those horses—they cost a pretty penny, I'm sure."

Brady, hatless, his sandy brown hair tousled, grinned back at me. "Afraid I'm getting myself into debt, Em?"

"Wouldn't be the first time."

"Yes, well, never fear. Your relatives pay me well at the New York Central."

"They're your relatives, too," I reminded him.

He shrugged. "Not really."

That was true. The Vanderbilts were my third cousins—or was it fourth—on my father's side. Brady and I shared a mother and our Newport heritage, but not my blood ties to the Vanderbilt family. "Well, they're treating you like one of their own. You've proved yourself to them, Brady, and I'm proud of you."

"You're just happy you don't have to come bail me out of the jailhouse anymore."

"Yes, that, too, certainly." I laughed, lifting my face to the warmth beaming down on us from a nearly cloudless sky. The moment might have appeared light to a casual observer, but the hope I had always harbored for my often incorrigible brother gathered into a tight orb wrapped in a prayer that his transformation to productive respectability would last. "How is Hannah?" I asked as offhandedly as I could.

I felt him staring at me, and grinning. I turned to gaze back. "Well? Have you seen her since you've been home?" Brady and I had both lived in New York the past year, though for the most part our lives and occupations had sent us in separate directions except when we met at Vanderbilt family functions. He had arrived in Newport a few weeks ahead of me for the summer Season, making the trip on our relative William Vanderbilt's steamer yacht. I supposed his carriage and horses had arrived on a cargo steamer.

"You think Hannah will keep me honest, don't you?"

The laughter left my voice. "I do, Brady. I think she's good for you."

Hannah Hanson and her brother had grown up with Brady and me on the Point, a harborside, colonial neighborhood that saw its origins in the seventeenth century. Hardly considered fashionable nowadays, the Point nonetheless forged strong bonds between those who lived there. Hailing from Newport's hardiest stock, we understood and respected one another in ways outsiders could not.

It had been one of the things I missed most in New York.

Brady gave the reins a light flick. Hammersmith Farm rolled into view, snuggled in acres of verdant lawn, its weathered shingles gleaming in the sunlight. His gaze lingered on the varied roofline of its many wings, presided over by a single, regal turret. "Hannah is no society girl."

"No. That's exactly what makes her so right for you."

"Does it? If you believed that, Em, you'd have married Derrick Andrews by now."

The comment stung, for all Brady hadn't meant it to. He was merely stating a fact. I hadn't married Derrick Andrews because doing so would change my life forever, substituting riches and luxury for the personal independence I presently enjoyed and valued above all else. "That's different. You're no Knickerbocker, and you never will be."

"Ouch. Touché."

"Brady, try to understand. I haven't married Derrick, not because I fear his world and my place in it, but because I cherish *my* world as it is, warts and all. It's *our* world, Brady. It's no insult when I say you'll never be part of New York's generations-old aristocracy, Mrs. Astor's Four Hundred. It's simply a fact, no matter how high your pile of money. They might appear to accept you now for Uncle Cornelius's sake, but you wouldn't be happy married to one of their daughters, even if you managed such a feat. They'd never let you forget you aren't one of them."

"Times are changing, Em. Slowly, but they are changing."

I pressed a hand to his coat sleeve. "Then let them change with Hannah."

Our debate ceased as we rounded the bend onto Ocean Avenue, not because of the sea-born wind that snatched the words from my lips and pounded in our ears, but because of the sheer exhilaration that filled me—oh, *always* filled me—at the strength and majesty of the Atlantic pulsing against our shores. It was like a heartbeat, pumping life into our island, and yes, sometimes death, but always the guiding force of our very existence.

"Oh, Brady, how I've missed this."

"It's only been since Easter. And before that Christmas, and before that—"

"Too long. And neither the East River, the Hudson, nor New York Harbor can take its place."

The carriage slowed slightly as Brady turned his attention to me. "You're not going back, are you?"

"I don't wish to discuss it now, but no, I don't think I'm going back to New York. Let me enjoy the view, and once we're home I'll explain everything."

As welcome a sight as the ocean had been, the tattered shingles, loose shutters, and hodgepodge roof tiles of Gull Manor raised a tender ache beneath my breastbone. My joy throbbed all the more fiercely when, from around the side of the house, a yapping brown and white spaniel came running, his mismatched ears streaming out behind him. The front door opened, and out stepped Mrs. Mary O'Neal, my house-

keeper and so very much more than that. Friend, grandmother, confidante. She had been my nanny when I was a
child, and Nanny she remained in my life and my heart.

My eyes brimmed and overflowed, blinding me so that
my foot missed the step down and I stumbled my way to the
ground, barely keeping myself from collapsing. I needn't
have bothered fighting gravity, for as my dear mutt, Patch,
reached me, he scrambled and leaped, knocking both of us
down into a heap of barking and laughter and the occasional
sob. Just as I dried my tears and finished hugging Nanny, my
outpouring began anew when a happily sniffling Katie, my
maid-of-all-work, declared in her singsong Irish brogue
how good it was to have me home.

Thus was my typical homecoming over the past year, and
I wouldn't have changed it for anything.

Katie brought tea into the parlor and then sat to join
Nanny and Brady in listening to my news of New York.
Young Katie Dylan had been with us these past three years
after being summarily dismissed from her position at The
Breakers, and only now did she feel comfortable enough
with my slack views on servant discipline—as my aunt Alice
would say—to occupy the same seating arrangement as the
rest of us.

"He lied," I said bluntly to Nanny's inquiry into the current state of my employment with the *Herald.* I thumped a
ragged spot on the cushion beside me for emphasis. "Again.
Mr. Bennett brought me to New York under the false pre-
tense of my covering real news stories, but that is never
going to happen. He hired me for my society connections,
and he wants me sniffing out sordid gossip. I've tried reason-
ing with him, but he only smiles and tells me I'm doing a
spiffing job. Nothing is ever going to change there. I can
only control where I live, and I'm choosing Newport."

Nanny's half-moon spectacles, sitting low on her nose, flashed in the light from the front windows. "What about the money?"

"What about it? Yes, it's more than I ever hoped to make working for the Newport *Observer*, but by the time I send funds to you for the running of Gull Manor and make my monthly donations to St. Nicholas Orphanage, I've barely enough left to pay for my own upkeep. New York is expensive."

"Even living with Alice and Cornelius?" Brady raised his eyebrows at me, and leaned to snatch another sandwich off the tray on the sofa table. "Those aren't shabby digs, after all."

"No, the Fifth Avenue house is lovely, but I have no desire to go on living there."

Brady shook his head sadly, as if at a hopeless case. "You are an odd one, Em."

"Don't pretend you don't know what I mean." I raised my voice an octave in my best imitation of Alice Vanderbilt. "Where am I going, with whom and when? And wouldn't I like to meet the Bransons' third oldest son? And, 'Oh, Emmaline, since you're not busy —I don't know how many times Aunt Alice has uttered that phrase when I was quite clearly working on an article for the next day's edition." I stopped to collect my breath and my thoughts, then went on more calmly. "I love them and I appreciate their generosity, but if I have to live another day under Aunt Alice's kindly thumb, I'll sew bricks into my petticoats and throw myself in the East River."

Brady wrinkled his nose. "With the way the ships toss their refuse overboard? Yuck. So what will you do here in Newport? Beg Mr. Millford for your old job back?"

"No, certainly not that." I frowned and compressed my lips. I kicked at the faded oval rug beneath the sofa table.

"Maybe. I don't know yet." Dubious expressions from the others bombarded me, but I pretended to ignore them. "I don't want to be writing society columns for the rest of my life, but I belong here. I know that now. Newport is home, and here is where I want to make my future. I'll figure something out."

"Of course you will, sweetie." Nanny patted my knee with a plump, wrinkled hand capable of bringing me more comfort than all the luxuries my Vanderbilt relatives could buy.

"Em . . ." An ominous note in Brady's tone made me wary. I waited for him to continue. "Newport will never do for your career what New York can do. Have you considered selling Gull Manor and moving permanently to the city? With Nanny and Katie, of course."

"No. Absolutely not." The very idea sent outrage coursing through my veins. "That is out of the question."

"We'd go with you to New York, if it came to that," Nanny said bravely, but I noted the tremor in her voice. Katie vigorously nodded, although trepidation peeked out from her summer blue eyes.

"Did no one hear what I just said? Aunt Sadie left me this house and a responsibility to go with it. If Gull Manor changed hands, would the new owners open the door when some abused and hungry young woman came knocking?"

Katie flinched, for she had been both when she came to me three years ago: with child and cast out onto the street, with nowhere to go and no one to help her. Except me, here at Gull Manor. I smiled at her and reached across the sofa table to squeeze her hand.

She smiled back. "I'm not the only one you've helped." She was right. Most recently had been a young lady named Flossie, who'd accepted my offer to help her leave a life of prostitution and start anew. She'd spent five months here, during which Nanny discovered her talent for baking. She now worked as a baker's assistant at a hotel in Providence. "'Tis sure Newport needs Gull Manor, Miss Emma."

"That's correct." I straightened and poured another cup of tea to shore up my resolution. "Newport is my home. If I'm to be a journalist, I'll do it here. I'll find a way, even if I have to buy a decades-old press, set up business here in our cellar, and deliver the papers myself."

Chapter 2

❧

As the name implied, Ochre Court occupied several acres on Ochre Point Avenue overlooking the Cliff Walk and the sea. Being only a few minutes' walk north of The Breakers, I left Barney and my carriage with my relatives' gatekeeper and walked up to the Goelets' home. I was to cover an afternoon ladies' tea in honor of Miss Cleo Cooper-Smith, whose coming-out ball would be later that night.

Wrought-iron gates stood open to a tree-lined drive that bisected the property perfectly in half and led, without a curve or wobble, to a circular drive in front of the entryway. The house, in the style of a French château of the Loire Valley, boasted deep, mansard rooflines and elaborate carvings crowning the dormer windows. A pleasing asymmetry of the house somehow presented an aspect of perfect balance that revealed the brilliance of the architect, Richard Morris Hunt.

The house stood regally against a gently clouded afternoon sky, its creamy stonework golden in the afternoon sun, its only shadows huddled beneath the porte cochere. An oppressive heat closed in around me, for I'd dressed, not in the latest daytime summer fashion, but in the female journalist's traditional garb of shirtwaist over a plain, dark skirt, with a matching jacket. My blue serge that once belonged to Aunt Sadie, but which had been updated numerous times by Nanny, served me well. Mrs. Goelet had made it clear I would attend today's functions in a professional capacity, pencil and notebook at the ready, and not as a guest. It didn't matter that her sister, Grace, and I enjoyed a close friendship or that we were all cousins by marriage. Mrs. Goelet considered me a mere step or so above a servant, and so while Ochre Court's open gates beckoned, it was to the side entrance that I traipsed.

I didn't much mind. In this, Mrs. Goelet behaved no differently than most other society matrons. After all, despite my relatives, I wasn't a member of the Four Hundred, that magical number of wealthy individuals who could comfortably fit inside Mrs. Astor's New York ballroom. Compounding my faults, I also earned my keep by describing their exploits in painstaking detail for the less fortunate to enjoy. While they welcomed the renown and the admiration of the masses, they viewed me as a necessary evil.

The housekeeper admitted me with an economy of words and warmth, and led me up the service staircase to the ground floor. She bade me to wait in a sitting area off the Great Hall, though she omitted to invite me to sit in any of the four wing chairs grouped there. I waited, standing, near the fireplace, carved of Caen stone, listening to the light, feminine voices echoing in the soaring openness of the Great Hall. From another direction came a hum, a creaking, and the mechanical workings of Ochre Court's elevator. The sound unnerved me. Even after a year in New York, I hadn't grown used to or fond of those claustrophobic boxes that conveyed humans up and down buildings with little more than a few cables between them and a fast plummet to the ground. Yes, I knew all about the safety brake invented by Elisha Otis, but knowing and trusting were two different things. My stomach dropped simply thinking about it.

The clacking of heels alerted me to the imminent arrival of Mrs. Goelet. She swept around the corner of the hall in black with deep violet trimmings, a sign of mourning her husband who passed away nearly a year ago. Her willingness to sponsor Miss Cooper-Smith in this way, before her official grieving period ended, attested to the sincere affection she must have for the young woman and her family.

Like the housekeeper, she, too, greeted me in a brisk manner. "There you are. Tea has started, but you aren't needed in there. Not now. I want you to view the drawing room in daylight and write down what you'll need to remember about the details." Her lips twitched in the faintest of smiles. "I intend to dazzle my guests tonight, Miss Cross, and I want you able to pick apart the minutiae in order to dazzle your readers."

"Thank you, ma'am. I appreciate that."

"I'm not doing it for you, girl," she said, not unpleasantly, but as a matter of course. One would never suspect the relation between this woman and her sister, Grace. On the surface, they could not have been more different. Some fifteen years separated them in age, and while Grace presently courted society's favor with her beauty, charm, and high spirits, Mary had settled squarely into middle age and all that that encompassed. Yet, when people referred to Mrs. Ogden Goelet in her youth, it was with a wistful admiration that evoked the poise and style of one of society's one-time legendary beauties.

She continued in a confidential tone. "I am launching Miss Cooper-Smith into society, and I wish to be certain there isn't a soul in this country who doesn't know her name after tonight."

"The *Herald* will make sure of that, ma'am."

"Indeed. Her mother was my dearest friend, and I promised her I'd do the best for her girls, and spare no expense." Emotion made her voice husky. I knew the story. Mrs. Cooper-Smith had succumbed to the Russian flu that took so many lives in Europe and this country, even here in Newport, early in the decade. Mrs. Goelet's eyes grew unfocused, and I guessed that for several moments she saw, not me, but the ashen face of her friend in her final moments of coherence.

Just as suddenly, her brusqueness returned. "Come with me."

I followed her, nearly trotting to keep up, across the Great Hall. I wondered about her last statement, that she would spare no expense. I understood her stepping in to perform a mother's role in launching a young woman into society, even opening her home for such a purpose, but must she pay for the event as well? Shouldn't that be Mr. Cooper-Smith's responsibility?

I knew better than to ask. There was no surer or faster way to find myself out on the sidewalk.

Those voices I'd heard continued emanating, I surmised, from the dining room. Our footsteps raised a clattering echo until we reached the rug beneath the seating arrangement in the center of the room, near the shallow, stone fireplace that had never seen a flame. I hadn't been in the house since the Goelets opened it several years ago and I had come on behalf of the *Observer*, but many of its features had ingrained themselves in my memory. Out of over fifty fireplaces in the house, only three worked, one of them being in the sitting area where I'd waited for Mrs. Goelet to greet me; the rest were ornamental only. In a house that saw use only in the summer months, why go through all the fuss of equipping fireplaces with flues? The chimneys visible along the roofline ventilated the coal furnaces far below us, which generated the house's electrical system.

I glanced up at the biblical mural far above our heads. Like The Breakers' Great Hall, this one rose three stories, surrounded by the open galleries of the second and third floors. Each story was distinct, with the first entirely lined in carved Caen stone, the second of rich, dark-stained teak, while the third-floor arches glimmered with gilding. Everywhere I looked, carved faces gazed back at me from their heights, like angels, or perhaps guardians to make sure I didn't deviate a step from where Mrs. Goelet wished me to go. I didn't dare defy them.

We stopped at the wide double doorway of a room facing the rear of the property and beyond, thick blue bands of sea and sky. A footman stood at attention beside the closed doors, and before she opened them, Mrs. Goelet turned to regard me. "I'm going to unlock the doors and let you in. No one else is to enter this room, and you are not to breathe a word of what you see to anyone before this evening's ball. Is that understood?"

My curiosity spiked, but I held my expression steady. "Yes, ma'am."

"When you are finished taking your notes, come out, close the door, and come find me in the dining room. Oh, and you are not to touch anything. Not a thing, Miss Cross."

"Understood, ma'am. Um . . . do you wish me to view the ballroom as well?"

"Mmm . . . A good idea, that. You can pass into the ballroom from the drawing room. Those doors are not locked. But you'll need to exit through the drawing room again."

After unlocking the doors, she left me to return to her guests. I glanced at the footman, who deigned to make eye contact. I turned the knob and stepped inside . . .

Into another time and place. The first thing I noticed was the springy crunch beneath my feet, and looked down to discover, to my bafflement, not the herringbone floor I remembered but a lawn of bright green clover. But no, that couldn't be right. I bent down and felt with my fingertips. This clover had been woven from silk.

No longer a drawing room, the furniture had been removed, and a garden planted in its stead. Potted trees, flowers by the hundreds, vines stretched across latticework surrounded me, and where walls and ceiling had once been, now were tapestries and silks in such an array of colors and patterns I felt vaguely dizzy. Heavy curtains festooned with garlands covered the rear-facing windows, extending into a canopy over a dais some six steps high. A throne occupied the center of the dais, surrounded by low stools, pillows, and small, cushioned chairs. Two pairs of columns covered in hieroglyphic designs held up the canopy in a setting for an elaborate, Egyptian-themed *tableau vivant*.

Good heavens, all this for a young woman's coming-out ball? Certainly Mrs. Goelet intended to launch her young ingenue in a manner that would not soon be forgotten.

I retrieved my pencil and notepad from my handbag and began to take notes. I wondered about the wisdom of climbing the dais, but Mrs. Goelet hadn't specifically told me not to. The steps appeared to be stone, though closer inspection revealed them to be cleverly painted wood. Up I went to inspect the throne, which turned out to be gilt over another metal, perhaps bronze, and covered in silken cushions. Though the side windows were uncovered, the curtains over the windows behind the dais darkened the room considerably. I longed to sample the surprise Mrs. Goelet had in store for her guests, but I didn't dare. Instead, I gingerly moved the draped sides of the canopy to reveal the wires artfully strung from the chandelier and electric sconces, cleverly concealed within the decorations, and connected to Edison bulbs hidden among the flowers and foliage.

Though once again I would be writing about a society

event, my pulse sped in anticipation. This was new; this was why the *Herald* had agreed to send me home, that I might report on something that had never been done before, not to this extent. Few homes were fully electrified; here in Newport, I knew of only one other—The Breakers. So far.

I spent a while longer poking around, examining the wiring, the lights, and the decorations. Mrs. Goelet wished to dazzle her guests, and they would not be disappointed.

I had just about finished in the room when a crash drew my attention to the ballroom next door. I'd assumed no one else was supposed to be in these rooms at this time. The adjoining doors were closed but not locked, and as I passed through, I heard the light whoosh of fabric brushing against fabric.

I stood very still in the Rococo ballroom and looked about me. Flowers and garlands festooned this room, too, but without the theatrics of the drawing room. Fresh roses, water, and porcelain shards littered the floor at the foot of a pedestal, set beside the tied-back curtain on the side of a doorway. Beyond the doorway was a sitting room, but from what I could see of it, it appeared empty. Was someone crouching in a corner? I moved to peer inside when I noticed the toes of a pair of embroidered satin house shoes peeking out from beneath the velvet curtain. I nearly chuckled aloud as I tiptoed over and swept the curtain aside. My quarry gasped and raised her hands to her lips.

"Caught you! Don't you know Mrs. Goelet has given strict orders that no one is to be in these rooms?"

As soon as the words left my lips, I wished to recall them. The young woman before me, about my age or perhaps a bit younger, cowered as if I might strike her. Petite in figure, she stood crookedly as if crippled by some malformation of the spine or legs, or perhaps both, with one shoulder higher than the other and an awkward angle to her hips. She stared back at me with large, almond-shaped brown eyes, generously lashed, above a pert nose framed by high cheekbones. She would have been exceedingly pretty, if not for the expression of fear and alarm that furrowed her brow and tightened her mouth.

Instantly remorseful, I reached out to gently touch her forearm. "I'm terribly sorry. I didn't mean to startle you. I heard the crash and thought someone was up to some mischief in here."

"I shouldn't really be here, I suppose." She whispered so low, I had to strain to hear her. "It's just that the ball is for my sister, and I wished to make certain everything was ready. That it was perfect for her. And then I heard Mrs. Goelet outside the door, so I ran and hid in here." She pointed down at the broken vase. "I only meant to come into the sitting room, but I stumbled . . . I . . ."

To spare her having to explain her faltering step, I hurriedly said, "It could happen to anyone." But then a pertinent detail occurred to me. "Wait a moment. How did you get in? Mrs. Goelet has a footman standing guard outside the drawing room."

A cunning little smile spread across her lips, which she raised a hand to shield. But in the moment I glimpsed it, I saw that she was indeed quite pretty. "I nicked an extra key and he agreed to look the other way."

"Did he now?" I couldn't help grinning. Yes, I'd find it hard to deny this waif anything, either.

"Cleo is my sister. Can you blame me for wanting to see firsthand that tonight will be a great triumph for her?"

"I suppose one can't blame you a bit. But perhaps we should start over. You must be Miss Ilsa Cooper-Smith." She nodded solemnly. "I am Emma Cross, and I'll be covering your sister's event for the New York *Herald*."

Her eyes became large again. "Your name is well known

to me, Miss Cross. What is it like, being a journalist, being a lady who works? Is it terribly hard?"

"No, it's wonderful." Or would be, if I were taken seriously. "Perhaps we should go. Mrs. Goelet will begin to wonder what's keeping me so long and come looking for me." I gazed down at the shattered porcelain and sad, sodden roses. "What's to be done about this?"

"Never mind. Let's be off. Someone else can worry about it." With that, she hurried as best she could with her halting, uneven gait, into the drawing room. I followed her and as we let ourselves back into the hall, she smiled up at the footman.

She preceded me across the Great Hall, following the voices of the women still enjoying their afternoon tea. I watched her go, noting, not her twisted torso, but her creamy silk tea gown with its bows and flounces and lace insets. Did she realize, I wondered, that the person held to blame for the shattered vase would more than likely be me?

Mrs. Goelet took me aside when I returned to Ochre Court that evening before the ball began. She made no mention of the broken vase. I could only assume it hadn't been a treasure, or perhaps Miss Ilsa had confessed to the accident to prevent a servant from being blamed.

"However things go tonight, Miss Cross, I want nothing short of a glorious write-up from you. You have the exclusive, and whatever you write in the *Herald* will be picked up by newspapers all across the country. Of course, things *will* go gloriously tonight. I simply wish to be sure you understand."

She spoke, of course, of the innovative use of electric lighting for the *tableau vivant*. "Yes, ma'am."

She looked past me as she mused aloud, "I promised her poor mother, God rest her, that I would see to Cleo's happiness, and much of that depends on tonight's success. I expect that child to be engaged before the month is out."

"Yes, ma'am." I hoped she wouldn't hold me responsible if her plans didn't come to pass. I also wondered if Mrs. Goelet had promised to see to Ilsa's happiness as well, but I kept that thought to myself. "Is there anything I should know ahead of time, ma'am?"

"Yes. Pay particular attention to Silas Griggson. He's highly eligible and he's interested. Should he have any hesitation, a mention in your article could give him the prod he needs. But I doubt he'll need any persuasion."

My stomach tightened at the name. "Silas Griggson will be here tonight?" I asked stupidly, as Mrs. Goelet had just stated as much.

"New money, to be sure, and rather coarse around the edges, but considering . . . well, he would be a good catch. Not that we'll rule out others at this point, but I've got my eye on Mr. Griggson for Cleo."

Even as I wondered what she had obviously omitted from her remarks, I clamped my teeth on the inside of my lower lip to prevent myself from voicing my objections. It was none of my business whom Cleo Cooper-Smith married. I thought of her sister. If Mrs. Goelet had intended shackling Ilsa to Silas Griggson, I might not have been able to hold my peace. But I'd been introduced to Cleo after my sojourn in the drawing and ball rooms earlier, and whereas Ilsa had captured my sympathies, Cleo, the younger of the two, inspired pure confidence that she could take care of herself.

"Now, you'll stand discreetly behind the receiving line, out of view of the arriving guests but where you can observe who is who."

"I'm sure I'm familiar with most of your guests, ma'am, but thank you, that will be helpful."

"Good." She surveyed my attire, her discerning gaze starting at my simple coif and slowly descending to my hems. Once again, I'd dressed simply, this time in a gray silk skirt and bodice with black satin trimming. "Good," she repeated. "You may wait in the office until it is time."

She left me to find my own way, which I did, passing numerous servants bustling back and forth between the butler's pantry and the dining room. I danced a bit of a jig to avoid collisions but reached the office at the front of the house without mishap. A giggle stopped me before I turned into the room. I turned and grinned at the sight of an auburn-haired beauty who beamed back at me.

"Darling Emma." Grace Wilson Vanderbilt, my cousin Neily's wife and Mary Goelet's youngest sibling, approached me with open arms. We embraced heartily, and then held each other at arm's length.

"You look wonderful, Grace," I said. "Motherhood certainly agrees with you." Grace had given birth to her and Neily's first child, a boy, back in April. "How is little Corneil? Is he here?"

"He's in Newport, yes, staying with Mama tonight. We'll certainly make time for you and he to become acquainted. Oh, he'll adore you, I simply know it."

"And I'll adore him. Nanny has knitted a lovely blanket for him."

"How darling of her. I'm sorry I wasn't here this afternoon to greet you, Emma. Has May been horrible?"

She referred to her sister by her family pet name. "No, she's been lovely."

"May, lovely? Now I know you're lying." Like her sister had done, Grace scanned my outfit, but without her sister's approval. "I see she has put you in your place. I'm terribly sorry."

"There is no need to be. I am here as a journalist for the *Herald.* There is no shame in that, and this is how I typically dress when I cover evening events in New York."

She looked unconvinced. "If you say so. But . . ." She

leaned closer to whisper. "Word has it you might not be returning to New York. Is that true?"

"Brady." I sighed. "He shouldn't have said anything yet. Honestly, Grace, I didn't know myself how intent I was on moving back home until the ferry ride over here yesterday. Before that, it had been a wistful yearning, but not a plan."

"I'd miss having you in New York most of the year," she said with a little pout.

"Grace, need I remind you that you and Neily spend most of the year in Europe?"

She shrugged that observation aside. "Come upstairs with me while I change for the ball. We can catch up."

"You sister wants me to wait in the office."

"Bother May. Come with me. I have questions for you."

My feet dragged, for I had a good idea what those questions might entail. I proved correct.

"Does that delicious Derrick Andrews know you're home yet?" she asked minutes later as her maid unhooked the back of her afternoon gown.

"Grace, surely you've already learned from Brady that I have not spoken to Derrick since I came home for Easter."

"But you'll see him soon, yes?"

I held up my hands. "I don't know. Perhaps he's busy. Perhaps he's in Providence." I knew the latter to be unlikely. Derrick and his father had had a falling-out, resulting in Derrick's being disinherited. I didn't believe it would last forever, but his father wished to make a point and assert his position as head of the family. Equally stubborn, Derrick had taken up permanent residence in Newport—in my former childhood home, no less—and purchased a floundering local newspaper with the notion of making it a success. So far, it didn't come close to rivaling his family's Providence *Sun*, but in only a year's time Derrick had managed to increase his subscription rate and double the *Messenger*'s number of pages.

"I believe I shall have to host a small dinner party very soon. Are you free on Tuesday night?" She went to sit at her dressing table to allow her maid to rearrange her hair.

I pursed my lips at her through the mirror. "Will Derrick Andrews be there?"

"Perhaps. I don't quite know yet. . . ."

Dearest, scheming Grace. I gave her a tentative yes and we left it at that.

An hour and a half later, she and I were back downstairs, she mingling with the guests, and I moving slowly through the Great Hall, ballroom, and the library, taking notes on those in attendance, what they wore, and, when I could detain them for a minute or two, where their recent travels had taken them. My role as a society reporter had taught me how much people enjoyed talking about themselves, even those who claimed to value their privacy. I spent several more minutes in the dining room. A buffet of French delicacies beckoned from the table, from *saucissons de Lyon* to *brochettes de foie de volaille* to *sole gratinéau vin blanc*, and so much more. It could never all be consumed, not even later, by the servants. So much waste. Yet my job was not to judge, but merely record.

On my way out of the dining room, I passed the great double fireplace rendered in pink marble, its twin hearths flanking a gilded head of the god Bacchus. A small line had formed, and one by one each guest rubbed the image's nose and made a silent wish. It was a tradition at all events here at Ochre Court.

Feeling rather foolish, I nonetheless waited patiently in line. When my turn came, I reached out, brushed the smooth, gilded nose, and made a quick wish that remaining in Newport would prove to be the right decision. Then I moved on, shaking my head ruefully at my folly.

Familiar faces filled the rooms. I greeted my Vanderbilt relatives, siblings Neily and Alfred and Gertrude, along with her new husband, Harry Whitney. My aunt Alva and her new husband, Oliver Belmont, had come with my cousin, Willy Vanderbilt, who had recently turned twenty. I wondered if he was among the hopefuls vying for Cleo Cooper-Smith's hand. If so, he could be in for a battle with his formidable mother, who had triumphed when her daughter, Consuelo, married an English duke. Did she have a princess in mind for her son?

Grace's brother, Orme Wilson, and his wife, Carrie, were there as well, along with Senator and Mrs. Wetmore. The latter pair greeted me warmly, Mrs. Wetmore even embracing me. I had done them a service last summer, and they once more expressed their gratitude. Along with the Wetmores, I noticed another full-time Newport resident, Max Brentworth, owner of the Newport Gas Light Company. Though certainly not old money, Mr. Brentworth's millions allowed him entrée into affairs such as this.

It wasn't long before my instincts for unearthing newsworthy gossip, reluctantly honed during the past year of working for the *Herald,* led me to my first puzzling encounter of the evening. In a corner of the ballroom, Colonel John Jacob Astor, in U.S. Army dress blues, stood woodenly by his beautiful wife, Ava, while she apparently spoke words that pleased him not at all. I watched the tension bead across his jaw as her lips moved rapidly, close to his ear. The tendons in her neck stood out, tense and strained, in her effort not to raise her voice. That in itself didn't fascinate me. Theirs had never been a happy marriage and this was not the first time I'd witnessed contention between them. No, what struck me as odd was the woman standing not far away from them, dressed all in black—not fashionable black silk but the crepe of deep and recent mourning. Here, at a ball?

Equally incongruous was that she didn't merely stand

near them, she stood facing them, as if waiting for the right moment to approach. For what, I wondered. To make small talk? Surely not. She hadn't passed through the receiving line earlier, nor was she a Newport summer resident, but I knew her previously from my time in New York. She was Mrs. Lorraine Kipp, widowed five years ago. Only a couple of weeks prior, she had lost her only son to the Battle of Santiago in Cuba. I particularly remembered the obituary running in the *Herald* because her son, Oliver, had died so young.

Mrs. Astor left her husband after a sharp, parting word. He might have been completely deaf for all the reaction he showed. Only after she had put several paces between them did he release a breath and relax his stance. In that moment, Lorraine Kipp clasped her hands primly at her waist and swept to him.

He looked no happier than he had during his wife's quiet tirade. His gaze darted here and there, anywhere but at Mrs. Kipp's sallow complexion framed by an abundance of silver curls. I felt half inclined to go to his rescue. As it was, I moved a few feet closer in my attempt to eavesdrop. Oh, yes, my year at the *Herald* had taught me well.

"You must do this for me, Colonel Astor. For Oliver. Please," Mrs. Kipp whispered as fiercely as had Ava Astor moments ago. Her lips were pinched, the skin around her eyes as crinkled as old parchment.

The colonel reacted no less uncomfortably to this latest onslaught. "I'm very sorry for your loss, Mrs. Kipp."

"Then say it."

"I just did, ma'am."

"No. You know what I mean." She grasped his coat sleeve with long, bony fingers. "Say it. Proclaim it."

"I cannot, Mrs. Kipp." He pulled away without warning, dislodging her hand from his arm. "Please excuse me."

"Colonel Astor, do not walk away from me, sir—"

Her voice had begun to rise before cutting off short. With a hand pressed to his brow as if to contain its throbbing, Colonel Astor made his way through the knotted throng of guests until he became enveloped in a group of officers and their wives. Mrs. Kipp blinked, moisture clinging to her gray lashes and darkening them. I understood the reason for her grief; her son had died in the war, but what could Colonel Astor do about it now? What could be changed? I couldn't bring myself to ask her. She had seen me—had skimmed a watery gaze over me—and knew what I did for a living. If she wished to speak with me, I certainly wouldn't walk away, but neither would I intrude on her privacy any more than I already had. She drifted away aimlessly, or so I thought at first, until I saw her once more hovering at the periphery of Colonel Astor's group.

I turned my attention away. I don't know why I felt responsible for her well-being, but I made a point of seeking out Ilsa Cooper-Smith. She stood alone near the wall, her crooked figure made less conspicuous by the draping of her gown. She'd pasted a carefully pleasant expression on her face as she observed the dancing I doubted she would enjoy tonight. I understood that look. It was one all young ladies learned, long before they ever arrived at their first social occasion. *All is well,* that look said. *I am perfectly content.* A true lady never allowed unhappy sentiments to intrude upon an evening's gaiety—no matter how miserable she might be feeling.

I wanted to go to her, to stand beside her in a show of camaraderie. After all, no one would be asking me to dance tonight either. But I had a job to perform, and another member of the Cooper-Smith family beckoned, though he had yet to realize it.

"Mr. Cooper-Smith, I'm Emma Cross with the New York

Herald." I held up my notepad and pencil as he turned from the circle of acquaintances with whom he had been speaking.

He eyed me warily. "Yes?"

"I'm here covering your daughter's ball, sir." I drew breath in preparation of asking him whether he and Mr. Griggson would be doing business here in Newport. While Richard Morris Hunt designed Ochre Court and many of the other mansions lining Bellevue Avenue, other architects had left their mark on Newport as well. My question for him was innocent enough, and indeed I had nothing against Randall Cooper-Smith. It was Silas Griggson I despised for his unconscionable actions. "If I may, sir, I'd like to ask you whether you are considering undertaking any projects in Newport—"

"That is hardly society news, Miss Cross. If you are here to cover my daughter's coming-out, then please do so. Excuse me."

"Mr. Cooper-Smith, another moment, please. My next question does pertain to your daughter. Word has it Silas Griggson is among her most favored suitors. Is that true, sir?"

He had already begun moving away. Now he slowly turned pinched features toward me, his eyes blazing. "Do not spread rumors, Miss Cross. It is a risky endeavor, especially in your line of business."

He didn't excuse himself this time, but turned on his heel and strode away, rather more rudely than Colonel Astor had been in escaping Mrs. Kipp.

Had he threatened me? Did he oppose his daughter's potential marriage to Silas Griggson? Why would he, if the two men were business associates? It set me wondering if Randall Cooper-Smith willingly took part in Mr. Griggson's projects. Did he, too, suspect Griggson had caused the collapse of a tenement on New York's Lower East Side? Or, worse, did he fear being discovered as blameworthy in the tragedy?

If he thought his evasiveness would put me off, he would

soon learn differently. But I hoped Randall Cooper-Smith had played no role in Mr. Griggson's perfidy, for Ilsa's sake if nothing else.

I spotted her again, and felt inexplicably relieved to see her smiling up at a dark-haired man of about thirty. His features were patrician, his nose long and slightly aquiline, his chin square and firm. He was unknown to me personally, but on the receiving line I had learned his name was Patrick Floyd. I noticed his smile made only rare appearances as Ilsa chatted away, and when his lips did curl in amusement, there seemed something almost painful in the gesture, though I didn't believe he wished to be away from her. On the contrary, he seemed quite settled at her side; one might even say protective in his stance beside her.

Knowing full well Ilsa was not my assignment tonight, I nonetheless drifted closer while continuing to take notes on those present and what they wore.

"If you would like to dance, Patrick, really, I wouldn't mind," I heard Ilsa saying. "Ask Cleo. I'd enjoy watching you."

He was a friend of the Cooper-Smith family, I surmised, or Ilsa would not have used his given name. My heart clenched at her encouraging him to dance with someone else, a clear reference to her own inability to do so.

"Nonsense, Ilsa. I have no desire to dance tonight. I'm barely out of mourning, after all."

Perhaps that explained those pained looks of his; a ball could only be a grim reminder of a lost loved one.

"You're very kind to remain here with me," she replied. "It's been more than a year since your wife left us, and while I understand you miss Matilda very much, no one would think the less of you for rejoining society in all its many facets. Including dancing. Really, Patrick, you needn't play the gallant for me. I am quite used to *not* dancing."

I wondered if his throat tightened the way mine did. Perhaps so. With a somber expression he turned his face to hers. "I play at nothing, Ilsa. I am perfectly content where I am."

She beamed up at him, and in that moment I perceived the unfortunate imbalance of their regard for each other. Did he realize her feelings approached love, were no less, certainly, than adoration, while his appeared those of a kindly uncle or older brother?

Assured, at least, that she would be well looked after for the time being, I moved away. My compassion dissipated as I did so, for Silas Griggson moved within my sights. His attire once again fit him like a second skin, his evening clothes of the finest materials and tailoring. Apparently, he countenanced only the best when it came to his own creature comforts.

I pulled up short. He stood with two other men, both much younger than himself and in military uniform. One of them was Sam Caldwell, whom I had met coming off the ferry yesterday. The other was Dorian Norris, whom I did not know personally, but by reputation only. He and Sam hailed from two of New York's oldest, if not wealthiest, families. I hoped they were only trading the usual pleasantries with Griggson. The Four Hundred tolerated men like him only because they found him useful. As a real estate developer, he had influence on the course of their investments, and that allowed him entrée into their drawing rooms and ballrooms.

But there were no drawing rooms or ballrooms in the tenement that collapsed last month. A half-dozen residents killed, dozens more injured, and the man held responsible— the construction foreman—dead.

Like every other New York newspaper, the *Herald* reported that the project foreman had ordered shoddy materials and pocketed the cash he saved. He denied it, vehemently. Griggson himself had posted the bail. Only days before his first court hearing, a tugboat captain found the foreman floating in the East River.

And yet here was Griggson, laughing with a pair of officers home from the war. . . .

My attention sharpened as the music ended and Mr. Griggson broke away from his young companions. He walked purposefully onto the dance floor, his target obviously Cleo Cooper-Smith. His cool smile exuded the hope—no, the knowledge—that he would partner her for the next dance. When he was within several feet of her he extended his hand. Another man had moved to Miss Cooper-Smith's side, his name undoubtedly written on her dance card, but at Griggson's approach he backed away. It would appear Silas Griggson wielded the same influence at balls as he did in Tammany Hall. Or did he? For as he came within reach of Miss Cooper-Smith, her expression showed distaste. She raised her hems and scrambled in the opposite direction.

Chapter 3

"What on earth just happened?" Miss Cooper-Smith might as well have shot Silas Griggson point-blank, for the look of horror that crossed Mrs. Goelet's face. She came up behind me, her voice so sharp I flinched. "Do something, quickly."

Startled, I whirled to regard her. "Me, ma'am? What can I do?"

Her gaze slid past my shoulder, and then she brushed by me to where Grace and my cousin, Cornelius Vanderbilt III, stood ready for the next dance. Mrs. Goelet rudely stepped between them. "Grace, I need you to speak with Cleo. She just openly snubbed Mr. Griggson. What *can* she be thinking?"

Grace was no more keen on intervening than I. "I barely know the child, May. She won't listen to me. You should speak with her. You're her patroness."

"She has grown weary of hearing my advice, Grace. She needs a fresh perspective to convince her of her best opportunities. Young girls can be so headstrong. . . ."

As they debated the issue, Mrs. Goelet on the verge of

panic and Grace firmly uncooperative, I sidled over to my cousin. Poor Neily looked uncertain and thoroughly out of his element, caught as he was in the machinations of women. Relief flooded his face as he caught sight of me.

"Can I get you anything, Emmaline? Punch? A bite to eat?"

I couldn't help smiling at his eager tone. "I don't think Grace would thank me for taking you away from her. Especially not now, with her sister attempting to enlist her help with Miss Cooper-Smith." Despite my words, I slipped my arm through his and drew him a few feet off the dance floor. "Tell me, what do you know about her? Does she wish to marry?"

"Doesn't every young woman wish to marry?"

I'd been studying Grace and her sister, and alternately, Cleo Cooper-Smith, who had joined her sister across the room. At Neily's observation, my gaze darted to his face. His question was a sincere one, as I could see by his bemused expression. "Most, Neily, but not all. And many of those who do wish a husband and children only do so because they've been told all their lives they should want such things."

"Not every woman is like you, Emmaline. Most can't take care of themselves the way you can."

My sights once more landed on the Misses Cooper-Smith, and I noted how very differently each young woman carried herself—not just physically but with a quality that spoke of confidence, or the lack of it. To Neily I said, "You'd be surprised what women are capable of when they make up their minds. I'm going to go talk to her."

"To whom? Cleo?" Neily asked to my back, but I continued walking, my notebook and pencil once more primed for note-taking.

"Miss Cooper-Smith, may I ask you another few questions?" I had interviewed her earlier during the afternoon tea. The young woman couldn't hold a candle to her sister Ilsa in terms of attractiveness. Despite her affliction, Ilsa's natural, effortless beauty had immediately struck me when I met her. There seemed nothing effortless about Cleo; on the contrary, every tilt of her head suggested she had spent time in front a mirror practicing to her best advantage. Yet it was an artificial brand of confidence that would fool many people, and I guessed most men, if asked, would have considered Cleo far more beautiful than her sister.

She offered me a just such a head tilt designed to impress. "What would you like to know now, Miss . . . uh?"

"Cross." I found it difficult to believe she had forgotten my name in the ensuing hours. Another affectation? "First, I see you are wearing Worth tonight, yes?" I hadn't really needed to ask. The pale, frothy confection of chiffon, tulle, and lace could have come from no other designer.

She inclined her head. "Of course."

"Then I assume you spent at least part of the spring in France, choosing gowns and being fitted?"

"Oh . . . uh . . . no." She colored slightly. I had inadvertently hit a bit of a nerve and she couldn't lie. Whether or not she had been in Paris this spring would be too easy to verify. "I was able to place my orders from New York."

"I see." What I saw, in actuality, was her discomfiture. Her answer struck me as odd, for nearly every debutante visited the Paris fashion salons for her coming-out wardrobe. But I changed the subject. Earlier she had told me she had been to Newport only once before, several years ago before her mother died. "What do you think of our city? Will you come back to visit?"

"I should like to." Her smile appeared genuine. "New York is so stuffy and dreary in the summer. Perhaps, if Mrs. Goelet is kind enough to invite me, I shall spend my summers here in the future."

Odd that a young woman on the marriage mart would assume dependence on a family friend for future visits. It made me wonder if Miss Cooper-Smith wished to marry at all. "It's wonderful of Mrs. Goelet to serve in your mother's stead tonight. You must be very grateful."

"Aunt May promised Mama she'd see me married." She gave a little head toss that made her glossy curls bounce. But she hadn't answered my question about gratitude. Perhaps she felt none, or considered tonight's festivities a matter of course.

Once again, the dissimilarities between the Cooper-Smith sisters struck me, for even with what little I knew of Ilsa, I felt assured she would have expressed her appreciation for Mrs. Goelet's kindness in no uncertain terms, and to all who would listen.

I turned to include Ilsa and the man beside her in the conversation. Before I could speak, however, an elegant blonde approached us, her smile haughty as she raised an eyebrow to Cleo. "Such a spectacular fuss over you tonight, Miss Cooper-Smith. You must be terribly flattered by it all." The young wife of a banker, Lucinda Russell didn't sound as if she approved of Mrs. Goelet's efforts, though I suspected envy colored her sentiments. Before Miss Cleo could respond, Mrs. Russell's attention shifted to her sister. She swept Ilsa with an appraising glance. "One would imagine your turn is next, my dear. Though, you really should have been first, shouldn't you? I do believe you're older than your sister, no?"

Ilsa blushed fiercely and stammered out an unintelligible reply, making me squirm on Mrs. Russell's behalf. Surely she knew of Ilsa's infirmity—the evidence of it was plain enough. And while I certainly hoped the young woman would someday marry if she wished, I could easily surmise that hers would be a quiet, private courtship free of the conjecture of others as to whether she could manage the running of a household, bear children, and take her place in society. Mrs. Russell's comments seemed deliberately engineered to wound, to point out Ilsa's physical and social shortcomings. Why such cruelty? Was there a history there I didn't know about? A feud, perhaps, between the families?

In a protective gesture, Patrick Floyd lifted a hand to cover Ilsa's where it rested in the crook of his arm. Her complexion began to cool.

But Mrs. Russell persisted. "Oh, but then a ball such as this wouldn't be quite the thing for you, would it?" She tsked, giving a sad shake of her head that renewed the fire in Ilsa's cheeks. My own blood turned hot, and I longed to utter a bitter reprimand.

The sight of Cleo's scowl made me brace for a swift chastisement, the thorough tongue lashing Mrs. Russell deserved. She delivered one, but not to Mrs. Russell. "Oh, Ilsa, don't be so tragic. You'll marry someday and we'll have a great to-do, so you needn't play the martyr. Isn't she wearisome, Patrick?"

The breath left me, and Mr. Floyd as well, for his chest heaved and his eyes flashed with ire. Mrs. Russell merely tittered in amusement, blind or perhaps indifferent to the tears that gathered in Ilsa's eyes and turned them to deep wells of sadness. She slipped her arm from Mr. Floyd's and limped away from us, and became lost within the crush. Another few strained seconds passed, and then Mr. Floyd tersely excused himself and strode off after her.

"Goodness, what did I say?" Mrs. Russell absently fingered the diamond bracelet encircling her gloved wrist. "Why, I certainly didn't mean to . . . Ah, well." To my utter astonishment, she drifted away without another word.

"Oh, Miss Cooper-Smith," I whispered, "do you think your sister is all right? I do hope—"

"Never mind," Cleo cut me off. "No one expects my sister to marry, but Mrs. Russell can't have realized it."

I rather doubted that, for the amusement in Mrs. Russell's voice during the encounter suggested she knew exactly what she was saying, and that she had purposely baited the hapless Ilsa. Why, I could not begin to imagine.

"You see," Miss Cooper-Smith went on, oblivious to my suspicions, "Ilsa suffers from extreme curvature of the spine and nothing the doctors could do, not even the braces they made her wear, made a difference." She lowered her voice. "It's so bad she'll never be able to have children, I'm afraid. So you see, there really is no point in her marrying."

"Yes, I . . . I see." But I didn't. I didn't see why she should never marry, or why she should be made to suffer insults without anyone coming to her defense. Waves of misery on Ilsa's behalf poured through me.

"It's grand of Patrick to keep her company, isn't it?" Something in Miss Cooper-Smith's voice suggested she wasn't as pleased as her words implied.

"Very gentlemanly of him," I agreed for want of something better to say. I shouldn't have asked my next question, but I couldn't help myself. "Is there some ill will between Mrs. Russell and your sister?"

Miss Cleo shrugged. "None that I know of. Lucinda Russell is a busybody and a shrew, and everyone knows it. Ilsa certainly knows it, which is why it vexed me to see her take the woman's teasing to heart. Now then, have you any other questions for me?" She spoke so brightly, so enthusiastically, I could only surmise she'd dismissed her sister from her mind.

I entertained no qualms, then, in posing my next query. "I understand your father and Mr. Silas Griggson often do business together, with your father designing many of the edifices Mr. Griggson's company builds."

"That's true, but what has that got to do with *me*?" She pushed out her plump lower lip. "You are here tonight because of me, aren't you?"

"Indeed, I am, Miss Cooper-Smith." I steeled myself to play the role of gossip columnist to the fullest. "But seeing the business relationship between your father and Mr. Griggson, would it not be an exceedingly advantageous match for you, Miss Cooper-Smith? Would not the union of your families create something of a construction dynasty in New York? And Mr. Griggson *is* here tonight, after all. One can only assume that he is among your many suitors."

"No—I—that is, you misunderstand . . ."

As if I had called across the room to the man, Silas Griggson came up from behind me. "You might certainly say that. Miss Cooper-Smith, I must insist the next dance be mine. And I am a man who is used to getting what he wants." As if to soften the claim, his lips pulled back from his teeth, yet his smile produced the opposite effect by revealing a pair of long, pointy incisors and reminding me of the mongrels that prowled the wharves in town. His very presence raised wary goose bumps across my shoulders, just as those half-wild dogs did.

Miss Cooper-Smith silently appealed to me for an assistance I was in no position to render. With little recourse, she placed her hand in his offered one, and then heaved a sigh of relief when Mrs. Goelet came striding through the crush.

Miss Cooper-Smith broke away from Mr. Griggson and trotted to her patroness. "It's time to prepare for the surprise, isn't it?"

Mrs. Goelet took in the scene before her, noticing Mr. Griggson still holding out the hand recently vacated by Miss Cooper-Smith's smaller one. Her smile was entirely for him, though she spoke to her charge. "My dear, I believe there is time for one more turn on the dance floor."

"No, no, I wouldn't want to keep our guests waiting. Everyone is bursting to know what awaits them in the drawing room. Do forgive me, Mr. Griggson." She could not have appeared happier or more relieved. So much for Mrs. Goelet's hopes of a match between her protégée and Silas Griggson; it was obvious the young woman had no interest in that direction.

As the two of them walked away, Mr. Griggson made a sound like a growl deep in his throat. His smile had vanished, a grimace in its stead. Some little imp in me pretended not to understand. I held my pencil to my notepad. "I'm sorry, did you say something, Mr. Griggson? May I quote you on your opinion of the ball?"

The ball continued another hour, minus several faces. Miss Cleo Cooper-Smith's was among them, along with Sam Caldwell and the other army officer with whom he had been speaking to Mr. Griggson earlier. Mr. Griggson appeared to have left the ball as well. Good riddance. I continued taking my usual notes while making the rounds of the various public rooms, stopping to sample delicacies off the dining room buffets, until a gong summoned everyone to the drawing room.

Mrs. Goelet stood in the doorway, waving everyone inside. "Move all the way in. We must make room for everyone."

Exclamations of surprise filled the air as the guests took in the trees and flowers and lush fabrics that transformed the ordinary drawing room into an Egyptian garden. The artificial clover once more felt springy beneath my feet as Mrs. Goelet gestured for me to move closer to the front, where I would have a good view of the proceedings. Candlelight threw a sunsetlike glow over the room. Curtains had been pulled across the dais, hiding the scene I'd viewed that afternoon.

The connecting doors to the ballroom had been opened to add a bit of space, and once the last guest had squeezed inside, Mrs. Goelet made her way to the dais. She held up her hands for silence.

"Ladies and gentlemen, on this very special night, in honor of our very special Miss Cooper-Smith, we have a most enchanting treat for you, something I am quite sure you have never seen before, not like this. Settle in, and behold. Maestro, if you please."

From beyond the room's open windows, music flowed from a chamber orchestra seated on the terrace. Mrs. Goelet moved away from the dais, coming to stand on my side of the room. At a nod from her, two footmen moved into place, each taking hold of a tasseled pull cord. At another signal from Mrs. Goelet, accompanied by an upswell in the music, the footmen tugged the cords and the curtains swooped open to reveal a nocturnal scene from the distant past.

Cleo Cooper-Smith stood front and center in a sleeveless white sheath embellished with cloth of gold trim and tiny seed pearls. A cape of similar, shimmering cloth of gold cascaded to a train behind her, while a jet black wig, winking with crystals—or were they diamonds?—and cut into blunt bangs fell sharply to her bared shoulders. Encircling her slender neck was a wide jeweled collar, while gold bracelets in the shape of asps, their emerald eyes glittering with cunning, curled around her forearms. Gold sandals laced around her ankles completed her guise of Cleopatra.

Around her, standing or lounging on the colorful cushions I'd seen earlier, were the individuals who had gone missing from the ball. Young ladies wore shoulder-baring sheaths similar to Miss Cooper-Smith's. The men, Sam Caldwell and his friend among them, wielded ornamental swords and looked fierce in their tunics and headdresses.

The guests behind me stirred with appreciation. The music continued. From the ballroom doorway entered a charming little girl dressed in a flowing gown of white silk organza and tulle. A wreath of white flowers encircled her golden curls, and her tiny hands clutched a posy of lilies and baby's breath—and a single red rose, still closed up tight. Like a drop of blood, the bud stood out in its cottony field. The child's blue eyes sparkled with excitement and the importance of her task, and a delicate blush suffused her porcelain-like skin. I knew this lovely child to be Mrs. Goelet's niece, Beatrice, the daughter of her deceased husband's brother.

Mrs. Goelet's own teenage son, Robert, followed Beatrice, proceeding at a dignified pace from the ballroom to the dais. He held a gold circlet studded with gems that shimmered like liquid in the flickering candlelight. When the pair reached the dais they solemnly climbed each step, Beatrice tottering slightly and Robert reaching out with one hand to steady her, until they stood directly in front of Cleo Cooper-Smith. Beatrice bobbed a wobbly curtsy and handed Miss Cooper-Smith the posy. Robert bowed to her. She lowered her head in return, and young Robert Goelet set the circlet upon it.

Out on the terrace, a single trumpet sang out a triumphant call. Robert took Beatrice's hand and moved off to the side, while shivering notes from the violins fueled the anticipation in the drawing room to a fevered pitch. My own stomach clenched in excitement, so caught up was I in the moment. The two footmen moved along the sides of the room, extinguishing the candles until all lay in darkness. Again, the throng stirred. I heard murmurs of expectation, even apprehension, behind me.

At a crescendo from the orchestra, broad daylight flooded the room as the Edison bulbs hidden within the foliage surged to life. A collective gasp burst from the guests. Ladies cried out, first in alarm, then delight. The scene on the dais glowed with a vibrancy that hurt the eyes, and, startled, I blinked. As I did so, Miss Cooper-Smith, duly crowned Queen of the Nile, backed toward the gilded throne, which glowed as if struck with the full force of a noonday sun. I knew that once Miss Cooper-Smith took her place, all movement on the dais would cease, allowing the audience to view the scene down to the minutest detail. She slowly lowered herself to sit on the sumptuous cushions and then reached with both hands to grasp the throne's arms.

Cracks like rapid gunshots echoed through the room. Sparks flew. Profound and utter darkness fell. Ladies screamed, then laughed, then cried out again. Mrs. Goelet called for quiet.

"It's all right, everyone, no need for alarm. All of you on the dais, stay where you are. We'll simply relight the candles . . . Good heavens, where is that electrician? He was to remain on hand. . . ."

Despite her reassurances, her dismay was obvious. All her meticulous planning, not to mention the expense of wiring the Edison bulbs to the room's existing electrical system, wasted. Even I felt an acute sense of letdown. They might continue with the *tableau vivant,* but the drama had been lost, the life of the event extinguished. My editor at the *Herald* wouldn't be happy, especially after paying my way home specifically for this event.

The footmen rapidly began relighting the candles. Suddenly, a young lady on the dais called out. "I think something is wrong with Cleo."

Mrs. Goelet whirled back toward the scene. "Cleo, are you all right? Poor dear, it was quite a shock, wasn't it? Cleo?" She raised her hems and hurried up the steps. "Cleo . . ."

Another of the sheath-clad young ladies, Mrs. Goelet's twenty-year-old daughter, named May for her mother, came to her feet and approached the throne, walking gingerly on the toes of her laced-up sandals. My own breath hung suspended in my lungs as a cold dread seeped through me.

Adding to the sense of dread, the room had gone as still as a sepulcher at midnight. Those on the dais remained where they were, craning their necks to watch, but, true to the form of a *tableau vivant*, no one budged from their assigned place until Sam Caldwell abandoned his post beside one of the columns. His sword at his side, he strode to the center of the dais looking the part of a sentry on patrol. The three of them—Captain Caldwell, Mrs. Goelet, and her daughter— converged around the prone Queen of the Nile. The captain leaned down and whispered Miss Cooper-Smith's name.

Mrs. Goelet reached out to touch her, one finger extended as if to nudge her from sleep. Until that moment, I'd been held in a daze like the rest of the guests behind me, but now a realization struck me.

"Don't!" I shouted, and scurried up the steps. "Don't touch her!"

With a look of alarm, Mrs. Goelet's hand fell to her side, and then she tilted her head, hearing, perhaps, the same sound that reached my ears. Despite the electric lights having been extinguished, an ominous humming arose from the throne, so low and deep I doubted anyone in the room behind me could hear it. Like a physical entity, the sound rippled beneath my skin and grazed my nerve endings. "The circuits must be shut off. We mustn't touch her before that."

"What are you saying?" Mrs. Goelet demanded. She reached for her daughter and wrapped her arms around her.

"Is Cleo all right?" came a small voice like the chirp of a frightened baby bird. Only then did I remember about Beatrice. Mrs. Goelet's gaze fell, horrified, upon the little girl.

"Beatrice, it's all right, dearest. Cleo's only fallen asleep. Silly Cleo." A woman in green taffeta pushed through the crowd and hurried to the dais. Without ascending the steps, she reached her arms out, beckoning to the child. Beatrice ran into them, whereupon her mama gathered her close and carried her from the ballroom. "You did splendidly, darling, just like a real princess. . . ."

With a mix of relief and trepidation, I stared at Miss Cooper-Smith's prone form. Her eyes were open, fixed on some point above her. She didn't move—not so much as a rise or fall of her chest. A reek of burned flesh sent me lurching back a step. "She is quite beyond our help," I said.

Mrs. Goelet fainted dead away. Somewhere in the room a woman screamed, and all hell broke loose.

Chapter 4

Within a half hour of that horrific occurrence, most of the guests, all shaken, some verging on hysterics, had fled Ochre Court. Those who remained gathered in the Great Hall, surrounding Miss Cooper-Smith's father, who appeared dazed and numb, and a distraught Mrs. Goelet, who had been roused with the use of smelling salts.

"First your father, and now this. I cannot take any more loss." Her feet threatened to give way, and her son and daughter hastened to flank her, each putting an arm around her. They hadn't changed out of their Egyptian garb, and presented an incongruent image with the formal surroundings of the Great Hall. "I promised her mother I'd look after her, see her to adulthood, marriage . . ."

"You did your best, Mama," her daughter murmured. "It's not your fault."

"Hardly your fault, Mama," her brother agreed.

"Thank God above I have you two . . ."

Servants circulated with tea and brandy. Mr. Cooper-Smith waved away both, but a tearful yet calm Ilsa accepted a snifter and held it to her father's lips. I spotted Grace and Neily near the fireplace. Colonel Astor and his wife, Ava, their differences apparently settled for the time being, were still there as well. I often forgot the connections between these families, for Colonel Astor's sister, Carrie, had married Grace's brother, Orme, making the Astors, Vanderbilts, and Goelets all in-laws.

Mrs. Goelet's brother-in-law, another Robert, knelt before the chair where Mrs. Goelet now sat. He held her hand and spoke quietly. Beatrice and her mother were not present. I assumed the child had been brought home, a short walk away.

"It was that man's fault. That electrician's." Mrs. Goelet sobbed into her handkerchief.

Her words sent shards of alarm through me. The electrician was a friend of mine, or, rather, the brother of my good friend, Hannah Hanson. We had grown up together on Easton's Point, and I knew Dale Hanson to be a hardworking, honest, and conscientious man. But I said nothing. Now was not the time, with everyone still in shock and overwrought. Yet, as Mrs. Goelet continued, I began to fear the consequences Dale might be made to bear. That he hadn't yet been found also boded ill for him, though I believed his absence from Ochre Court would be easily explained.

"He'll pay for what he's done to our poor Cleo. He will—" Tears choked off the rest, running down Mrs. Goelet's cheeks and splashing on her lap.

Jesse arrived with a uniformed policeman, followed by the coroner and a pair of assistants.

"Dear God," Jesse murmured after climbing the dais and using rubber tongs to move aside the sheet that had been draped over Miss Cooper-Smith's body. At first her father and some of the other men had wanted to move her off the throne, but I had cautioned them to touch nothing before the police arrived. Despite this being an accident, due to the nature of her ghastly death there would need to be a report and a routine investigation.

Jesse let the sheet fall to cover the body. He came down the steps and approached me. "Can you tell me what happened?"

"I honestly don't know. The light bulbs were switched on, and . . . and it happened. It was awful."

A commotion in the Great Hall caught Jesse's and my attention. There came angry shouts and running feet, and then Dale Hanson burst into the drawing room at full speed.

"They say she's been electrocuted. It's not possible. It could not have happened." Dale was a large man, blond and good-looking in the way many people of Nordic descent are, with coloring that implied robust good health. Except tonight his complexion was gray and white terror ringed his blue eyes. "What the devil happened?"

He stopped several feet shy of the dais and stood gazing up at the figure swathed in white linen. He shook his head over and over. "She cannot be . . ."

"Dale." Jesse had to repeat the name several times before Dale finally turned toward him. "Tell me what happened. Did you fully test the wiring before tonight?"

"Several times." Dale hung his head in bewilderment. "I swear, Jesse, I . . ."

"Were you drinking?" The question came, not from Jesse, but from a man standing in the doorway. Silas Griggson stepped into the room, and with a grim expression crossed to us. "Has anyone checked on this man's whereabouts before the ball? Did anyone see him drinking?"

"Dale Hanson is no drunkard." I stepped in Mr. Griggson's path. "He's a good man. I can attest to that. I've known him all my life."

He eyed me coldly. "Excuse me, Miss Cross, but who are you to vouch for the moral integrity of any man?"

Dale was at my side in an instant. "Don't speak to her that way. Emma Cross is as decent a woman as was ever born."

Mr. Griggson's icy regard remained steadfastly on me. I refused to blink or waver. "I am speaking from experience, sir. I have never seen Dale Hanson inebriated and I have never seen him behave in anything but a responsible manner. Isn't that so, Jesse?"

Jesse didn't respond, didn't back up my claim, and I realized he couldn't, not in his official capacity as investigating detective. He must remain impartial, or at least appear so.

"Well, what are you going to do about this?" Mr. Griggson now demanded, turning his enmity on Jesse.

"I am going to determine what happened here tonight."

"And are you going to arrest this man for murder?"

I gasped. "Don't be ridiculous."

"Where has he been?" Griggson persisted. "He should have been here in the event something went wrong. Why is he only now showing up?"

"I walked over to Forty Steps," Dale said defensively. "I didn't think I'd be needed."

"You hadn't the stomach to witness your own crime. Murderer."

"If it's a murder that has taken place," Jesse interrupted, "then many others besides Mr. Hanson will come under suspicion." Griggson's complexion darkened, but before he could respond, Jesse added, "As it is, what happened will be termed an accident until evidence suggests otherwise. I'd prefer you to leave, sir, while we continue with our work."

"Why, I . . ."

Jesse held up a hand. "I can have you arrested for obstructing police business."

"And I'd see you tossed out on the street by tomorrow."

Jesse smiled. "Not the first time I've been threatened with that." He turned away from Mr. Griggson and climbed the dais steps. Silas Griggson stared at his back, his nostrils pinched, lips parted, his breath coming in rapid spurts. I confess that when his eyes narrowed, a chill went through me, raising goose bumps and a resolve to warn Jesse to watch his back around this man.

"Sir," the police officer called. "We've found something. One of the main cables is stripped and wrapped around all four feet of the throne."

"What? That can't be." Dale scrambled up the steps. When he reached the throne he leaned down to see what the police had discovered, and in doing so placed his right hand on one of the gilded arms of the piece.

"Dale, no!" I shouted, but too late. The current once more made its jarring crack and sparked. Dale yelped and stiffened, and Jesse reached for him, closing his hands around Dale's upper arms. He, too, cried out, his arms stiffening as if the joints and ligaments suddenly solidified. His eyes filled with terror, and with the realization of his mistake. Then, somehow finding presence of mind, he gave a great heave and broke both Dale and himself free of the electricity's grip.

Their legs giving way, both men sank to the dais. Once again, the stench of burning flesh permeated the air. I coughed and sputtered; my stomach roiled. I swallowed and held my breath, fighting for control as I mounted the steps and fell to my knees between the fallen men.

I'd paced the waiting area of Newport's tiny hospital for what seemed an eternity, in reality perhaps forty minutes or so. Each time I passed the doorway into the lobby, I craned my neck to see past the front desk, searching for any sign of my friend Hannah, a nurse and Dale's sister, coming from the main examination room.

Jesse was in that room. Jesse, whom I had known for as long as I could remember. His thirty-odd years put him rather squarely between my parents' age and my own. He had first been my father's friend, coming to sit with him in our rear garden in the evenings to trade news and stories of the day. During most of those years I had been little Emmaline, Arthur and Beatrice Cross's precocious daughter. But gradually that had changed. First my parents had emigrated to Paris along with others of their artistic circle, leaving me to the guidance of Nanny and my aunt Sadie until I entered adulthood. Then circumstances began to throw Jesse and me together in ways that made it necessary for each of us to depend on the other.

I'm not certain when Jesse began to see me differently. I only know that one day I was no longer a little girl in his eyes, or in his heart. At first, the sentiments I'd glimpsed in him made me look away, for I despaired of ever returning his regard, not in the way he wished. That, too, gradually changed. I began to see him not as a family friend or kindly neighbor, but as a man in his own right. That didn't necessarily make anything easier or clarify my choices for me. Even now, pacing up and down the waiting area, I could not say with any authority what my future or my heart held. I only knew I wanted Jesse whole and alive and with a long future ahead of him.

Hannah's blue dress and white pinafore apron came into view. She hurried to me. The strain of events showed in her face, yet the calm façade of a professional nurse remained firmly in place. "They're both very lucky, Emma. Dale took the worst of it, since he touched his hand directly onto the arm of the throne. What was Mrs. Goelet thinking, using gilded metal with all that electricity?"

I shuddered at the memory of Dale's blackened fingers, while at the same time basking in the relief that neither man would die. "Will he lose any part of his hand?"

"We don't yet know." Her composure slipping a fraction, she made a fist and gripped it with the other hand. "He'll certainly have nerve damage that could be permanent. Oh, Emma, if he loses some or all of his fingers, or his dexterity, he'll also lose his means of earning his livelihood."

At a loss for comforting words, I embraced her, whereupon she visibly collected herself. "I'm so sorry. You want to know about Jesse, too."

I very much did, but I said, truthfully, "I'm concerned about both of them."

"Of course. Thank you. Jesse isn't in any danger of losing fingers, or even of permanent nerve damage, we don't believe. There is pain in both arms and he can't hold them steady, but that should pass in time." She paused, and again relief for Jesse welled inside me, nearly making me giddy. "Dale knows better than to touch an object connected to a live cable. This shows how completely anguished he became at Miss Cooper-Smith's death. He blames himself."

Before I could reply, the street door opened. A gust of warm wind swirled about our ankles, followed by Silas Griggson as he stepped in from outside. He wasn't alone. Behind him came two police officers. Scotty Binsford, who'd grown up on the Point along with Hannah and me, cast me sheepish look from beneath a lock of tousled brown hair that had escaped his police helmet.

Silas Griggson spoke first. "I want that man, that electrician, taken to the jail as soon as he is physically able to be moved."

Hannah, obviously caught off guard, made a sound of distress.

Griggson's right eyebrow arced into a sharp peak. "Is that a problem, Nurse?"

"Where and when Dale Hanson is moved is entirely up to his doctor," I said while Hannah gaped at him. I couldn't blame her.

"And to the police," Griggson corrected me. "Whom I have brought with me to make certain the man doesn't attempt to escape. He is directly responsible for my fiancée's death, and he will pay for it."

At a tearful gasp from Hannah, I slipped my hand into hers. "You are making two highly questionable claims, Mr. Griggson. While I am terribly sorry about Miss Cooper-Smith, fault, if there was any, is yet to be determined. And forgive me if I missed a development, but at no time did that poor young lady, or anyone else, indicate an engagement between the two of you."

"We would have been engaged by the end of the evening." Both his voice and his glare challenged me to contradict him. I didn't. I merely stared back in my own attempt to convey the message that I didn't fear him, though perhaps I did, a bit. He was first to tear his gaze away, swinging about to address the officers. "Well? Don't you have work to do?"

They looked uncertain and silently appealed to me. I said, "Why don't you go and talk with Jesse? Hannah, would that be all right now?"

She nodded and found her voice. "He's still in the examination room. You know the way."

They moved to go, but Silas stopped them with the flat of his palm. "You are not here to talk. Hanson may not have *meant* to kill Miss Cooper-Smith but he is responsible just the same. There was a half-empty bottle of rum found hidden among his tools. He's guilty of gross negligence."

Hannah gasped, but Scotty said evenly, "We're here, sir, to

make sure you don't disrupt the hospital with your demands."

"How dare you."

"Chief Rogers made that clear to us before we left the station with you. You're welcome to take it up with him." Scotty issued a grim little smirk at me, and led his partner to the rear of the building.

"We'll see about this." Mr. Griggson's face contorted. Without another word he exited the building.

Hannah let go a breath. "I fear that man won't rest until he sees my brother in jail. I don't understand how a bottle of rum could have been found with his tools. Dale doesn't drink, not like that, and certainly never while he's working."

"I don't believe Dale had anything to do with what happened to Miss Cooper-Smith, but I very much believe someone is determined for him to take the blame."

"Yes, that awful man who was just here. But what are we to do?" Even as she spoke, the answer to her own question dawned in her expression. Her eyes filled with hope. "Emma, would you . . . ? For Dale's sake?"

I understood her query. This would not be the first time I had snatched the reins of an investigation. There were times when forces in Newport stood in the way of the police doing their job as one might wish. They were not at fault. With a word and a pile of bills placed in the right palm—often a palm far removed from Newport—powerful men could silence inquiries and force a convenient judgment. It had almost happened to my brother, Brady, three years ago, except that I had refused to sit idly by in my parlor while circumstantial evidence sent him to the gallows.

Silas Griggson was just such a powerful man. . . .

"Of course I will," I said resolutely to Hannah, and to myself. "For you and Dale both. And for Jesse. I'll find out how and why Miss Cooper-Smith died tonight."

"Follow that man. I've no doubt he'll lead you to the answers."

"Perhaps." It would have been all too easy to focus solely on Silas Griggson, an individual with little or no conscience, who seemed more than willing to sacrifice others for profit. I stared into the blackness outside the nearest window. My teeth clenched so tightly my temples began to ache. I forcibly relaxed my jaws. "I won't rest until I'm certain of what happened."

After Scotty and his fellow officer left the hospital, I took their place at Jesse's bedside. He had been moved to the ward upstairs, rather against his will, but his doctor wished to observe him for the night at least. Dale occupied a bed at the other end of the ward, while the beds between them lay empty. He had been given a dose of morphia to ease the pain. He lay on his back, snoring lightly, his bandaged hands and forearms resting on top of the blanket.

Hannah brought me a stool, and I sat holding Jesse's hand, carefully, mindful of his injuries. Unlike Dale, no scorch marks marred his skin, but I felt the weakness in his fingers and the tremor of his palm against mine. This worried me, but I didn't let him see it.

"Do you think Silas Griggson will pressure the department to charge Dale?" I asked him, already certain of the answer. But if Jesse feared for his future as a detective, the best way to distract him was to engage him in what he did best.

His answer was blunt. "Yes. But that won't stop us, Emma."

"Us?" I smiled down at our clasped hands. "You would never have said *that* three years ago."

"Three years ago I would have told you to stay out of it, that poking your nose where it doesn't belong is dangerous."

"But you've learned I can take care of myself, haven't you?"

"I've learned there is no arguing with you. You're far too stubborn." He didn't mean it; the fondness in his expression assured me he didn't.

"It's fairly certain this was no accident tonight. Someone murdered Cleo Cooper-Smith."

"Yes, but why? She was how old? Nineteen?" When I nodded, he sighed and shook his head. "What can one so young possibly have done to warrant cutting her life short?"

"Perhaps the question is what did she know that necessitated her silence, and who would stand to gain from her death."

He studied me, his gaze gently caressing my features. "You have some ideas about that, don't you?"

"I didn't come all the way to Newport just to cover this coming-out ball. True, that's why the *Herald* sent me, but I came with another purpose in mind. Jesse, several weeks ago, a tenement on the Lower East Side collapsed. Several people died, and dozens more were injured."

"My God, how awful."

"The project foreman took the blame, but before his case went to court, someone bailed him out of jail . . ." I paused to gather a breath, and yes, perhaps for dramatic effect as well. "And the next day, his body was found floating in the East River."

"Sounds like the work of one of those cutthroat gangs New York is famous for."

"I don't know about that. But I do know whose company built that building and employed that foreman. Silas Griggson's."

His gaze locked with mine. "And the connection to Miss Cooper-Smith?"

"Her father is an architect who often works with Mr. Griggson."

He looked down at our joined hands and swore. "So this Griggson tops the list."

"For now," I said. "What bothers me is that it seems too easy."

"But it's a start." He glanced up sharply. "A building contractor nowadays would probably have at least a rudimentary understanding of electricity. Voltage, current, circuits. Someone had to have known what they were doing. So . . . you followed Griggson to Newport. Why? Why not simply wait until he returned to New York to investigate his activities?"

"Because I'm afraid he might have taken it into his head to buy property here in Newport, with the intention to build. Whether or not he had anything to do with Cleo Cooper-Smith's death, I don't want that man here. I certainly don't want anyone else to suffer for his shady dealings."

"I don't want *you* suffering for his shady dealings either." His fingers trembled as he tightened them around mine. He tried to hide his grimace of pain. I pretended not to notice, yet neither of us was fooling anyone. He laughed softly. "Whatever brought you home, Emma, I'm glad. I've missed you." Then, perhaps deciding he'd admitted too much after what had basically been a yearlong separation, he added, "Newport has missed you."

"And I've missed Newport. Silas Griggson and Miss Cooper-Smith's coming-out ball weren't the only matters that brought me home." I steeled myself to reveal my recent decision, which became more of a reality each time I voiced it. "The *Herald* doesn't yet know it, but I'm staying, Jesse. I'm not going back to New York."

He beamed at me with an emotion that pinched my throat

and stung my eyes. Hannah shooed me away soon after with strict orders that Jesse get some sleep. His deep-throated "Good night, Emma" echoed inside me all the way down the stairs and into the lobby, whereupon I walked half-blindly into the arms of Derrick Andrews.

Chapter 5

"What are you doing here?" I asked after Derrick steadied me and his hands came away from my shoulders, leaving traces of warmth where they had rested.

"I came to see how Jesse's doing." He bent his head to me, his dark hair and eyes seeming to fill my vision. "And to see you."

"How did you know . . . ?" I hadn't given him notice of my returning to Newport, and he hadn't been at Ochre Court earlier. Movement behind Derrick caught my eye. "Brady."

"Hello, Em." His hat in his hands, Brady leaned around Derrick's shoulder and grinned.

Derrick smiled. "When were you going to let me know you were home?"

"All in good time," I said, with a prick at my conscience. "There was no rush, you see. I'm planning to stay."

"Permanently?" The eagerness in both his voice and his expression prevented me from trusting my voice in that moment. I nodded.

Any reason for reticence about my decision had passed. If Brady, Hannah, Nanny, and Grace all knew I'd decided to move back to Newport, then all of Newport probably knew by now as well. A disconcerting notion struck me. James Bennett, owner of the *Herald* and the man who directly hired me on, was also currently in Newport. He hadn't attended Mrs. Goelet's ball either, but how soon before my decision reached his ears? I preferred to tell him of my plans myself and resolved to call at his summer cottage, Stone Villa, tomorrow. "It was good of you to come to check on Jesse."

"Yes, well, he and I have settled some of our differences in the past year."

"Only some?"

"I'm afraid there are some matters on which we'll never see eye to eye." A lift of his eyebrows indicated that one of those matters stood before him now.

I silently thanked Brady when he changed the subject. "How are Dale and Jesse doing?"

"Hannah says the doctor thinks Jesse will be all right in time. Dale's fate isn't clear. His life isn't in danger," I hastened to add, "but only time will tell how much damage was done to his hands."

"Can we see them?" Brady asked.

"Dale was sleeping when I left, and I'm not sure if Hannah will allow Jesse any more visitors tonight. Brady, go up and talk to her. She's putting up a good front, but she's terribly upset about what happened." I lowered my voice. "Dale is being blamed. Even framed, I fear."

"Then what happened wasn't an accident," Derrick said rather than asked.

I regarded him. "Are you asking as a newspaperman, or as a friend?"

Another waggle of those dark eyebrows. "Both."

Before I could respond, Brady spoke. "I've been called back to New York, Em. I've got to head back in the morning."

"Oh, Brady. I've only just got home."

"I know. But you know how things are with the old man being ill."

He referred to my uncle, Cornelius Vanderbilt II, who had suffered a stroke two years ago and showed few signs of recovering. As head of the Vanderbilt family *and* the New York Central Railroad, his incapacity created a large, exceedingly hard-to-fill gap in the daily running of the family's affairs.

"Then you had better go up and see Hannah." I gave him a little nudge, and he headed for the stairs.

Derrick offered his arm to me. "Can I drive you home? You can tell me what happened on the way."

"I have my carriage here."

"You're going to make poor Barney walk all the way back to Gull Manor at this late hour? Leave him. I'll bring you home, and meanwhile have my valet collect your gig and bring it over to my house."

"You mean *my* house," I murmured. I still hadn't quite forgiven him for purchasing my childhood home on the Point when my parents quietly put it up for sale three years ago. Had I known, I would have bought the property myself. Somehow. Although with what funds, I had never precisely determined. And I suppose my parents had realized that. My father, an artist, came into money sporadically, and that summer they'd fallen short. They hadn't had the time to wait for me to devise a plan; besides, I already owned Gull Manor. I understood their decision, yet my heart still ached when I thought about it.

Derrick replied with a lopsided grin. I sighed and decided

my roan hack, Barney, deserved a good night's sleep. I would also reach home eons sooner than if Barney, who knew only one slow speed, brought me. "Thank you."

"We'll bring your horse and carriage home in the morning. Come."

Though it was well after midnight, Newport's streets were alive with summer residents coming and going from parties and events. Carriages lined Bellevue Avenue outside the Casino and choked driveways inside the gates of the grand cottages farther along. I was thankful not to have to pass by Ochre Court, which sat on Ochre Point Avenue to the east of Bellevue. Along the way I explained to Derrick what happened. He listened with very little comment, his profile tense in the moonlight.

At the wide turn where Coggeshall Avenue joined Ocean Avenue, the horse seemed to know where to go without Derrick prompting him. That made me curious. "Do you come out here often?"

"A bit." Did I detect a note of evasiveness?

"To swim?" I gestured toward the dark outlines of the pavilion and cabanas of Bailey's Beach, hunched against the ocean.

"Actually," he said, "Nanny sometimes invites me to dinner."

"She does? She never told me that." I didn't know whether to be amused or annoyed. Clearly, Nanny had wished to keep Derrick firmly entrenched in her—and by association, my—life, while I was away. "She knew I'd be coming back, didn't she?"

"Either that or she hoped I'd follow you to New York." He paused to adjust the reins. "Or one of us would. I hear tell she invites Jesse to dinner, too. Just not on the nights she invites me."

But for a single lantern in the parlor window, the house was dark when we arrived. Dear Nanny always provided a light to guide me inside. Derrick stopped the carriage close to the front door. An awkwardness suddenly came over me as I prepared to leave him.

"Well, thank you."

"I'll see you soon, yes?"

"You'll see me in the morning, remember? You and your valet will bring Barney home."

"Ah, yes. Have you thought of replacing him?"

"Barney? I can't afford to keep two horses, and I couldn't possibly part with him. What would become of him? Why, someone might . . ." I shuddered to think of the fate that befell aging horses that were no longer of any use to anyone. Why, it would be akin to sending Nanny packing someday, when she was no longer able to cook her wonderful meals or offer her sage advice. Nanny would always have a home at Gull Manor, and Barney would always enjoy a warm stall here as well. I adamantly shook my head. "I'm content to travel as slowly as Barney could wish."

Derrick gave a soft laugh. "All right. Good night, Emma."

"Good night." I started to step down, but he caught my arm, leaned in, and grazed my lips with his.

Contrary to my observation that Derrick would see me in the morning, I awoke to rather different circumstances.

"Have you seen your surprise yet?" Nanny asked when I padded into the morning room for breakfast. At my blank look, she gestured for me to turn around and retrace my steps to the front hall. "You'll want to see this."

As I might have expected, my carriage, with its faded canvas roof and crinkling leather seat, sat on my driveway in front of the house. Derrick and his valet had apparently gotten a very early start, had been here and gone again. What I had not expected to see hitched to my old vehicle, however, was the handsome dark bay carriage horse. They made a most unlikely match. A note sat on the seat, held in place by a rock the size of my palm. It said, simply, "His name is Maestro."

Once the initial surprise subsided, I experienced a spark of alarm. "But where is Barney?" Without waiting for anyone to answer me, I circled the house, my dressing gown flapping out behind me. Upon reaching the small barn in my rear garden, I flung open the door and stopped short, once more held motionless in surprise.

Dear Barney raised his head above the wall of his stall to peer at me as he continued chewing a mouthful of fresh hay. Had Katie been out to feed him already? Perhaps, but it seemed Barney's fairy godmother had visited him as well. Or his fairy godfather, I should say. Bales of hay that hadn't been there yesterday had been stacked along one wall, along with sacks of oats and another of apples I knew hadn't been charged to my household account.

I had told Derrick I couldn't afford to keep two carriage horses, and he had solved my problem for me. Not sure how I felt about that, I stood for some moments taking in the scene while weighing the expense of his gesture against what monies I knew were available for such extravagance. Barney stamped a foot and snorted, breaking the spell of uncertainty that held me. Not the uncertainty itself, mind you, but, roused from my immobile state, I went to Barney and scratched behind his ears.

I didn't turn at the sound of the soft, slippered tread or the squeaking board. Nanny came up behind me and slipped an arm about my shoulders. "Such a lovely thing to do. Wouldn't you agree, Emma?"

I stifled a sigh. It *was* a lovely gesture. However much I valued and fervently protected my independence, I couldn't deny that.

"Please don't say you're going to return it all—the horse, the supplies. Derrick's kindness." At the gentle admonishment in her tone, I turned to her and shook my head.

"No. To do so would be foolish and self-defeating. I made a promise I'd find the person who killed Cleo Cooper-Smith and framed Dale Hanson. Derrick has made that task so much easier."

"A pity he didn't include a new carriage."

"Nanny!"

"I'm only saying."

"Maestro goes back to Derrick as soon as I've completed my errands. With my sincere thanks, of course." Barney nudged my shoulder, prompting me to pivot once again and stroke his neck. "Don't you worry, old friend. No one will forget you. We'll need Katie to exercise him every day so he doesn't grow bored and . . . well . . . sad. It doesn't do to deprive an individual of his occupation."

"I can do that," Nanny said. "He's such a gentle soul. He and I move at the same unhurried pace nowadays. Don't we, boy?"

My throat tightened. I could not envision my world lacking either Nanny or my loyal horse. I placed an arm around her and laid my cheek against her shoulder, wide, cushioned by her plumpness, and still the bastion of comfort it had been all my life.

After telephoning over, I returned to Ochre Court shortly after breakfast. This time I went to the front door, and Grace let me in, having spent the night to comfort her sister. She must have been watching for me, for I saw no sign of the butler upon stepping inside.

"May is in bed," she told me. "And likely to stay there all day today."

"How are her son and daughter?" I removed my hat and driving gloves and handed them to a footman who appeared from seemingly out of nowhere.

"They're holding up remarkably well. Neither were particularly close with Cleo. Not even young May, oddly enough. She and Cleo were the same age."

"That is odd, considering the friendship between their mothers. I wonder why that was."

"I really couldn't say." I heard something in her voice, a bit of reluctance perhaps, to reveal too much. I considered pressing her, but then remembered her relation to the Goelets. She might be my friend and sincere in her desire to be of help, but her first loyalties would lie with family.

"And little Beatrice? Have you heard anything about how this affected her?"

Here Grace smiled. "Her mother telephoned a little while ago to say Beatrice is happily playing with her dolls and has made no mention of last night other than to congratulate herself once again on a job well done. Three-year-olds are remarkably resilient, I understand, and terribly pleased with themselves at the slightest accomplishment. But tell me, where to first?"

I had explained on the telephone the purpose of my visit, including the accusations made against Dale Hanson. Through Brady, Grace had a passing acquaintance with his sister, Hannah. While she maintained that Brady would do better to set his sights on some less-well-to-do heiress, she tolerated Hannah as "a girl with a good head on her shoulders."

At my request she took me into the ballroom and through into the drawing room. Everything looked as it had yesterday—the artificial garden, the dais, the Egyptian stage setting. And the throne, of course, its gilded finish charred and pitted.

I took a magnifying glass from my handbag, but first looked about me with my naked eyes. The silken clover no longer retained its spring beneath my boots, as it had been quite trampled last night. So many people had traipsed through the room that I couldn't hope to find anything as identifying as a footprint.

I climbed the dais steps and knelt beside the throne. Before I touched anything, I listened for the telltale humming of active circuitry. It had been turned off last night, but I couldn't dislodge from my mind the image of Jesse and Dale touching the throne and nearly being electrocuted.

Reassured at hearing only my own breathing and Grace's occasional steps brushing through the clover, I reached out a tentative fingertip and touched the wiring wrapped around one of the front legs of the throne. I noticed two things immediately. The first had already been noted by the police, that the rubber insulation had been stripped from the wiring where it came in contact with the throne's metal leg.

As far as I knew, the second hadn't yet been noted, but this wire appeared thicker than those connected to the surrounding Edison bulbs. I got to my feet and went to the side of the dais to examine those wires, and yes, they did appear thinner, which meant the current running through the throne would have been stronger than that needed for the bulbs.

Someone had indeed known what they were doing. I returned to the throne.

Crouching low, I held my magnifying glass over the stripped wire. It appeared some kind of blade had been used to cut away the rubber, leaving jagged edges. The job appeared hurried, perhaps slightly frantic. That suggested whoever had done this feared discovery, and wished to be done and away as soon as possible.

The cut marks providing me with little other information, I searched around each leg, hoping for some clue—a thread, a button, anything the culprit might have dropped. I found nothing.

And then an idea sent me crawling from leg to leg, examining the direction in which the wire had been wrapped each time. I discovered a counterclockwise motion had been utilized. I pretended I held a length of wire in my right hand, the one I favored. My instinct was to wrap in a clockwise direction.

Did that mean a left-handed person had rigged the wiring? I sat up.

"Did you find something?" At Grace's question, I started. I'd been so intent on my examination I'd forgotten she was still in the room watching me.

"I'm not certain. I need to review everyone who had access to this room yesterday." I contemplated the wiring again. Having been camouflaged by the vividly woven rugs covering the dais, it had been easy to miss. Dale Hanson and his assistant had installed the Edison bulbs three days ago. Most of the decorating had already been completed by then. Could this errant wire have been wrapped around the throne legs when I came here yesterday afternoon? Or had the deed been accomplished after that, perhaps even during the ball itself?

That meant the individual could have been a workman, servant, or any of the guests, male or female. I sat back on my haunches and thought about that. Something seemed off, and then it occurred to me that the vast majority of both workmen and footmen were right-handed. In the case of workmen, right-handedness was a matter of safety, as most tools, fine tools in particular, were made for right-handed men. In the case of footmen, uniformity when serving at the table dictated they be right-handed as well. Could I safely rule out both categories of men? Perhaps not entirely, but this potentially narrowed down the field considerably. Dale, I knew, was right-handed.

What about women? I had learned that women are hardly immune from the passions that prompt an individual to commit murder. Mrs. Goelet's tea yesterday had been attended by some of Newport's most respected doyennes and their daughters. It seemed unlikely one of them could be guilty, but I had been fooled before.

A name escaped my lips before I could stop it. "Ilsa."

"What's that, Emma?" Grace came closer to the dais. "Did you say Ilsa? What about her?" When I didn't answer, Grace set her hands on her hips. "Surely you don't think she had anything to do with her sister's death."

I wished I could call back my ill-advised utterance. "Of course not," I assured her. In truth, I didn't . . . and yet, on what basis could I rule her out? "She was in here yesterday afternoon, when no one was supposed to be. I found her in the ballroom while making notes on the decorations. I startled her, and she knocked over a vase. It was odd," I added weakly.

"Did she give you a reason for being here?"

"She said she wished to ensure everything was perfect for her sister."

"There you are then. They are—were—quite close from what I understand. I never knew either of them very well, I'm afraid. Their mother was May's friend and nearly twenty years older than I. She and I enjoyed only a passing acquaintance."

Ilsa's presence in the ballroom could have been innocent enough. Before I accused anyone, I needed to learn more about Cleo—her habits, her interests, her goals. Silas Griggson claimed they were practically engaged, but that seemed dubious at best. Did she love someone else? Or, like me, did she long for independence?

"Grace, do you know if Cleo kept a diary?"

"I couldn't say. Ilsa might know. They were both staying here for the festivities, though their father is staying in town. I believe Ilsa's upstairs in her room, or with May, perhaps. Would you like me to check?"

"No, please don't disturb either of them. Rather, would you show me to Cleo's room?"

"May probably wouldn't like that," she said and then winked. "So we'll go quietly. Follow me."

She led me up the main staircase to the open gallery that looked down upon the Great Hall. We hurried along a section of it, and then down an enclosed hallway that branched off to a separate wing. Grace tried a knob and to our luck discovered the door unlocked. We slipped inside and closed the door.

"I believe Ilsa's room is right next door, so we must be as discreet as possible unless you want her here asking questions."

I shook my head. "No, indeed. At least, not yet."

"What are we looking for?" Grace asked brightly, obviously warming to the task. Grace always did enjoy a bout of intrigue, as long as it didn't come accompanied by any true danger.

I went to the dressing table and began opening drawers. The very act sent me spiraling back to last summer, when another death had necessitated rummaging through the victim's private effects. "As I said, a diary," I replied, "should we be so fortunate. Or anything, really, that sheds a bit of insight into who Cleo Cooper-Smith was."

A small leather case yielded facial powders, rouge, tinted lip balm, and even a tiny bottle filled with some blackish liquid. Thickened elderberry juice, I surmised, which could be brushed on the eyelashes to darken them. "It seems Cleo was not opposed to enhancing her appearance."

Grace came to peer over my shoulder. "She was rather young for that," she observed. "One would suppose she used them on the sly." She touched her fingertips to her own cheek. If Grace used cosmetics, as I guessed she did, she applied them artfully and subtly.

I continued my perusal of the dressing table, finding nothing of particular interest. I moved next to one of the two dressers and asked Grace to search through the other.

"It feels wrong to be doing this," she said with a little trill in her voice. "And yet exciting at the same time."

"We're doing nothing but seeking justice for Cleo. As for excitement, Grace, let's hope we don't encounter too much of that." Having exhausted the dresser without finding anything but the usual trappings of a young lady, I threw open the armoire. Dresses and gowns of the very latest designs met my eye. Most spoke of House of Worth, though I believed I detected creations by Redfern and perhaps Rouff as well. I carefully thumbed through as I would the pages of an ancient and precious book. Something struck me as not quite right. My hand stilled as I continued to contemplate Cleo's wardrobe.

Grace came up beside me. "What is it?"

"These gowns . . ." I turned around and returned to the dresser I'd just rifled through. Sliding open the top drawer, I once again viewed underclothing, gloves, and handkerchiefs. Much of it was no better than my own. "The gowns don't match the rest," I said.

"What do you mean?"

"The quality. Her gowns are the finest, yet nothing else boasts the same superiority." I turned to face her. "We haven't found any jewelry. At least, nothing of value. Doesn't that strike you as odd?"

"Now that you mention it."

"Do you know anything about the Cooper-Smiths' finances? Are they as wealthy as these dresses would imply?"

"I always believed them to be, at least fairly so. They *are* a Four Hundred family, an old one."

"Her father works as an architect," I pointed out. And as I had learned, "old money" did not always mean current money.

"Emma, unlike our counterparts in, say, England, American gentlemen work. I know another architect, Mr. Phelps Stokes. He designs buildings for the love of it rather than for money. His inheritance is sufficient to allow him to pursue such interests."

"Still, this lack of jewelry could be significant. These fine dresses could be an attempt to hide the fact that the family finances are not what they should be." Could this be why Mrs. Goelet had set her sights on Silas Griggson for Cleo? A self-made man such as he would not resent a bride's lack of fortune the way members of the Four Hundred would.

Across the room, the end tables on either side of the bed beckoned. "Let's check these," I said, gesturing. I opened the drawer above, sifted through, and then opened the cupboard below. As I reached in, Grace stopped me.

"Emma, come here." Grace backed away from the gaping drawer in the cabinet across from me. She held a small wooden box and stared down at something in her other hand. "See what I've found!"

I quickly circled the bed.

"I think these are diamonds." Narrowing her eyes, she held the small setting of several stones up to an electric wall sconce. "Yes, most definitely diamonds. They were in this box and shoved into a corner. But the setting is broken. See how the links at either end have been pulled open. This appears to be part of a larger piece, most likely a necklace. Here, you look."

She poured the glittering segment into my palm. Several diamonds dangled from what I judged to be a platinum chain. I agreed with Grace; this did seem to be part of a larger piece of jewelry. So where was the rest?

We went through the room again, and into the bathroom that adjoined Ilsa's bedroom on the other side. We found nothing that helped solve the mystery of the diamond setting.

"Perhaps you're correct about the Cooper-Smiths' finances." Grace perched at the edge of the bed. "In truth, I've seen it before, where the family of a young woman on the marriage mart will spend their last pennies on her trousseau to hide their penury. It's even possible May paid for Cleo's wardrobe. She loved Cleo's mother that much. Should I ask her?"

"Do, but be discreet. We don't want to distress your sister any more than necessary."

Grace smiled. "Leave it to me. I know just how to go about it."

My thoughts drifted back to Ilsa. "Can you tell me about Ilsa's affliction? I know she suffers from curvature of the spine."

"Yes. She was normal enough as a young girl. The twisting of her spine began as she entered her teen years. Her parents tried back braces and hot springs, but nothing helped."

I suppressed a shudder at the thought of back braces. My cousin Consuelo Vanderbilt had been required to wear a brace of sorts, a metal rod attached to a belt at her waist and a strap around her head, whenever she sat at her lessons as a child. She had suffered from no such affliction as Ilsa Cooper-Smith, however. Her mother, my aunt Alva, had simply wished for her to develop perfect posture. Consuelo had, along with a simmering resentment toward her mother.

"Has Ilsa ever displayed any bitterness?" I asked.

Grace considered a moment. "Not bitterness, no. I'd say resignation. Sadness, most assuredly."

"What was she like as a younger girl? Do you know?"

"Thoughtful." Grace smiled. "Studious. She loved to read."

"And Cleo?"

"Humph." Grace's eyebrows twitched; her mouth took on an ironic slant. "Not studious. Cleo was the more adventurous one. She seemed to crave excitement and loved to be around people."

"The center of attention," I suggested.

"Positively. But that's obvious in the kind of coming-out ball my sister planned for her. Had it been for Ilsa, May would have devised a much more sedate, intimate event."

I thought back to the ball, and how Ilsa remained off to the side, an observer rather than a participant, despite being the sister of the guest of honor. "There was a man at the ball who stayed beside Ilsa—"

"Patrick Floyd. He's a family friend of theirs."

"He seemed rather devoted to Ilsa. Is there an understanding between them?"

"Between Patrick and Ilsa? Heavens no. Ilsa isn't expected to ever marry. Her condition precludes her ever having children. She's been told it could kill her, poor dear."

"I know, and I'm sorry about that. She seemed rather enamored of him, but perhaps I misread the situation. He happened to mention being in mourning."

"Patrick was widowed only a year ago. His wife, Matilda, died quite suddenly. There were rumors at the time . . ." She trailed off, her lips compressing. "But I shouldn't repeat rumors."

"Actually, Grace, perhaps you should. Anything you know about the guests last night could help reveal the truth about what happened."

Grace seemed to debate this inwardly before nodding. "Some people insinuated that Matilda Floyd might have taken her own life."

I gasped; I hadn't expected any such thing. "How did she die?"

"It was a gas leak in her bedroom. Her husband was away at the time. Apparently, she went to bed one night and never woke up again. The gas line was found open with no flame."

"Was anyone else in the house with her at the time?"

"Only the servants, as far as I heard."

"An accident, or a deliberate act," I said more to myself than to Grace. "Do you have any idea why she might have committed suicide?"

"I'm truly loath to say, Emma. I never believed the whispers. He seems to be a perfectly lovely gentleman. You saw how he rescued Ilsa from the ignominy of being a wallflower."

"It was gallant of him, to be sure." I remember Ilsa saying just that—that Patrick needn't play the gallant for her. "But you mentioned whispers. Given what his wife might have done, I can only assume those whispers involved stains on Mr. Floyd's character. Am I correct?"

With a great show of reluctance, Grace nodded. "Some people believed—wrongly, I'm quite sure—that Patrick might have been dallying with another woman. That he had gone away that week to be with his paramour. But please don't repeat this to anyone."

I answered her with silence, for it was a promise I couldn't make, not if I found a link between Patrick Floyd and Cleo Cooper-Smith's death. I had learned in recent years that murder rarely occurred as an isolated incident. Rather, death seemed to follow death in a chain of violence, and this news about Mr. Floyd's wife felt too coincidental given the circumstances.

"Grace," I said, speaking slowly as thoughts took shape in my mind, "the woman Patrick might have been dallying with . . . Could it have been Cleo?"

"Good gracious, no." The idea not only took Grace aback, she seemed angered by the suggestion. I realized my logic had perhaps taken a sizable leap and started to apologize, but she had more to add. "I don't suppose you would know, but Cleo was practically engaged in the spring. His name was Oliver Kipp—perhaps you've heard of the family?"

"I have, and I know Oliver Kipp recently died in the war." The image of the young man's mother, Lorraine, trailing after John Astor last night and making mysterious demands of him flashed in my mind. "He and Cleo were engaged?"

"Not quite, but society assumed they had intentions toward each other. They had formed an attachment the previous year, before Matilda Floyd died."

While I conceded Grace's point that it was unlikely Cleo would have been involved with Mr. Floyd, I also acknowledged a third death linked to Cleo Cooper-Smith. True, Oliver Kipp had died far away on a battlefield in Cuba, but the coincidence made it impossible for me to dismiss it as irrelevant.

I had learned a lot here in a short time, information that

would require a return to Ochre Court, but which would also send me in other directions. Willing or not, Colonel Astor, Mrs. Kipp, and Patrick Floyd might provide information I needed.

"Would it be all right if I kept this for now?" I indicated the broken setting. Where was the better part of the piece, and to whom did it belong? Had Cleo come to possess it by less than honest means? Perhaps a trip to one of our local jewelers would set me on the trail to the answers. "I'll be sure to return it."

"Of course."

I left her after that, making my way down the service staircase. A woman waited for me at the bottom. She wore the black dress and starched linen apron and cap of a housemaid.

"Miss Cross, might I have a word?"

Like my own housemaid, Katie, this woman spoke with a pleasing Irish cadence. She was about my age, with raven black hair and vivid green eyes that darted side to side as she beckoned to me.

I nodded, and she introduced herself. "I'm Nora Taylor, miss, and I've a bit of information that might interest you concernin' Miss Cleo."

I, too, scanned the immediate vicinity to see if we might be overheard. Detecting no one close by, I said, "Yes, go ahead."

"I heard arguin' comin' from her bedroom yesterday mornin'." She fidgeted with the pins on her apron. "I don't know who she was havin' words with, but from the sounds of it, either her sister or her maid. The missus would never raise her voice like that, especially not to a guest, and I cannot think of another soul it could have been."

"Are you certain they were arguing? Could they have merely been excited about the ball?"

"The voices sounded riled up to me, miss."

"Can you be sure it wasn't Mrs. Goelet's daughter?"

"Oh, no, miss. Like her mam, Miss May wouldn't treat a guest so ill. I've been servin' the family for three years now, since I first landed in New York, and I've never heard an unkind word from Miss May's lips. She's a kindly girl, that one."

"And had you heard Miss Cleo arguing with anyone else since she's been here?"

"That I have not, miss. That's why it struck me as odd."

My hand went instinctively to my handbag. The broken piece of jewelry lay nestled within. Could it have provoked the argument Nora overheard? "Did you hear anything specific?"

"Well, no, not exactly, miss. The walls and doors are thick in this house. The words were muffled and all."

This information made me wish to climb back up the stairs and question Miss Ilsa and her sister's lady's maid. But I couldn't bring myself to do so, not this soon while their grief remained so fresh. Besides, what young woman didn't sometimes argue with her sister, or her maid? I'd overheard my cousin, Gertrude Vanderbilt, scolding her own maid countless times at The Breakers. Never had it led to murder or anything more than a quiet sulk for either of them.

"I know that electrician fellow's being blamed for Miss Cleo's death." Nora's eyes narrowed.

"You don't believe it?"

"I don't know what to believe, miss. He's an agreeable fellow. And people like him, and like me—we take the blame for most things, don't we?"

"Yes, Nora, I'm sorry to say you're right about that."

"I believe you want to do somethin' about it, don't you, miss?" With a sheepish look, Nora lowered her chin and peeked out at me from beneath her lashes. "I heard about what you did last summer, miss, helpin' catch that wicked murderer and all. If I can help you now, I will."

"Thank you, Nora. If you think of anything else, please telephone me. Tell the operator you wish to be connected to Gull Manor."

"I will, miss. You can be sure of that."

Before I left Ochre Court, I used the telephone. Then I left Maestro and my carriage on the property in favor of walking over to Spring Street and taking the trolley into town. The street rail brought me to Broadway, where I alighted outside the hospital on Friendship Street.

My telephone call had established that Jesse hadn't been released yet, and I must admit to a sense of relief that my visit would not take place in the intimacy of his home. He and I had never been alone in such a way, never unchaperoned by family and friends, or his fellow officers at the police station, or pedestrians on the street. Seeing Derrick and experiencing my reaction to him assured me now was not the time to encourage an understanding with Jesse.

The nurse manning the front desk waved me through and I went upstairs to the men's ward. I found Hannah sitting at Dale's bedside. His bandaged hand lay on top of the sheet. He appeared to be sleeping.

"How is he this morning?"

"In a lot of pain. The doctors are keeping him sedated." She reached up to finger the edge of her starched linen nurse's cap, then clutched her hands together in her lap. "We're still not certain about the extent of the damage. Only time will tell."

Fearing any assurances would sound hollow, I pressed her shoulder before moving down the aisle to Jesse's bed. The grin he flashed at my approach faded as he correctly read my expression. He sat up, the covers drawn to his waist, a dressing gown secured over his nightshirt. Once I settled on the stool beside his bed, he asked me what I'd learned since last night.

One by one I reviewed each name Grace and I had discussed, along with their relationship to Cleo Cooper-Smith. He seemed particularly keen on learning more about Patrick Floyd, although not for the reason I might have thought.

"His wife died a year ago," he mused aloud. "And he is well acquainted with both Cooper-Smith sisters."

"Yes, a family friend. He stayed by Ilsa's side during the ball because she isn't able to dance."

"Did he dance with Cleo?"

"Not that I saw, although Ilsa urged him to. She said she would enjoy watching him. She seemed rather enamored of him."

Jesse's chin tilted. "And he of her?"

"No, not that I observed. Kind and affectionate in a brotherly way, but I would not venture to say he returned her feelings, if indeed I read them correctly. Ilsa suffers from extreme curvature of the spine and can never have children. This makes marriage an unlikely prospect for her."

"One never knows. Someday she might meet that rare man who either doesn't wish to have children, or who has children from a first marriage."

"I hope so. A guest last night, a Mrs. Lucinda Russell, made a comment that Ilsa's coming-out ball should be next. This distressed Ilsa greatly, but it was what her sister said that drew tears. Cleo told Ilsa not to be tragic, not to be a martyr. Then she turned to Mr. Floyd with a comment about how wearisome Ilsa can be."

"That's hardly sisterly accord."

"Yet Grace Wilson said they were close." I frowned, trying to reconcile loving sisters with the cruel words Cleo had uttered. "I suppose sisters are apt to argue sometimes."

"Especially when a man stands between them."

My gaze, which had wandered to the window beside Jesse's bed, darted back to his face. I saw nothing facetious or ironic in his expression. He had meant what he said.

I, however, couldn't fathom such a thing. "Are you implying Ilsa killed her sister over Patrick Floyd?"

"It surely wouldn't be the first time jealousy led to murder."

"Oh, but—" My intended protest died unspoken. Ilsa had been in the drawing room yesterday afternoon, and had admitted to gaining entry on the sly. Cleo's unkindness at the ball had driven Ilsa away—perhaps to be sure her plan to electrify the throne would work? I didn't like having to do it, but I told Jesse what I had witnessed.

"And here I was thinking Patrick Floyd might have some connection to Cleo's death," I concluded, leaving the rest unspoken.

"And so he might, through Ilsa. And his wife . . . perhaps Ilsa wanted her gone as well. How did she die?"

"Gas inhalation. The flame on an open sconce had gone out sometime after she went to bed that night."

"Or had been extinguished deliberately. I don't suppose Miss Ilsa was in the Floyds' house that night?"

"Not according to Grace. She told me some people suspected suicide, that Mrs. Floyd had caught her husband in a dalliance." I told him about the argument Nora Taylor had overheard the morning before the ball.

"The net tightens," he replied. When I cast him a quizzical glance, he explained, "Around Miss Ilsa."

"We can't assume Cleo's argument was with her sister. As Nora pointed out, it might have been with her maid. She couldn't hear clearly enough to make a positive identification, other than that Cleo argued with another woman. And then there is this." I snapped open my bag and drew out the diamonds Grace had discovered in Cleo's nightstand. I explained how this broken piece comprised the only bit of valuable jewelry she appeared to own.

He held it in his palm. "We'll need to find the rest. It's certainly possible this argument had to do with this."

"Yes, but I can't question Ilsa, not yet."

"Give her a day or two. But no more. If she's guilty, I want to keep her off her guard."

The edge in his voice drew my scrutiny to his profile. The boyish features I'd become so familiar with and found so endearing were set and stony, almost cruel. I wondered why. This couldn't be the first time he'd been wounded in the line of duty.

Perhaps not, I realized, but never before had he sustained an injury with the potential to end his career. A police detective without full use of his hands. . . . A seeping dread turned my insides cold. What if I could no longer ply my trade, and I lost not only my ability to earn the funds I needed to survive, not only my independence, but a thing I loved. Though I had not yet achieved my dream of reporting on hard news as Nellie Bly had done, journalism ran in my very veins, a vital part of who I was.

What and who would I be if that were taken from me? What and who would Jesse be?

I reached out and ever so gently placed my hand over his. He flinched convulsively, startling me, before visibly forcing himself to relax. He even attempted a smile, albeit an empty one. The hollow reassurances I hadn't allowed myself to convey to Hannah now sprang from my lips. "You'll be fine, Jesse. This is temporary. I'm sure the doctors—"

"The doctors can do nothing but wait," he snapped. It was my turn to flinch. Remorse immediately softened his expression. His eyes darted down the ward to where Dale lay in his numbed torpor; to where Hannah sat staring adamantly down at him, willing him to heal. He lifted the hand I had touched, the fingers weak and trembling as they beckoned to me. "I'm sorry, Emma."

My fingers closed lightly around his, and for the briefest moment, their shaking stilled. "Don't be."

"Find out all you can about the sisters," he said, the vulnerability of a moment ago gone, or at least hidden beneath his policeman's exterior. I promised him I would, and promised to visit him again soon.

Chapter 6

I stopped at one of the local jewelers in town and showed him the diamonds. After studying the individual stones through his loupe, he confirmed the authenticity of the stones, declaring them of clear, quite good quality. He also agreed with the assessment that I had brought him a piece of a necklace, ruling out a bracelet due to the way the diamonds dangled from the chain connecting them. Beyond that, he could provide little insight, though he offered to repair the piece should the rest be found. I thanked him for his time and caught the eastbound trolley out of town.

Jesse's haunted expression accompanied me as I went. His words did as well. I couldn't bring myself to believe Ilsa had murdered her sister, but I did believe she might have information that could help expose Cleo's killer. I believed their father had such information as well, based on his evasiveness at the ball. I found it odd he hadn't been at Ochre Court earlier. Why hadn't he been on hand to comfort Ilsa? Was he so distraught that he'd leave his remaining daughter alone in her grief?

I wanted to learn more about his connections to Silas Griggson, both business and personal. Did he hold Griggson responsible for the tenement collapse? Would he continue to design structures for Griggson's company? Did he suspect, as I did, that Silas Griggson ordered the death of the foreman blamed for the incident?

If so, surely Randall Cooper-Smith could not have approved of his daughter marrying the man. I needed to speak with him, but the same constraints that kept me away from Ilsa prevented me from approaching her father, for now. But as Jesse had said, it helped to catch people off guard.

My visit to the hospital had supplied me with yet another reason to find Cleo's killer. I fully believed both Dale and Jesse would recover—I *had* to believe it, as there was simply no fathoming the future otherwise. Jesse's uncertainties and his shaking fingers spurred me on with wave after wave of anger. No one harmed those I cared about without fully reckoning with me.

After collecting Maestro and my carriage, I set out from Ochre Court and headed south on Bellevue Avenue, toward home. I made a stop along the way, however, one that unsettled me the moment the peaked roofline came into view. I routinely passed this house, but for the past three years I did so while averting my gaze and hurrying Barney along as much as he could be hurried.

Redwing Cottage hadn't changed much since my last visit here in the summer of 1895. The weeping beech had grown, sweeping a greater portion of lawn, while the Japanese maples provided deeper shade than they had then. The house itself, a traditional New England shingle style with a turret and wraparound veranda, had not changed at all, except perhaps for a fresh coat of paint. I shivered as I brought Maestro to a stop near the front door, and hesitated before stepping to the ground.

A voice that bordered on the edge of hysteria shrieked in my mind as the details of that day flickered and flashed like the sunlight sifting through the trees. A murder at my Vanderbilt cousins' nearby home, The Breakers, had eventually led me here that summer afternoon, a day much like this one with high, dazzling clouds racing across a silken sky, while bracing breezes skipped across Aquidneck Island from the Atlantic Ocean to Narragansett Bay. That day had forced me to accept an unpalatable truth about human nature and robbed me of whatever innocence had followed me into adulthood.

A deep breath helped banish the voice and the memories. Redwing Cottage no longer housed the dangers present then. The owners never returned to Newport nowadays, but instead rented the property to a different tenant each summer. Steadfastly, I walked up the steps and used the knocker to announce my presence. The door opened upon a footman in livery who seemed unimpressed as he looked me up and down.

"Yes?" His tone implied he considered ordering me around to the servants' entrance.

"I am Emma Cross, here to see Mrs. Kipp, please."

"Is she expecting you?"

"No. The tragic business at Ochre Court last night has sent me here."

He didn't pretend not to understand my reference. "Then you will understand that Mrs. Kipp is indisposed and not receiving."

I met the closing door with the flat of my hand. "Announce me anyway. I might be able to save Mrs. Kipp from an interview with the police." At his dubious look, I explained, "I am not here in any official capacity. I merely have some questions for her about the victim. I believe they were acquainted."

He stepped aside to allow me to enter. After a brief absence, he returned to lead me up the stairs to an all-too-familiar room—a room where I had once made myself comfortable and enjoyed a light lunch with an old friend. The furnishings then had been of white wicker and bright florals, making this space resemble a conservatory with its airy views of the ocean beyond the cliffs. The décor had been replaced with darker colors, heavier pieces. Despite the more somber atmosphere, I breathed easier.

The woman I'd come to visit sat near the open windows, her thick gray hair piled high on her head and held there by a wide scarf. Though not wearing mourning crepe, she nonetheless presented a dreary aspect in an ill-fitting tea gown of dark, nondescript colors. She turned weary eyes in my direction.

"Good morning, Mrs. Kipp. Thank you for seeing me."

"Did I have a choice?"

I didn't answer that directly, but said, "It's important, or I would not have disturbed you."

"I know you by reputation, Miss Cross." The fingers of her right hand plucked absently at her gown. Yes, I had made a point of noticing: her *right* hand, while the left draped the arm of her chair. "Have you come to learn some sordid fact about me to splash across the pages of the *Herald*?"

I'd heard such accusations before, but for some reason this time it stung. Such was not the renown I aspired to. "Not at all, Mrs. Kipp. I am . . ." I thought a moment, and settled on the truth. "I am assisting the local law enforcement with Cleo Cooper-Smith's death."

"I thought it was an accident."

"Evidence suggested it might not have been."

"And you think I killed her?" The passionless question took me aback. She didn't seem to care either way.

"I merely wish to ask you some questions about Miss Cooper-Smith and your son."

Ruddy color suffused her face and a tick above her right

eye surged to life. So changed was she from her apathy of a moment ago, I feared she might order me out. Before she could, I swept closer and began to lower myself into the chair opposite her. "May I sit?"

She turned to stare out the window. "If it'll help facilitate your errand and send you on your way, then yes."

This inhospitable reply sufficed, and I sat. "I understand your son and Miss Cooper-Smith were all but engaged last spring. Is that true?"

"What difference does it make, Miss Cross? My son is dead."

"It might make a good deal of difference, ma'am. Don't you find it a bit too much of a coincidence that both Oliver and Cleo are deceased, only a couple of weeks apart?"

A slight shrug of one shoulder formed her answer.

"Please, did they have intentions toward each other?"

"I thought so at one time, until that witch ended it." The tick pulsed, drawing her right eyebrow down sharply over her eye. "She didn't deserve him, and she doesn't deserve to be mourned, Miss Cross. Cleo Cooper-Smith killed my son, just as surely as if she had pulled the trigger at point-blank range."

I didn't understand, and perhaps unwisely said, "He died serving his country. How can that be Miss Cooper-Smith's fault?"

"She drove him to that battlefield." Her voice rose with each word. She continued more quietly, but no less vehemently. "She led Oliver on, only to then tell him he would never be wealthy enough or important enough for her. He was going to make a fine officer—he was at the top of his class at West Point. He was studying law as well. And his inheritance, though not as vast as some, was nothing to sniff at. But that greedy trollop broke his heart. He dropped out of the academy, signed on with Colonel Astor, and rushed off to war. Now he's dead, and the fault lies squarely at Cleo's feet. It's time the world knew what kind of despicable person she was."

But if wealth constituted Cleo's first priority in marriage, then why did she appear to snub Silas Griggson? Even if he repulsed her, wouldn't she have dangled him along until and unless someone equally as rich but more appealing came along?

Another question from last night continued to nag. "Mrs. Kipp, I noticed you trying to speak with Colonel Astor at the ball, but he seemed to cut you off short."

"That's none of your business, Miss Cross. It's got nothing to do with Cleo."

I didn't believe her. After all, not only did she claim Cleo sent Oliver off to war and to his death, but whatever demands Mrs. Kipp attempted to make of Colonel Astor were urgent enough to send her, a woman in deep mourning, to a social event held in honor of the very woman she claimed to despise.

"Mrs. Kipp, is there anything else you can tell me about Miss Cooper-Smith and her acquaintance with your son?"

"Such as what?"

"What first drew them together? What did they have in common?"

"In common?" Her lips turned down. "Nothing, other than they were two young people with mutual acquaintances. They attended the same functions, were thrown together frequently enough that they noticed each other. Isn't that how matches are made, Miss Cross? No one worries about commonality. Goodness, if that were a concern, who would ever marry?"

Her cynicism rankled, yet I had heard it all before from my own wealthy aunts, often in the context of finding me a husband. "In that case, in the days and weeks leading up to their parting, did you notice a difference in your son's demeanor, something that might have been a clue that all was not well between them?"

"No. Cleo's rejection was quite sudden. One day they seemed happily attached, and the next he was running off to war. I've no doubt his state of mind—his broken heart—made him an even greater target during battle. If only . . ." Her hand—again, her *right* hand—fisted and her voice plunged to a whisper. "If only that girl had died sooner, perhaps my boy would still be alive."

At home that evening, I completed my article for the *Herald*. Or I should say I finished my *first* article for the *Herald*. This would be no simple description of a noteworthy social event, but an ongoing story. I would give my employer so much more than he asked of me, and more than my readers would expect. In the past, when I worked for the Newport *Observer*, I'd fallen into the habit of tempering my articles. Mr. Millford, the editor-in-chief, had hired me to be a social columnist and any time I had tried to step beyond the boundary he set for me, I'd receive a pat on the head and an admonishment to leave the more distressing news to fellow reporter Ed Billings.

Humph. Ed Billings's articles contained far more fiction than fact, but that hadn't mattered to Mr. Millford. Perhaps I should have heeded his warnings, but stubbornness and yes, ambition, had prevailed. When I finally strayed too far off the proper path, deliberately disregarding my suitable place as a woman, he summarily fired me.

That is what had sent me to New York, only to discover James Gordon Bennett, owner of the *Herald*, wanted a more sensationalized version of the same role I had played at the

Observer. Well and good, but no more. What had I to lose? In my view, nothing of significance. True, I needed funds to run my household, to keep us clothed and fed, and to help do the same for the orphans of St. Nicholas Orphanage in Providence, but I would find a way. We would not starve. But neither would I continue to compromise my principles.

As I sat at my desk before the window that overlooked a rocky Atlantic coastline, my resolve hardened. No longer would I hold back. My articles would contain the facts—all of them. As new details came to light about what happened to Cleo Cooper-Smith and why, I would write subsequent articles until this story reached its natural conclusion—with justice and an arrest.

When I finally went to bed, it was with a new sense of satisfaction. Still, I didn't sleep well. Mrs. Kipp's parting words ran through my dreams, turning them into a series of repetitive, obsessive reckonings to which I found no solutions. *If only that girl had died sooner, perhaps my boy would still be alive.*

More than ever, Oliver Kipp's death seemed intricately linked to Cleo's. But how? What happened between them? What happened two weeks ago in Cuba? While Lorraine Kipp might have been able to answer the former question, I doubted that bitter woman could provide much insight into the latter. No, for that I needed to speak with someone who had been there. A fellow soldier. Colonel Astor. Sam Caldwell. But would either agree to speak with me? Would Colonel Astor shrug me off as he had done Mrs. Kipp at the ball?

I wouldn't give him the chance. In the morning, early, I made a telephone call to the offices of the Newport *Messenger* and asked to speak with the owner.

"Andrews here."

"Derrick, it's Emma."

Before I could explain the purpose of my call, he blurted a series of questions at me. "What is it? Are you all right? Is everyone out at Gull Manor all right? It's not about Jesse, is it? Or your friend's brother?"

"I haven't heard an update on Jesse or Dale, and the rest of us are fine. I need a favor today, if you can leave the office for a time."

I heard a soft laugh. "I own the place. Of course I can leave. Where are we going?"

"Beechwood. I have some questions for Colonel Astor, but I'm afraid he might not be forthcoming with me. I thought if you came along and pretended to interview him about his battalion's experiences in the war, I might get the answers I need."

"About what, may I ask?"

"What happened to Oliver Kipp in Santiago two weeks ago."

"He was a casualty. The *Messenger* ran his obituary."

"So did the *Herald*. But I fear neither of us knows the true story. I'm convinced there's more, and that it's somehow connected to Cleo Cooper-Smith."

"I don't see how that can be, but I'll help you. Not at Beechwood, though. I have it on good authority that Colonel Astor took up residence at Fort Adams with the rest of his men that are in Newport. I could meet you out there in . . . shall we say an hour?"

"Thank you. That would be perfect. Oh, and Derrick? Thank you for Maestro. It's very sweet of you, but it's only temporary. As soon as this investigation is over, I'll return him to you."

"You needn't."

"Yes, I do. You know I do."

Grumbling made its way over the wire. And then he said, "Well, if you must know the truth, the creature has no liking for me. Whenever I go near him, he takes a chunk out of my sleeve. He's costing me a fortune in coats. One of these days he'll chew off half my arm. You'll be doing me a great favor in keeping him."

Dressed once more in the dark, businesslike garb of a reporter, I drew Maestro up at the outer gatehouse of Fort Adams, at the southwestern tip of Aquidneck Island. On a peninsula that jutted into Narragansett Bay, the fort commanded wide-open views of Newport Harbor, the west coast of Aquidneck Island, Conanicut Island across the way, and the brisk channels where the Atlantic fed into the bay.

As I stepped down from my carriage to speak with the guard who came out to greet me, a unit of infantrymen marched past, disappearing into the fort's shadowed entryway. Built decades ago to protect our deep water harbor and the naval gateway to both Providence and Boston, Fort Adams ironically had never seen a moment's action. Not a shell, not a bullet, not even an implied threat. The place had been heavily fortified during the War Between the States, but in my lifetime only minimal forces had been stationed here.

I had visited with my father a time or two, my hand firmly in his, my eyes wide with wonderment as I'd taken in the sheer size and scope of the sprawling battlements. I'd felt impossibly small in the middle of the grassy parade, and filled with fear that, should my father's hand suddenly release mine, I'd become irretrievably lost. I had held on so tightly my fingers had ached.

In the comings and goings of carts, buggies, and men on horseback, a familiar face caught my eye. Derrick pulled up behind my own carriage and alighted in a bound. His features held an expression I'd seen on him often in the past, a combination of eagerness for adventure tempered by concern for my well-being.

"What are you getting up to now?" he asked in lieu of a proper greeting.

"Good morning to you." I touched the brim of my hat, stiffly and staunchly resisting the tug of the wind that seemed never to cease here. I turned back to the guard. I had already introduced myself as a reporter for the *Herald,* a circumstance that had seemed to impress him, for he had pulled himself up taller and puffed out his chest. "This is my associate, Mr. Derrick Andrews of the *Messenger,*" I told him now. "We are each working on stories about the Astor Battery. May we have entry to speak with the colonel?"

"I can't guarantee he'll see you, but you can go on in."

I had thought as much. Once again, Fort Adams had passed through a war without direct threat, and security would be relaxed. Derrick and I left our carriages by the guardhouse and proceeded on foot inside.

The sunlight dazzled my eyes as we emerged from the entry tunnel onto the parade, larger than any enclosed space I'd ever seen or could imagine. My fingers curled, and I only just stopped myself from reaching for Derrick's hand. Directly before us, the unit I'd seen marching into the fort now moved in formation, hoisting their weapons one minute, dropping them to their sides the next in time to a drill sergeant's rhythmic commands. Farther along the field, other battalions drilled, while men streamed in and out of countless doorways along the tall inner walls.

"Goodness," I murmured, feeling out of breath, "where do we start?"

"We ask someone."

"Who?"

Derrick grinned and rather than answer me, raised a hand and said, in his most authoritative tone, "You there. I need assistance."

A young private with pale blue eyes and a sunburned nose stopped in his tracks, changed course, and approached us. He could not be more than seventeen, and I found myself relieved he was here and not on the battlefields of Santiago. "Yes, sir?"

I bit back a smile. I'd forgotten that men of Derrick's class possessed the natural skill of commanding men whether they wore a uniform or not. From their earliest days in the schoolroom, they were instructed on the subtleties of cultivating authority of tone, posture, and expression. Taught to dominate with a mere lift of an eyebrow. The young private wasted no time in escorting us to the officers' lodgings along the northwest wall. Through the overlooking windows, I spied parlors one might have found in any of Newport's finer homes, albeit smaller. At one window, a small face surrounded by a cloud of golden hair pressed itself close to the glass, peeking out. I waved and was rewarded with a chubby hand waving in kind, accompanied by a little burst of laughter.

After knocking on a door, the private announced us to the servant who answered, who in turn announced us to her employer. Colonel John Jacob Astor IV, only son of *The* Mrs. Astor, was a classically handsome man whom one could just as easily imagine holding court in the drawing rooms of European nobility as here in these military surroundings.

He seemed happy to see Derrick—they were of course acquainted—and shook his hand. He seemed rather less appreciative of my presence, if familiar with my identity. He did not call his wife to the door, which brought to mind their tiff at the ball. Neither did he invite us to come in and sit, but rather stepped outside, asking if we would mind very much walking with him as we asked our questions. He seemed all too happy to discuss the Astor Battalion, and before long his pride in his men became apparent. In reply to Derrick's questions, he discussed the circumstances and strategy that led to the Battle of Santiago. He even spoke about the casualties and the men he lost, but when Derrick finally broached the subject of Oliver Kipp, Colonel Astor hesitated.

His gaze, direct, piercing, and unused to apologizing for anything, pinned itself to me. "This is one matter unsuitable for a lady's ears. I wouldn't wish to unduly distress Miss Cross."

After all else he'd been willing to elucidate about the war, he suddenly worried about my delicate sensibilities? And yet, this neither surprised nor frustrated me, for I'd fully expected to be dismissed at some point.

I had my response ready. "I thank you for your consideration, Colonel. Perhaps Mr. Andrews will be so kind as to provide me with the pertinent details later?"

Derrick played his part equally well. "I should be happy to share anything you find important to your article, Miss Cross, minus the more harrowing details."

"Thank you." I raised my chin to the colonel. "Would it be permissible for me to stroll along the parade and observe the goings-on? I believe my readers would be thoroughly fascinated by the workings of such a large fortress."

"Indeed, Miss Cross, if you'll be mindful of keeping out of the way." John Astor fingered his mustache as he peered down the parade. "I believe you'll find my own battalion drilling near the south end."

"Oh, how fortuitous. I should very much like to observe their formations. Thank you, Colonel." With that I swept away, but not before the slightest of winks at Derrick. Fortuitous, indeed; I had hoped the colonel's pride would extend to wishing to see a full write-up about his men in the *Herald.* I would not disappoint him, but neither would I be disappointed in my journey here today, or so I hoped as I made the long walk down the field.

I didn't need to ask anyone to point out the Astor Battery, for I recognized Captain Samuel Caldwell barking orders to the perfect rows of soldiers before him. I watched and waited, taking notes here and there, until the captain finally called out for the soldiers to be at ease. Fearing he might walk off the field, I hurried over to him, raising more than a few eyebrows and speculative titters among the ranks.

"Why, Miss Cross!" He seemed genuinely pleased to see me. He shook my hand in a light, gentlemanly grip. "What are you doing here?"

"Have you forgotten my position at the *Herald*? I'm here to inspect the troops, if I may." I let my smile fade and took on a more somber tone. "How are you, Captain, after so tragic an occurrence at Ochre Court?"

"I should be asking you that question, Miss Cross. It was a terribly sad business at the ball the other night."

"Yes, and if I allow myself to dwell on the particulars, Captain Caldwell, I'm not very well at all. But Miss Cooper-Smith was your friend. You knew her much better than I."

He hesitated over that assessment, and then nodded. "She will be greatly missed."

"Tell me, are your families connected? Did you and she grow up together?"

He again seemed slightly flustered, before offering a sad smile. "Most of the New York families share a long history together. Cleo and I had only a passing acquaintance as young boys and girls will do, but I certainly considered her one of ours, if you see what I mean."

"I believe I do. I'm so very sorry for your loss."

"Uh . . . thank you." A frown gathered between his brows. I sensed his growing discomfort as he asked, "Is there something I can do for you?"

"Oh, yes. Forgive me for suddenly appearing out of the blue like this. I came with a colleague in the newspaper business, who is right now interviewing Colonel Astor about his experiences in the war." I slipped my pencil and notepad from my handbag. "I thought perhaps I might ask you a few questions as well, if it wouldn't be too impertinent of me."

"Impertinent? Not at all, Miss Cross." A pink hue suffused his cheeks.

"Splendid. Tell me about the battalion, then. Oops!" I dropped my pencil, and watched Captain Caldwell bend over to retrieve it. He did so with his right hand. I didn't suspect the young man of being involved in Cleo's death, but even so I was glad to rule out as many people as possible.

"Thank you so much." I gestured with the end of the pencil. "I see that Colonel Astor has given you great responsibility and authority with his soldiers."

As men will do when talk turns to their particular prowess, he warmed to the discussion and provided me with the inner workings of the military unit, which I found fascinating. As we talked, another officer strolled over to us. I recognized him from Ochre Court, as he had been one of Colonel Astor's circle of acquaintances, as well as having assumed the part of an Egyptian guard during the tableau. I looked inquiringly at Captain Caldwell, hoping for an introduction. He didn't disappointment me.

"My fellow officer, Lieutenant Dorian Norris."

I allowed the newcomer to take my hand. "A pleasure," I said, and he smoothly returned the compliment. I knew the name Norris. His family was an old one, with a fortune that had originated in fur trading early in the last century. We again exchanged condolences about Miss Cooper-Smith, while I also noted that both officers wore their swords on their left sides—an indication of right-handedness.

After a very few minutes, I broached the subject I truly wished to discuss. "I understand several of your comrades did not return from Cuba . . ." They obliged me by mentioning several names, speaking in reverent tones of heroics and sacrifice. One name in particular was not mentioned, however, until I brought him up myself. "Oliver Kipp was among them, wasn't he? Hadn't he been engaged to Miss

Cooper-Smith? It's difficult to fathom such tragedy surrounding two young people with seemingly bright futures
ahead of them."

A glance darted between them, and I sensed a wall rising
between us. I hastened to breach it. "Perhaps I misunderstood their intentions. Mrs. Kipp seemed to imply they had
formed an attachment. I do wish to have my facts straight
before I return to New York." My implication, of course,
was that I intended to include details about the pair in my articles for the *Herald*. If they in turn assumed I would devise
such details to suit the voracious appetites of my readers, so
much the better. I waited for them to correct any misconcep-
tions they believed I had formed.

The younger of the two, Lieutenant Norris, tugged his
sleeves lower and cleared his throat. "That was true, yes. For
a time. But before we all signed up with Astor's Battery,
Oliver ended things with Cleo. At least, that's what I'd heard
at the time. I myself was not privy to the confidences of either of them."

"*He* ended it?" My surprise was genuine. According to
Mrs. Kipp, Cleo had broken Oliver's heart. Had Oliver
spread a different story among his male friends to save face?
"Is it true he dropped out of West Point to sign up?"

Sam Caldwell compressed his lips and nodded. "It was all
quite sudden and surprising. Oliver might have attained the
rank of captain had he finished his studies and training, but I
suppose the call to serve his country in the war proved irre-
sistible for him. As for Miss Cooper-Smith, they certainly
seemed as attached as any couple I've known, so yes, it astonished me when they halted their plans."

I noticed Lieutenant Norris nodding in agreement as the
captain spoke, suggesting both men had known Oliver Kipp
well enough to be familiar with his personal life.

"One wonders, then, if perhaps events beyond their control separated the pair," I said with a pensive tilt of my head, "since by all accounts it appears the couple had been very much in love."

Lieutenant Norris frowned. "Why all these questions about Oliver Kipp, Miss Cross?"

"Anyone connected with Miss Cooper-Smith is of interest, Lieutenant."

"We thought you were here to inquire about the war," the lieutenant persisted.

"And Astor's Battery," Captain Caldwell added.

"And so I am. But the stories are connected, aren't they? After all, Oliver Kipp died a hero's death on the battlefield of Santiago, did he not? My readers will appreciate anything you gentlemen can tell me about that."

Yet another look skipped between them, and Captain Caldwell blanched.

"I . . . uh . . ." He absently touched the brim of his cap. "I didn't exactly see what happened."

"But you were there. You must have heard from others what happened," I coaxed him. I turned to the other young man. "What about you, Lieutenant? Did you witness what happened?"

"I'm afraid not," he said stiffly. "In the midst of battle, all is confusion and smoke, noise and desperation. And . . . the death of a comrade is painful to speak about. I'm sure you can understand that, Miss Cross."

His sudden hostility, though subtle, was nonetheless palpable. I nodded and lowered my gaze. "I do. But I am not wrong, am I? Oliver Kipp died a hero?"

"Of course he did. If you'll excuse me, Miss Cross, I must return to the men." Sam Caldwell tipped his hat to me and strode away. As he reached the men he shouted an order that quickly returned them to formation.

"I suppose I should let you go as well, Lieutenant," I said to the other man. He was looking past me, his attention diverted to somewhere along the fort's south wall.

"Excuse me, Miss Cross." Before I could reply, he set off at a brisk pace. I turned to follow him with my gaze, and realized I was not the only woman to visit Fort Adams today.

Chapter 7

Although officers and their families enjoyed residences at the fort, I immediately saw that this newcomer was no officer's wife. In fact, even from a distance I recognized her—from Ochre Court.

The woman in the sensible dark dress carried a basket over one arm, and as Lieutenant Norris reached her, she moved aside a colorful fabric drape. He took something from the basket—a baked good of some sort, I surmised—held it beneath his nose, and took a bite. The woman laughed, the sound barely reaching me. Arm in arm, they turned to stroll along the edge of the parade, until they blended into the shadows and commotion of the south wall.

I might not have given the matter a second thought, except the woman in question served as lady's maid to none other than Ilsa Cooper-Smith, as well as Cleo, before she died. I had encountered her in passing several times on the day of the ball, though we had not had occasion to converse.

A lady's maid visiting an officer of good family? Perhaps Ilsa sent her here with treats for the soldiers. That seemed unlikely, under the circumstances. Besides, they were walking arm in arm. Though common sense declared her appearance here too much of a coincidence to be connected with Cleo's death, I reminded myself that I had waited a day to come to Fort Adams for exactly that reason.

Deciding to follow them, I hurried in their direction. True, I'd lost sight of them in the deep shadows and steady stream of soldiers, but I trusted I would come upon them shortly. I had my excuse at the ready: I had seen Miss Ilsa's maid and wished to convey a message to her.

Except that I didn't come upon them. When I reached the area where I believed I'd find them, they were nowhere in sight. Several doorways entered the three-story structure. I judged which of them had mostly likely been their destination and ventured inside. Cool, damp darkness closed around me. I blinked as my eyes grew accustomed to the scant light. Several corridors fanned away in different directions. Several soldiers hurried along one of them, and I appealed to one of them for assistance.

"Excuse me, I suppose I shouldn't be here, but I'm looking for a lieutenant and a young woman."

He looked scandalized. "You must be mistaken. There shouldn't be any young women in this part of the fort, ma'am. Yourself included, if you'll excuse me for saying. It's not safe. You'd best go along now."

"Yes, thank you. I'll go . . ." Luckily, he breezed by me and kept going, apparently trusting me to retrace my steps. I most assuredly did not, but ventured deeper into the building, lured on by the very sort of voices I shouldn't have been hearing, according to my helpful soldier.

They were little more than whispers, but I heard enough to identify one as male, the other as female. Were they merely the endearments of circumspect lovers? That I couldn't say, for the actual words disintegrated as they traveled the stony corridors.

As I went, the sounds of the bustling fort began to fade, and I realized I must be in a little used area during the day, or perhaps not meant to be used except in times of siege. I remembered from my youthful foray here with my father that Fort Adams was not only the largest, but one of the most impenetrable fortresses ever built. I believed myself to be in the southeast quadrant, where a system of tunnels, bastions, ditches, and tenailles rendered invasion virtually impossible.

Led on by the whispers, I passed several doorways and forks. The seeping chill told me I was descending deeper into the bowels of the structure, and I was grateful I'd worn my somber skirt and jacket rather than a summer frock. Once again, I stopped to listen and this time heard nothing but the whoosh of air rushing through the subterranean byways and the occasional drip-drip of moisture. I had obviously gone too far and turned to make my way back. Proceeding at a confident pace, I reached a second fork. Here I hesitated. From which way had I come?

I had no inkling, and so chose the one I believed most likely correct and hoped for the best. It wasn't long, however, before the increasing damp and cold dashed those hopes. Worse, the tunnel narrowed, the ground roughened, and the ceiling dropped until I had to hunch or risk hitting my head on the arching stonework. I turned around again, only to find myself in yet another cramped space whose walls stretched into utter darkness.

My heart began to pound in my throat and reverberate against my temples. Images of crypts formed in my mind, of being trapped beneath stone and earth, cut off from light and air. I was well and truly lost within this maze, and I had no one to blame but my own stubborn foolishness.

Or did I? It occurred to me that I might have been lured here. Had Lieutenant Norris and Ilsa's maid seen me pursuing them? Had they led me deep beneath the fort with their whispers, only to double back themselves and leave me to wander aimlessly?

But surely, surely the way could not be so impossible. Men were sent down here, and they returned to the daylight, didn't they? So did my common sense reassure me as I pressed my hands to my bosom to calm my erratic heart.

In an attempt to gain my bearings, I stood motionless and held my breath, for even that slight sound created deafening echoes in the confined space. And then I heard the voices again—except no, these were different. No longer did the high tones of a woman make their way to me, but instead the rumbling murmurs of two men. How could that be? I heard nothing else: no footsteps, no rustlings or other noises to suggest they were somewhere close by. Only their voices, hissing and hollow, flowing with the air that continually swept the tunnels.

As my eyes further adjusted to this more profound darkness, a hint of light formed several yards ahead of me. I went to it to discover a shaft, high on the wall where it met the arched ceiling. The light remained negligent at best, but fresh air brushed my cheeks. Such shafts must be a regular occurrence along the tunnels; hence the ever-flowing air. *At least I would not suffocate.*

Another memory came to me, and suddenly I realized I had stumbled down into Fort Adams's ingenious listening tunnels, a little known defense system wherein anyone positioned here would be able to hear the enemy attempting to breach the outworks.

Still, I should not be able to hear anything as subtle as conversation, yet the voices continued to travel down the shaft. They must be directly above me, then, in the tenaille between the outer walls. Once more holding my breath, I stood on tiptoe and tilted my head to place my ear as close to the shaft as I could reach. Instinct prodded me to call out for help, but another tendency, honed by my experiences over the past three years, cautioned me to remain silent and listen. It proved the better course.

"Stop worrying, will you?" Anger punctuated the command. "You'll . . . into trouble."

". . . questions . . . lead to no good."

"She's . . . to ask questions. Doesn't matter."

"Too close . . ."

I clenched my teeth in frustration. Who stood above me? What were they discussing?

"No one . . . expose the truth . . . besides . . . accident . . ." The anger had left this voice, replaced by a placating tone.

"Suppose . . . she does . . ."

". . . Won't, I tell you . . . promise . . . if you'll . . . keep silent."

The voices faded, and I heard nothing more, not even their footsteps although I assumed they had left the immediate area. Who were they? Sam Caldwell and Dorian Norris? I had visibly agitated them with my questions about Oliver Kipp's death. Had that been what one of the voices termed an accident? At the same time, however, there had been another reference to the *truth*, which negates the notion of an accident.

Or could they—whoever they were—have been talking about Cleo's death, or something else entirely? What other *accidents* had occurred recently? I could think of none significant enough to send two soldiers seeking the privacy of a grassy tenaille between the battlements. Had something happened here, at the fort? And about whom were they speaking when one of them mentioned a *she*, and *questions*? Me?

With such answers unlikely to appear to me out of the cool, inky dampness, I once more set my attentions on remaining calm and finding my way out. While I searched, I could not have said how much time passed. On the one hand, panic crouched inside me like a wild dog ready to spring, while on the other, the voices echoed over and over again in my mind as I tried in vain to sort out their meaning.

Forcing myself to stay calm and pay closer attention to the minute changes in the elevation of the hard-packed earth beneath my feet, I found it possible to plot a course upward and, I prayed, outward. Which is not to say frequent dips and sudden changes in direction didn't threaten to drown me in despair. I kept on until a far-off glimmer of daylight prompted me to suck in a great gulp of air and hasten my steps.

I emerged winded, stumbling, and blinded by the sunlight. I didn't care. Relief flowed through me like my uncle Cornelius's finest brandy, deliciously soothing while at the same time fortifying. The grass beneath my feet might as well have been the most luxurious of carpets.

"Emma! There you are."

I turned toward the voice, glimpsed dark hair, darker eyes deepened by concern, was swept up in the scent of shaving soap and hair tonic, and felt the breath leave me at the crush of strong arms. My legs sagged and I relished the hard cushion of Derrick's chest against my cheek.

"Where were you? I've been looking for you. I was worried."

I pointed. "In there."

I felt rather than saw the shake of his head, sensed rather than heard his exasperation. "Why?"

"I'll tell you, but not here. Not now." Blinking, welcoming the return of my vision, I scanned the parade. Men continued bustling about, units drilled, officers shouted orders. Nothing had changed in my absence, except that Astor's Battery no longer occupied the area, and Captain Caldwell and Lieutenant Norris were nowhere to be seen. I lamented an opportunity lost. If not for my attempt to follow Lieutenant Norris and the maid, I might have questioned some of the foot soldiers of Astor's Battery about Oliver Kipp's death. Perhaps another opportunity would present itself.

I stepped away from Derrick, forcing his arms to fall away. Perhaps I moved too brusquely, for his expression fell. Ignoring the questions in his eyes, I said, "Let's be gone. We'll go to Gull Manor. We can talk there."

I silently thanked Derrick for not mentioning my subterranean foray to Nanny. The experience had drained me and I had no energy left to bear her well-meaning admonishments. I wanted only to sip her strong Irish tea and sink into the comfort of my tattered parlor sofa.

Derrick sat opposite me, Patch's head against his knee. In quiet tones I told him what had lured me into the tunnels and what I heard while there. My frustrations once more surged at my inability to identify the voices or draw conclusions from their conversation.

Then it was Derrick's turn. "Colonel Astor was more forthcoming than I'd expected."

"Was he willing to speak about Oliver Kipp? Captain Caldwell and Lieutenant Norris certainly were not."

He nodded pensively. "I could see it pained him to do so. Understandably. Oliver froze in battle, and then for some unknown reason simply stood up in the line of fire."

"What? By all accounts he died a hero's death."

"Not all accounts," he said softly. He stroked Patch's ears.

I took in this revelation, or tried to. I considered again

what those voices had said. *No one . . . expose the truth . . . accident . . .* If they were speaking of Oliver, they might only wish to protect his memory, to allow him his hero's death in the minds of those who had cared about him. His mother . . .

"Oh, Derrick. At the ball, Mrs. Kipp had adamantly tried to speak with the colonel, but he cut her rather bluntly."

"I would expect so. He confided that she wants the reports to reflect his heroism with full honors, but Astor being Astor, he refuses to falsify records."

"That poor woman." I frowned, remembering my conversation with her. "She blames Cleo. Says she broke his heart and drove him to join up, and if not for her, Oliver would still be alive." I sipped my tea and drew a deep breath. "She said, 'If only that girl had died sooner, perhaps my boy would still be alive.'"

Derrick stared down at the floor. "Mothers will say things."

"I know. But we can't discount the comment. Not in light of what happened to Cleo."

"Do you believe Lorraine Kipp has the know-how to rig an electrocution?"

This got my back up and I said, forcefully, "The only person involved who has true technical know-how is Dale Hanson, and I do not believe he is guilty."

"Nor do I." He spoke apologetically, then met my gaze. Something in his expression had turned wistful. "Emma, what happened back at the fort?"

The sudden change of subject took me aback. Part of me knew exactly what he meant, but the part of me that instinctively guarded against admissions of the heart pretended ignorance. "What do you mean? I told you what happened."

"No. Why did you pull away from me so abruptly? Have you decided . . . ?"

"I've decided nothing." The words snapped out of me. Even Patch lifted his head to stare. I closed my mouth, breathed, and continued more calmly. "That is the point. Please don't make me repeat all my reasons for my indecision. And we were both distraught at the time."

He shifted in his chair, looking uncomfortable. "Could you not accept the concern of a friend?"

"Yes, certainly. But it was more than that and you know it. It would be wrong of us—wrong of *me*—to allow my fears to become an excuse for intimacy. In the past three years since we met, we have been apart for two of them, you in Italy and me in New York."

He laughed softly. "And so once again we are to start over."

I drained my teacup and set the cup and saucer on the table before me, perhaps with a too-loud rattle. "You needn't do anything you don't wish to do. I have tried to make that clear. I'm simply not ready. I'm sorry, but I am not. My career—"

"I never do anything I don't wish to do."

I sat back. "No, of course you don't."

"And neither do you," he said with resignation. "Nor would I wish you to."

"But . . ." I prompted.

"Pardon?"

"I believed I heard a *but* in your tone."

He regarded me with his typically lopsided smile. "But I thought perhaps seeing Jesse in such dire straits might have—"

"Might have made up my mind for me? No. I won't let extenuating circumstances force me into rash decisions. I'll act with a cool head, thank you."

His face unreadable, he gently disengaged from Patch, rose, and circled the table to sit beside me on the sofa. Taking my hand, warming it with both of his palms, he leaned close. "A cool head you say?"

I laughed, even as a delicious sensation crept through me, and I silently admitted he had a point. He straightened without waiting for an answer and became all business. "So then, what's next?"

Happily, I covered my discomfiture with a ready answer. "I'll be returning to Ochre Court. I want to speak with Cleo and Ilsa's maid and find out what she was doing at the fort."

Nanny soon poked her head into the parlor to announce lunch was served.

"I've got a nice butternut squash soup and apple crumble for dessert," she said, and crooked her finger. "Come along, you two."

It did my heart good to see how watching Derrick enjoy her cooking lit up Nanny's lined face. I also relished Derrick's enjoyment, sincere as it was, knowing full well he had grown up with the finest of Parisian chefs, yet was more than willing to sit at our kitchen table and eagerly accept seconds of Nanny's plain New England cooking.

That afternoon when I returned to Ochre Court, I once more went to the side door. The housekeeper didn't seem pleased by my reappearance, but she nonetheless called up to Ilsa's maid and asked her to come belowstairs. The woman then escorted me into the upper servants' dining room to wait. Only a few minutes later, the sandy-haired woman I had seen at the fort, and here prior to that, turned the corner into the room. "Yes? Miss Cross, is it? What can I do for you?"

She didn't bother hiding the impatience in her questions, obviously wishing me to know she had other things to do. I understood. A lady's maid's duties allowed for very little free time during the day. And yet . . .

"You were at Fort Adams this morning."

She had been fingering a loose strand of hair, but now she

dropped her hand and drew herself up. She looked me up and down as quick as you please, and apparently made her judgment. "I don't see as that's any of your business."

"Were you there on an errand for your employer?"

"Again, Miss Cross, I don't see how—"

"Did you see me there? You and Lieutenant Dorian Norris? That *is* who you went there to see, is it not?"

"I have work to do." She turned about, then froze in the doorway when I spoke again.

"I'm sure I don't have to remind you a young woman is dead, Miss . . ."

She turned slowly around. Crimson stained her cheeks. I'd at least gotten her attention. "It's Tate. Camille Tate, not that it's any concern of yours."

"Perhaps not, Miss Tate. I'd be happy to refer this matter to the police."

"My being at Fort Adams has nothing to do with what happened to Miss Cleo." Despite her obvious reluctance, she approached the table where I sat and looked down at me.

I held her gaze. "Did you see me there?"

She shook her head. "No. I never saw you."

"Are you certain about that? You and the lieutenant disappeared awfully quick. Where did you go?"

"We didn't go anywhere. Women aren't allowed inside the buildings." She angled her chin. "In your line of work, Miss Cross, you should know that."

I decided to let the matter drop, for now. "What were you doing there, then?"

"I had the morning off while Miss Ilsa was resting. It's no one's business what I do on my time off, not yours nor the police's."

"Are you certain about that? If you're traced to the events that led to Miss Cooper-Smith's death, it will most assuredly be the police's business."

With a loud scrape, she pulled back a chair and slumped down into it. "All right, yes, I went to see Dorian. Lieutenant Norris, that is. I brought him some muffins the cook here baked. But please don't say anything. I'll get in trouble."

"For taking the muffins or for visiting the lieutenant?"

She blew out a breath, floating that loose strand beside her face. "Both. You see . . ." She leaned forward, her hands clasped. "Have I your discretion, Miss Cross?"

"As far as I am able," I replied in an admittedly imperious tone. I had her, and I knew it. Perhaps she deserved to be unnerved. I hadn't dismissed the possibility that she and Dorian Norris purposely lured me into Fort Adams's tunnels.

"Dorian and I . . . we've been courting since before the war started," she said. "Oh, it's not like it sounds—a maid and an officer. We intend to marry, Miss Cross. But . . ."

"Yes? Have you encountered an obstacle?" I knew quite well there would be many obstacles to such a marriage, but I wished to hear it from her.

"His parents would never approve, and since they control his allowance, we've had to wait and keep everything a secret. Then the war delayed our plans even more. And Cleo—Miss Cooper-Smith—she wouldn't have approved either. Nor Miss Ilsa." She sat back against the chair, allowing her shoulders to sag. She expelled another breath laden with resentment. "Lady's maids aren't supposed to have romantic interests. We're supposed to be at our mistress's beck and call always, for the rest of our lives or until we're dismissed and tossed out on our ears."

She would never have dared display such bitterness before her employers or even her fellow servants, but I couldn't fault her for it. The wealthy set rarely stopped to think of the happiness or even the welfare of their servants; they expected a life of ease and convenience and it was the servant's job to provide it—at whatever the cost.

I folded my hands on the table before me. "What can you tell me about Oliver Kipp's death?"

Crimson once more spread like a red tide through her cheeks. "Nothing."

"Come now. Surely Lieutenant Norris has confided in you about what happened."

"Only that Mr. Kipp died in the battle."

"Then why does everyone, yourself included, balk at the question?"

"I'm not balking. I don't know anything."

"So you admit there is more to know."

"I'm not—"

It was my unfortunate luck that at that moment, one of the bells on the board right outside the door jingled. Camille jumped up and hurried over to see who had rung.

"That's Miss Ilsa. I have to go." With that, she scurried away.

Assuming she was lying, I went outside the room to view the board. The bell rang again. The placard beneath it read GUESTROOM 2. It very probably was Ilsa Cooper-Smith summoning her maid.

The housekeeper must have been keeping an eye out, for she approached me now with pinched lips and a disapproving expression. "Will that be all, Miss Cross?"

I hesitated. It couldn't have been more apparent that Camille had been lying than if she wore a sign to that effect on her forehead. And yet, I had once more made note of which hand she favored—her right. Did that rule her out? Perhaps not; perhaps I'd been wrong in my assumption about the individual who wrapped the wire around Cleo's throne.

"No," I said, much to the housekeeper's obvious dismay. "You know I'm here because of what happened to

Mrs. Goelet's guest?" I purposely phrased it that way—Mrs. Goelet's guest—to appeal to the woman's loyalties.

She nodded. "I do. Mrs. Goelet is still quite beside herself. If you're about to ask to see her, I'm afraid I cannot allow it."

Though I wondered about the validity of a housekeeper's power to restrict her mistress's visitors, I did realize she could summon any number of footmen to block my entrance to the upstairs rooms. "It's not Mrs. Goelet I wish to see. In fact, I don't wish to see anyone at the moment." I lowered my voice, as much to prevent others from hearing as to invite the housekeeper into my confidence. I had a hunch this astute and no-nonsense woman would sense something in Camille that garnered her disapproval. "Would you allow me to take a look at Miss Tate's bedroom?"

"Why? Has she done something untoward?"

A secret engagement would certainly qualify as *untoward* in this woman's view, but I decided to keep Camille's secret for now. "She tended to Miss Cleo Cooper-Smith, and I am assisting Detective Whyte with the investigation, at least until he has recovered from his injuries."

She nodded in solemn comprehension. "Follow me."

I admit to hesitating when I realized she headed for the elevator. However, she didn't pause as she opened what resembled an ordinary paneled door, then slid a collapsible gate to one side and stepped in. Setting aside my trepidation of the conveyance, I hurried to catch up to her, though when she gripped the lever and set the box in motion, my fingers curled into fists until my nails bit into my palms.

She slowed the car and gradually brought it even with the third-floor threshold. The gallery here consisted of low, elaborately gilded archways that shielded much of the activity here from the floors below. But it was along a secondary hallway, one that appeared reserved for upper servants, that she briskly led me. She stopped before a door and opened it with all the authority of her position as housekeeper.

"I'll have to remain with you, Miss Cross."

"That's perfectly all right." I went into the room, which contained only one bedstead, dresser, and a washstand. With a look at the housekeeper, who gave a nod of approval, I began going through the dresser. The usual things revealed themselves to me, and I found nothing to incriminate Camille in any way. The washstand could hide nothing, as it contained no drawers or cabinets. I quickly examined the walls for any sign of an opening panel, but there were none. Then I turned to the bed.

The housekeeper surmised my intent, for she moved from the doorway to stand at the other side of the mattress. As one, we knelt and slid our hands beneath the mattress, as far as they could go. We began at the iron headboard and worked our way down. My outstretched hands came in contact with nothing but linens. But the housekeeper went still about a yard from the footboard.

"Miss Cross."

She held a velvet drawstring bag, of a deep midnight blue color, and was working the strings open. I rose and circled the bed. Before I saw what spilled across her palm, I had already guessed what it might be.

"I knew there was something about that girl that couldn't be trusted." The housekeeper held out her hand to me. A platinum chain dripped diamonds across her fingers. "Mrs. Goelet and Miss Ilsa will hear of this right away. That little thief—"

"Please say nothing for now." I reached for my handbag where I had set it on the bed, opened it, and drew out the broken setting I'd found in Cleo's room. When I held it next to the larger piece, there could be no mistaking that they belonged together. "Look at this. I found it in Miss Cleo's room."

"Why, Camille not only stole it, she broke it, too. Even so, the stones must be worth a fortune." She looked me directly in the eye. "Tell me why her treachery should not be revealed this very minute, and the brazen hussy hauled off to jail."

"I need to discover what this means first," I said. "If Camille stole it from her mistress, and Miss Cleo discovered the theft, it could very well have been a reason for Camille to commit murder."

The woman's hand flew to her mouth. "Murder?"

I made a snap decision. "Surely you've heard the whispers that Miss Cleo's death was no accident."

She hesitated before nodding. "Isn't that all the more reason to expose Camille's theft?"

"The only thing we know for certain about this necklace is that it cannot belong to Camille. Since I found the broken fragment in Miss Cleo's room, we can safely assume it belonged to her. But someone could have put the necklace here in attempt to frame Camille. Or Camille might have stolen it, but it could still have nothing to do with Miss Cleo's death. Either way, the less information that reaches the murderer's ears the better. We don't want to alert him or her that we have any leads."

"Oh, yes, I do see. Then what do we do with it?" She issued a challenge with a lift of her eyebrow. Clearly she didn't quite trust me, not entirely.

To put her mind at ease, I said, "Perhaps we should leave it where you found it, for now. Keep an eye on Camille. If she leaves the house, check to see if the necklace is still here. If it isn't, telephone me at my home. You may leave a message if I'm not there. I live with my housekeeper and maid-of-all-work. I trust them both implicitly. Oh, and . . ."

She guessed my reason for trailing off. "I'm Mrs. Hendricks."

"Mrs. Hendricks, please also keep a close eye on Miss Ilsa."

She had poured the necklace back into the bag and leaned over to slide the parcel back beneath the mattress. At my words she looked up and froze. She asked no questions and I saw no need to explain. We both knew I had placed on her an onerous burden.

Chapter 8

✦

Katie finished bringing out dinner and took her own seat at the table. I ran a lax household in my aunt Alice Vanderbilt's opinion, but ever since Katie Dylan had come to me—after being dismissed by Aunt Alice's housekeeper at The Breakers—I had come to think of her more as a younger sister than merely my maid. She had been pregnant and terrified three years ago, and after losing the child, both devastated and relieved. And all the more devastated because of her relief.

I asked Nanny what she knew about Camille Tate. She sliced off a thin piece of pot roast and set it on her plate. "Very little. She's not a Newport girl."

"That much I know. But has there been any talk about her?"

Nanny chewed and shook her head slowly. "Nothing to make you blink twice. But no one enters this city without my circle knowing about it."

Nanny's circle, as she called it, or network, as I thought of it, consisted of servants from nearly every notable house in Newport. Most of them had grown up here in the city, and

Nanny had known them for decades. Tidings about the social set, good and bad, traveled this network in the same way an ocean breeze sweeps the island. They had little need of telephones, which most of them didn't entirely trust anyway. At the markets, apothecaries, and tradesmen's shops, on the sidewalks and trolleys, stories and rumors forged their trails, invisible to all but those along this trusted route. The servants knew things about the quality they themselves didn't know about each other.

"Stealin' a diamond necklace . . ." Katie sipped her water, drawn from our well beside the house. "How can she ever think to get away with a thing like that?"

"If she stole it, and it wasn't placed in her room to incriminate her, my question is did she steal it before or after Miss Cooper-Smith died?"

"And carryin' on with an officer," Katie continued as if I hadn't spoken. "Someone ought to remind that lass of her place, and soon."

I studied Katie as she continued eating as if she had said nothing out of the ordinary. Her linen cap hardly contained her spiraling auburn hair, and a faint dusting of powder had done little to hide her freckles. Though I valued her place in my household, I hoped someday she would meet a man and make a life for herself. I set my fork on my plate. "Katie, have you considered that perhaps Camille and Lieutenant Norris aren't carrying on, as you say, but truly care for each other?"

She gave me a dumbfounded stare. "He's a Knickerbocker, isn't he?"

I nodded. "But what has that got to do with a young man's feelings, or a young woman's worthiness?"

"But she's a thief." Katie looked to Nanny for consensus, but Nanny only watched us with a vague expression.

"*Maybe* she is a thief. As I said, I don't know for certain. Besides, that's another matter. We're talking about who may consort with whom. I see no reason why a perfectly respectable young woman of limited means cannot marry a respectable young man of abundant means, if they both wish it."

"But you know what they say about such women, Miss Emma. They call them gold diggers. Like . . ."

I raised my eyebrows at her. "Like whom?"

Katie lowered her chin and stared down at her plate. "Never mind. I spoke out of turn."

I continued studying the top of her cap and the fiery blush just visible on her downcast face. It didn't take many guesses to realize she had been referring to my own friend and cousin's wife, Grace Wilson. Despite Grace's family being vastly well off, she and her sisters—and even their brother, Orme—were the objects of some very unkind accusations merely because their father had amassed the family's wealth, rather than some ancestor several generations removed. Society gossips called them the *Marrying Wilsons*, because each sibling had married prosperously. For myself, I saw no difference between that and my aunt Alva forcing her daughter, Consuelo, to marry a duke, or my cousin Gertrude marrying Harry Payne Whitney. Though the latter couple had found happiness and the former had not, neither had married initially for love.

"Katie," I said gently, and waited for her to look up. "If you were to meet a Knickerbocker and the two of you wished to marry, I would not raise a whisper in objection."

Her blush deepened, became alarmingly scarlet. "It'll never happen," she murmured. "A nice merchant or tradesman would be lovely, though."

As the meal progressed, I brought up the other things I had learned. "I'd like to know more about Patrick Floyd's wife and how she died."

"That I do know a bit about," Nanny said. "There wasn't a servant in that house who believed it was an accident."

"Could one of the servants have been at fault, either intentionally or unintentionally?"

Nanny gave my question a moment's serious consideration, then shook her head. "The only person who would have been in the room with Mrs. Floyd before she retired for the night would be her personal maid, a woman who had been with the Floyds for several years and came to them with impeccable references."

"Do you know where she went after Mrs. Floyd's death?"

"I'm told she's taken the year off. Mr. Floyd paid her a handsome severance fee. I don't wonder why," she added with a knowing glint.

"What does that mean?"

"Well . . ." Nanny leaned a bit over the table toward me. "I heard from Mrs. Fish's second-floor maid who heard it from her cousin, who worked as a footman for the Floyds in New York, that they all suspected a dalliance on Mr. Floyd's part."

"Yes, I know."

Nanny looked disappointed that she hadn't shocked me.

"But with whom?" I sighed. "Could it have been Cleo Cooper-Smith?"

Katie looked up at that. "Why her?"

"Only because these people seem so interconnected. And then there's the fact that she had been practically engaged to Oliver Kipp. His mother told me she broke it off, but his fellow soldiers, the captain and the lieutenant, claim he did." With my fork, I moved potatoes around on my plate. "Perhaps he discovered she had not been true to him, that she wasn't the unspoiled girl he had believed."

"Because she had been carrying on with Mr. Floyd a year ago?" Nanny pursed her lips in obvious skepticism.

"Maybe they were *still* carrying on," I countered. "Nothing I've learned so far about Cleo Cooper-Smith suggests she had been an innocent, proper young lady. A broken engagement, a piece of a broken diamond necklace hidden away in a bedside cabinet . . . She had secrets, and I believe she had some sort of plan she never had time to implement."

Katie, her plate empty, stood up. "I'll start clearin' the dinner things and get dessert."

I waited for her to leave through the pantry before saying to Nanny, "I suppose I shouldn't discuss such matters in front of Katie. It makes her uncomfortable, dear soul."

"What you shouldn't do, Emma, is put ideas into her head. A Knickerbocker, indeed." Nanny once more pursed her lips, this time with a shake of her head.

I opened my mouth to defend my position, but no words came out. Hadn't I counseled Brady not long ago against setting his sights on marrying a woman of that class, because he'd never fully be accepted as one of them? What about my own qualms about ever being truly welcomed into Derrick's family? Unfortunately, Nanny was right. My reassurances to Katie had been idealistic at best, misguided at the worst. As for Camille Tate and Dorian Norris, how they proceeded was their business, and mine to neither approve nor judge.

The ringing of the telephone saved me from having to respond at all. I eagerly hurried away.

In the hallway, I ducked into the alcove beneath the stairs and grabbed the ear trumpet from its cradle. "Yes? Emma Cross here."

A throat clearing erupted from the device, prompting me to whisk it away from my ear. From several inches away, then, I heard, "Emma, it's Joe Millford. Do you have a moment?"

My former boss? What could *he* possibly want? I pulled

the ear trumpet back in place. "What can I do for you, Mr. Millford?"

"I was wondering if you might stop by the office sometime soon. I'd like to speak with you."

My heart began racing and my pulse points thumped. I sucked in a deep breath and let it out slowly. I willed myself to remain calm as I responded, "I suppose I might be able to manage that, sir. Do you have a time in mind?"

"Tomorrow morning?"

I was close to hyperventilating. I pressed my free hand to my mouth and breathed through my fingers to slow my rate of respiration. "I do believe I have might some free moments in the morning, yes."

"Good, glad to hear it. See you in the morning, then. I'll tell Donald I'm expecting you."

Need I say I slept very little that night? A year ago, Mr. Millford had summarily fired me for crossing a boundary he, and many others, felt no woman had a right to cross. The results I had achieved hadn't mattered a whit. And in the end, he hadn't been protecting me from myself, as was his claim, so much as protecting his male sensibilities from the notion of a woman daring to presume what might be best for herself.

So then . . . what could I expect from him now? That Mr. Millford might offer me my job back as society columnist? That he might offer me a position as a real reporter, covering all manner of news in town? The lift of my spirits at the latter and the sinking of my stomach at the former left me tossing and turning well toward morning.

I'm also rather ashamed to admit how much time and care I put into preparing for this meeting. Several outfits lay across my bed, along with a selection of hats, gloves, and brooches. Nanny came to help, and her suggestions of something fem-

inine yet professional, fastidious yet indifferent, only confused me more.

"Look your best, but don't look as if you tried too hard,"
she clarified. She made a quick assessment. "Wear your blue,
with the houndstooth scarf, the onyx brooch, and the gray
silk hat with the burgundy ribbon."

I studied each of her selections and then, pushing other
items out of the way, arranged them together on the coverlet.
I grinned. "You're right. That will do nicely."

"Of course I am. Let's get you dressed and on your way."

Before I left Gull Manor, I stepped around back to visit
Barney. Katie had already put him on his lead in the yard,
where he could stroll around the old scarlet oak tree and
munch crispy dandelion greens, sedge grass, and the long,
pointy leaves of the deep purple buddleia. He lifted his head
as I approached. Did I only imagine it, or did his liquid brown
eyes hold a mournful quality, tired and sad? I ran my hand
down his warm neck, and he swung his head around to rest
his chin on my shoulder. I felt a deep sigh rush out of him.

"What is it, boy?" Suddenly alarmed, I stepped back to
fully view him. I checked both eyes for clarity, his mouth,
his nose. I wrapped my arms around his neck and pressed
my ear against him to listen to his breathing. At the slam of
the kitchen door, I turned around to see Katie coming out
with the laundry. "Katie, how has Barney seemed to you?
I'm wondering if I need to call Dr. Sheehan."

She set her basket down in the laundry yard and crossed
the lawn to me. "I don't think a veterinarian can cure what
ails our Barney, Miss Emma."

"What do you mean?"

"He's been moping since yesterday, when Maestro showed
up. If you ask me, he's feeling left out. And as if he's no longer
needed around here."

This revelation sent my chin dropping. "You mean he

thinks he's being replaced?" Katie nodded, and I shook my head. "That can't be. He can't reason like that."

"Can't he, miss?"

I turned back to Barney, who had once more dropped his head to nibble at summer lush greens. "Good heavens, I would have thought he'd be relieved not to have to make the long trudges into town and back." I combed my fingers through his mane. "Well, don't worry, boy. No one is putting you out to pasture. But you do need a rest. Let's let Maestro take over for a while, and then we'll see."

"Don't worry, miss. I'll come out and visit with him as often as I can while you're away from home."

I thanked her and, with a pang of guilt I hadn't expected to feel, hitched Maestro to the carriage. Carroll Avenue took me north to Lower Thames Street, where commotion slowed my pace to a crawl. A crowd of some thirty men had gathered in front of the gates of the Newport Illuminating Company not far from the offices of the *Observer*. Some of the men were shouting while others held signs and a few waved fists in the air. Most were dressed in the corduroys and coveralls of workmen. Inside the gates, several men in dark suits and derbies hovered uncertainly, sometimes seeming to answer the shouts, other times conferring with one another.

Had the company that electrified our street rail system, and that had begun slowly replacing gas and coal power with electricity, laid off these workers? I brought Maestro to a stop and listened.

A young man stood at the fringe of the crowd. He occasionally lifted his voice to chant with the others, but his efforts seemed half-hearted at best. I waited until I could catch his eye and waved him over.

"Yeah, miss?" He removed his cap as he spoke.

"Can you tell me what's going on here?"

"Sure, miss. These are all men from the Newport Gas Light Company."

"I see. But what's the problem?"

"Electricity's the problem. It was one thing when they decided to run the trolleys on electricity. The old horse trolleys were slow and undependable. But now they want to start replacing the gas lines in homes. We say it isn't fair. Electric systems'll put the gas works out of business."

"I noticed you don't seem too enthusiastic about being here."

He shrugged. "I came because my workmates are here, but I'm planning to apprentice with an electrician, so I won't be left behind like some of the others."

"But so many houses are still dependent on gas for lighting and heat. It's going to be a very long time before gas is no longer needed, if ever."

"I suppose, miss." Obviously no longer interested in discussing the matter, he had resorted to being polite.

"Well, thank you." I fished in my handbag for a coin, but he shook his head and moved away. I clucked to Maestro to continue on. It was as I was stepping down outside the *Observer* that I remembered that Max Brentworth, owner of the Newport Gas Light Company, had been a guest at Mrs. Goelet's ball.

Did he, too, resent the advent of electricity in a town where he had for years enjoyed a veritable monopoly on lighting and fuel?

But to sacrifice a young woman's life? Surely not. But what if he hadn't meant for Cleo Cooper-Smith to die? Her death could have been a miscalculation. He might have believed she'd receive merely a shock and recover quickly enough. Meanwhile, all those watching might have been warned away from introducing electricity into their homes. I myself wondered at the safety of wires crisscrossing inside the walls of a home. In a structure such as Ochre Court or The Breakers, or some of the newer cottages presently being built, where the floors and walls were of marble, there might not be the same danger. But fires and electrocutions were known to happen, especially when too many circuits were crossed and too many appliances used at once.

Perhaps it seemed unlikely, but I had no choice but to add Max Brentworth's name to the list of possible suspects in Cleo's death. Mr. Brentworth, or someone who worked for him.

With a tug at my carriage jacket and a deep breath that squared my shoulders, I pushed my way through the door of the Newport *Observer*. Donald Larimer, the bespectacled front desk clerk, glanced up with an expression of inquiry. Upon seeing me, that neutral expression became more than a little interested, not to mention speculative.

"Miss Cross, how good to see you after all this time."

"It's only been a year, Mr. Larimer. I trust you've been well?"

"I have, thank you. How is New York? Do you like it there?" His eager tone spoke of dreams of possibly trying his own luck in the city someday.

"I've missed Newport," I said evasively. "Is Mr. Millford in?" I knew quite well he would be, but, no longer an employee, I couldn't very well go barging into his office unannounced. Mr. Larimer pushed a button on his desk and spoke into a cone attached to a length of rubber tubing connected to a box on the wall. "Miss Cross to see you, sir."

From the receiver on the box came, "Send her right in."

I clutched my handbag to keep my hands from trembling with excitement. Mr. Millford stood as I entered his office and he hurried around the desk. "Emma, it's good to have you back."

Was I back? Did he mean in Newport, or at the paper? "Thank you, Mr. Millford. It's good to be home." I left him to wonder, as I did, if by home I meant the city or these offices.

"Please, sit." He gestured to one of two leather armchairs in front of his desk. After resuming his own seat, he set his elbows on the desktop and leaned toward me. "Can I get you anything? Coffee?"

"No, thank you." I folded my hands and waited. If there was anything I'd learned about Mr. Millford while working here, it was that remaining silent was the best way to prompt him to speak his mind.

He leaned back, his gaze never wavering from mine, his smile never slipping. I had the distinct impression we were gingerly dancing around each other. "I've been thinking," he finally said so abruptly and so stridently, I winced.

"Yes?"

"Emma, I've been following your career at the *Herald* and I don't mind telling you I'm more than a little impressed. I'm prepared to offer you a full page in the *Observer*. How would you like to work here again?"

My insides buzzed with anticipation. "What do you have in mind, sir?"

"I know I can't entirely compete with the *Herald*. I simply don't have those kinds of resources. And I would hope you'd be willing to travel a bit from time to time."

"Travel?"

"Not far. To Providence, Boston, the occasional trip to New York."

My eyes widened. Was he asking me to be a traveling correspondent to our neighboring cities?

"You see, I don't want to limit you to Newport. I think you can certainly handle a wider scope."

It was all I could do not to laugh and clap my hands. "I can, Mr. Millford. I certainly can. Travel is no object, as long as I can base myself here in Newport."

"Yes, yes, surely. You'll be here full-time during the summer weeks, of course. But once the cottagers move on, I would want you hot on their trails."

A portion of my excitement ebbed. "Hot on their trails? You mean . . ."

"Yes, Emma. I want you to do what you've been doing for the *Herald,* but the *Observer* won't bury your columns somewhere in the middle of the paper. Oh no. You'll be right inside, page two, with a teaser on the front page. And in your own name, no more initials, if that's what you want. I intend to make you the biggest society gossip columnist in the Northeast. What do you say?"

Without giving Mr. Millford an answer, I left the *Observer* and walked. Or perhaps *strode* was the correct term, for my long paces propelled me along the sidewalk half-blindly. Other pedestrians stepped hastily out of my way as I passed. My heart ached. If only I hadn't brought such great hopes to my meeting with Mr. Millford. I hadn't even realized how lofty those hopes had soared until faced with the truth.

A society reporter. A gossip columnist. That was all I'd ever be. Perhaps Nellie Bly had been right; I didn't want it badly enough and wasn't willing to do whatever it took to achieve my dream.

No, she hadn't exactly said that to me. She had *asked* me how far I would willingly go, and then she had counseled me to marry a rich man. As I passed the bustle of Commercial Wharf, a potential answer came to me. The most obvious answer. Not only did I know a rich man willing to marry me, he owned a newspaper as well. How easy it would be to change my life.

Easy, if I had been willing to compromise my integrity, my convictions. My stomach sank, taking with it the shreds of my fortitude. There it was then, the answer to Nellie Bly's question, and the line I had drawn for myself, which I would not cross. Could not.

Could I? The question came as a faint murmur from a place deep down inside me, where there were no convictions or resolutions born of experience, but rather those naked, undeniable longings that defied logic or wisdom or patience. A place easily silenced or at least ignored when one felt in control of one's destiny, but not now, not when faced with the utter repudiation of all I had been working for and based my life upon. I was a woman; therefore I must be relegated to something less, something secondary, than the goals I had set for myself.

Why, then, shouldn't I do the expected thing, the *womanly* thing, and marry for advantage? Nellie Bly had, and she claimed happiness in her decision. I could, in all likelihood, make a success of such a marriage. I could make Derrick Andrews happy.

But there would always be that admonishment inside me reminding me of what I had done. Always that deep place inside me I would grow to despise.

Doubling back, I collected Maestro and my carriage and went on my way.

Chapter 9

"Yes, I'd like to see Mr. Randall Cooper-Smith please, if he's in."

The upstairs desk clerk at the Newport Casino raised his eyebrows as if I had made a lewd suggestion. However, he sent an assistant down a hallway to knock at Mr. Cooper-Smith's door. In addition to the second-floor reading rooms, card rooms, and billiard rooms, the Casino also offered accommodations to single men. Not for the first time, I wondered why Mr. Cooper-Smith had chosen to stay here rather than with his daughters at Ochre Court. Perhaps he simply enjoyed a quieter and less feminine environment. In light of what happened, however, it made no sense for him to maintain this distance from his grieving daughter.

He appeared moments later and I asked him to take a turn with me outside in the courtyard. Beyond the horseshoe pavilion, a tennis match was under way. The restaurant's outdoor porch bustled with lunchtime activity.

Mr. Cooper-Smith walked with his hands clasped behind his back. "What may I do for you, Miss Cross?"

He sounded impatient to be elsewhere. He had been brusque with me at the ball, warning me not to spread rumors when I brought up a potential engagement between Cleo and Silas Griggson. I had further questions about that, certainly, but I also wanted to know more about her relationship with Oliver Kipp. I knew I must proceed carefully if I were to learn anything from him.

"I'm terribly sorry for your loss, sir."

His brow creased. "Yes, thank you."

"She was a lovely young woman, so full of potential."

He let go a sigh. "Miss Cross, if you have come merely to offer your condolences, you might have saved them for the funeral. Whenever that takes place," he added in a tight murmur, referring to the fact that the police had not yet released her body.

"Sir, I want justice for your daughter—"

"Justice? They have the man responsible for her death. That imbecile electrician."

"He may not have caused . . . what happened," I said, trying to use diplomatic phrasing. Did Randall Cooper-Smith have no idea his daughter might have been deliberately murdered? "I—"

"I don't understand what this all means to you, Miss Cross."

"Mr. Cooper-Smith, I am in a position to help the police with the investigation."

"You? A woman? What can a woman possibly do to help the police? The very idea." He gave a half snort, half snigger. He seemed determined to be difficult. Was it grief making him so, or something else, perhaps a disinclination to reveal—what?

"Be that as it may, sir, I do have a couple of questions that could help the police. Did your daughter have enemies?"

"Enemies? Don't be absurd. She was a beautiful, vivacious young woman. Barely more than a girl."

"Beautiful young women often, through no fault of their own, inspire jealousy."

"That may be so, but I never heard anyone speak an unkind word about Cleo."

"Then can you think of anyone who might stand to gain from her death?" This was the question I had most wished to ask; the two previous ones had been merely to get me to this point. I hadn't been able to shake the image of all those lovely gowns in Cleo's bedroom, yet with a stark lack of jewelry other than that broken piece of necklace.

"Stand to gain?" What little patience he had shown thus far began to wane. I knew my time with him was limited. "How?"

"Had she an inheritance, for instance? Something another relative might inherit in your daughter's stead?"

"No, nothing like that."

"She had no inheritance at all, then?"

"I didn't say that. But nothing to prompt anyone to commit murder. Anything she might have had will go to her sister."

An interesting choice of words. *Anything she might have had . . .* As if he spoke only theoretically, but that his daughter in fact had possessed nothing of great value. What about the necklace? I didn't know if it had actually belonged to Cleo, or how she had come to possess it. I might have asked him, except that doing so would certainly spur Mr. Cooper-Smith to action. He'd claim the necklace and no doubt have Camille arrested for the theft. I preferred keeping that secret for now, with the prospect of Mrs. Hendricks catching Camille attempting to dispose of the piece.

But I was fairly convinced the Cooper-Smiths had no fortune to boast of. If they had, why wouldn't Mr. Cooper-Smith have rented a house or at least a spacious apartment in town rather than take a bachelor's room here at the Casino?

And wouldn't he have covered the expenses for his daughter's coming-out, rather than allow Mrs. Goelet to do so?

No, it made more sense to me that the family struggled to meet its expenses, and Cleo's costly gowns were meant to distract from that reality long enough for her to catch a man either old enough and rich enough not to care, or one who was too young and naïve to figure out the truth until it was too late.

"Is that all, Miss Cross?"

I blinked away my speculations. "Almost, sir. Can you tell me about your daughter and Oliver Kipp. Were they—"

"Oliver?" He sputtered and coughed. "What's he got to do with what happened to my daughter?"

"Sir, please, I don't mean to upset you. But it's come to my attention that they were practically engaged before the war started, and that they suddenly parted ways."

He looked as though he might deny it, then thought better of it. He most likely realized I had my information from people who had known them both. "They were little more than children, Miss Cross. Children often make rash decisions. Once they realized they were not suited, they agreed to part."

So this made yet a third version of the story. According to Mrs. Kipp, Cleo had broken things off. Lieutenant Norris and Captain Caldwell claimed Oliver had ended things. Where did the truth rest, and had Silas Griggson played any part in what happened?

That last question startled me. *Could* Silas Griggson have had a hand in parting a pair of young lovers? As far as I knew, he had played no role in the war, but that didn't mean he hadn't influenced the young couple to separate.

I chose my words, not to avoid upsetting Mr. Cooper-Smith, but rather to elicit a response. Had he been more forthcoming, I would not have resorted to such harsh tactics, but I felt he left me no choice. "Yet so soon after ending things with Oliver, she was to be engaged to Mr. Griggson."

His face turned fiery. "I don't know where you got such an outlandish idea. Silas Griggson is decades older than my daughter."

"That is not so unusual, and I got the idea from Mr. Griggson himself. He told me he and your daughter would have been engaged by the end of the evening, had fate not intervened." I said this last as gently as I could. I wanted answers, but I had no desire to torture a grieving man.

"Wishful thinking on Silas's part. Miss Cross, I'd advise you to stop digging up trouble. I know how you society reporters are, full of your own self-importance and eager to profit from the suffering of others. My daughter's death was due to the callous disregard of a drunken electrician, nothing more. If you wish to be of use, convince the police to release her body so she may have a decent burial, and I can return to New York."

He walked off, leaving me to stare after him. The tips of my ears burned; the pit of my stomach felt as though it churned with molten lead. In terms of my career, he hadn't said anything I hadn't already agonized over. But to have my very sentiments hurled back in my face, as hot as a branding iron, felt as though my conscience had disengaged from the rest of my being to cast its scorching judgment on me.

But I had already changed my future. I would not return to the *Herald,* nor would I occupy the same position at the *Observer.* And whether Mr. Cooper-Smith wished it or not, I would not rest until I'd achieved justice for his daughter. Even if that meant exposing whatever he seemed determined to hide.

One person I wished to question remained elusive. I had not seen or heard any word of him since the ball, and it seemed as if he had disappeared from the island. That was, until he knocked on my front door later that afternoon. Katie answered it and came to find me in the kitchen, where I was helping Nanny shell peas for dinner.

"A gentleman to see you, Miss Emma. A Mr. Griggson."

I tossed down a handful of pods, removed my apron, and hurried to the front of the house. Silas Griggson stood near the front parlor windows, his back to me. He turned around when he heard me, and the look on his face had the odd effect of making me feel as though I were the visitor and he was graciously receiving me.

"Ah, Miss Cross. I hope you'll forgive my sudden intrusion. Perhaps I should have sent my card first."

"That's all right, Mr. Griggson. Have you come about Miss Cooper-Smith?"

"Ilsa?"

I shook my head, puzzled that he would name the elder sister. Surely he knew by now that I had been assisting in the investigation. "No, Cleo. Do you have some information that might be helpful to the police?"

"About an accidental death? Or, rather, a death brought on by the negligence of a workman, I should say."

So, like his business associate, Randall Cooper-Smith, he was going to play that game. But unlike Cleo's father, Mr. Griggson seemed unperturbed to speak of her death, especially for a man who claimed they would have been engaged. I gestured for him to sit. I took a seat across from him and waited for him to go on.

"I am here about quite another matter." He held up a hand—his right. "This house."

"Gull Manor? What about it?"

"I've come to make you an offer on the place."

"You want to buy my house?" I couldn't quite absorb what he was saying. The conversation made no sense to me.

Of all the houses in Newport a man like Griggson could buy, why this one? He could afford to build another Ochre Court if he wished. "My property is small by most standards, Mr. Griggson, and the house is really quite ordinary."

He smiled, a stretch of his lips that did little to reassure me. "Oh, I don't intend to live here, Miss Cross. A client of mine is interested in property across the road. He'd like me to build him a tidy little cottage on the rise."

"Then . . . ?"

"I'm going to knock this place down. I can't have this sprawling monstrosity blocking my client's view of the ocean."

"Monstrosity?" Could this day possibly become any worse? Fury raged through my very veins, through every fiber of my being until Griggson's features wavered and blurred. "My house is not for sale," I said through clenched teeth.

He had the audacity to laugh. "Everything is for sale, Miss Cross. One has only to make the right offer."

"You've wasted your time. There is no offer that could induce me to sell." I stood. "And tell me, Mr. Griggson, do you plan to build this new showplace with the same substandard construction as your New York tenement buildings? The one that collapsed, for instance?"

The change in his smug expression was like watching water turn to ice. When he spoke, his voice cut like the whisper of the sharpest steel. "That tragedy was hardly my fault, Miss Cross. If you must know, Randall Cooper-Smith is to blame. His calculations were faulty, his blueprints flawed. Yes, I allowed a foreman to take the blame rather than destroy the family of the woman I wished to marry. I'm beginning to regret that decision. Perhaps it's time I told the authorities the truth."

The truth. Could this be what Mr. Cooper-Smith feared being revealed? Or had Mr. Griggson threatened Mr. Cooper-

Smith and his daughter? I certainly couldn't take this man's word for anything.

"Perhaps it *is* time for the truth, Mr. Griggson, about a number of things. You claimed you and Miss Cooper-Smith were to be engaged. But I wonder if perhaps she snubbed you that night. I can't imagine you would have appreciated that very much."

"Snubbed me?" He attempted to stare me down, but I glared right back. He shook his head. "Hardly. Not that our Cleo was a stranger to the notion."

"Are you talking about Oliver Kipp?"

"No, indeed, Miss Cross. Whatever happened between Oliver and Cleo was over with months ago. No, it's Norris she threw over recently."

A jolt of surprise went through me. "Lieutenant Dorian Norris?" Griggson merely nodded. Was he lying, attempting to throw suspicion onto another man? I didn't doubt he would try, if he felt cornered.

But what about the maid, Camille Tate? If Griggson spoke the truth, Dorian Norris would have been dallying with two women at once. Which could mean either Dorian or Camille might have wanted revenge against Cleo.

As these thoughts filtered through my mind, Griggson watched me closely. "What does any of it matter now? Come now, Miss Cross. Don't let your pride stand in the way of a windfall. I'm prepared to make you a generous offer. What does a single woman like you need with a house this size?"

"You know nothing about me or my needs, Mr. Griggson."

"I know you're a stubborn woman. That's for sure." His laugh set my teeth on edge. "Or perhaps you like to strike a hard bargain. Is that it? You want to make me squirm a bit. All right. Name your price."

My spine stiffened. "Mr. Griggson, you will never own

this house. *Never*. What's more, I intend to discover exactly who and what caused the tenement collapse."

"As you wish, Miss Cross." His eyes narrowed dangerously. "But you have no idea who you are dealing with." He held up a hand when I started to protest. "I know all about your illustrious relatives and how fond they are of you. I also happen to know that old man Vanderbilt has been reduced to a dribbling idiot. He can't be of any help to you."

If I were capable of breathing tongues of flame, I would have. "My uncle Cornelius is more of a man in his present condition than you will ever be, Mr. Griggson."

He waved dismissive fingers at me. "Whatever you care to believe, Miss Cross. But you cannot begin to imagine the kinds of connections I have. Believe me when I tell you I *will* own this property. This house will not stand much longer."

His prediction sent chills down my back, until I remembered that I, too, had connections even beyond my Vanderbilt relatives. I had a United States senator in my debt, and I felt certain George Wetmore would be more than happy to intercede on my behalf. "Please leave my home, Mr. Griggson. *Now*."

He lurched into motion, closing the space between us with such speed, I recoiled. His hand shot out toward me and I feared he would strike. In that instant, his cuff shot upward on his wrist, his right one, and a tiny tattoo, a star rendered in bold black ink, peeked out from just above his pulse point.

And then I saw the card extended to me from between his thumb and forefinger. "This is where I am staying. I'd advise you to change your mind and contact me. This is not over, Miss Cross. And I'd advise you to have a care." He shoved the card into my hand.

Despite the control I had maintained over my expression, he left me shaking in both fear and indignation. I glanced down at the card. An address had been handwritten, a location on Webster Street not far from Ochre Court. I flung the card to the sofa table. Then I hugged my arms around me and stood immobile, as if by moving I might set Mr. Griggson's abominable plan in motion. The very thought of my precious Gull Manor being taken away from me, yanked from my grasp, made me almost physically ill. The rumble of his carriage down my drive snapped me from my inert state. Gathering my skirts, I ran through the house calling Nanny's name, until I found her in the kitchen, and she wrapped her ample arms around me.

"Good morning, Miss Cross." The next day, the *Observer*'s young delivery boy waved to me where I stood on my front step and skidded his bicycle to a stop. "Did you hear yet what's happening over at The Elms?" he asked eagerly as he reached into his basket for my newspaper.

"Seeing as it's only seven in the morning, Ronnie, no." I took the rolled-up paper from him. He was obviously bursting with this latest news. "Why don't you tell me about it?"

"I saw it with my own eyes as I was delivering papers along Bellevue," he said in a rush. "More trouble with gas workers just like in town yesterday, except this time it was right on the sidewalk in front of The Elms."

The Elms was no more than a construction site, a colossal, rectangular hole in the ground from which rose the skeletal steel beams that would support the future structure. Edward Berwind made his fortune in coal, was one of the richest men in America, and had made it no secret his new home would not only be among Newport's largest, but would sport the latest in electrical innovation. So confident was he in the future of electricity, he ordered no backup systems, such as gas, installed. But the house would be dependent on no one for its power, for enormous coal furnaces, which would burn twenty-four hours a day, would generate the electricity on site.

"I would imagine gas workers are none too happy with Mr. Berwind's plans for the house. But is he even there to hear their complaints?"

"Beats me, Miss Cross. But the electricians laying out the underground wiring are taking an awful tongue lashing from the others. And a few mud balls were tossed."

"Oh, dear, this threatens to become ugly. Newporter against Newporter." In fact, it almost sounded to me as if someone were instigating the trouble. I still maintained that gas would go nowhere, that it would remain an important source of power for the city. "Ronnie, did you by any chance notice Max Brentworth on hand? Do you know who he is?"

"I do, and now that you mention it, I did see him."

I thought so. "What was he doing, exactly?"

Ronnie scrunched up his features as he thought about it. "Not much, that I saw. Just sort of standing around, watching. Sometimes he spoke to one or two of his workers."

"I don't suppose you overheard what they were talking about?"

"Well, not much. But I did hear him say he couldn't stand around all morning, because he has an appointment at The Breakers at ten o'clock."

My eyes opened wide. "The Breakers, you say?"

"That's right. Then I had to move on." He puffed up his chest. "I can't be late delivering my papers, after all."

"Indeed not, and I shouldn't keep you any longer. Before you go, though, would you like one of Mrs. O'Neal's buttermilk biscuits?"

His face lit up, and after leaning his bicycle against the house he hurried inside ahead of me.

After breakfast, I strolled to the edge of my property, out

onto the narrow headland that was surrounded on three sides by the water. It was where I went to think, to sort out myriad threads that tangled in my mind. Max Brentworth had much to lose should gas power suddenly fall out of use. Instigating his workers to protest the building of a house powered solely by electricity might bring attention to the matter, might even cause some property owners to have second thoughts, but would hardly sway a man like Edward Berwind from his intentions.

But an accident—in this case the death of a young woman—would surely spread fear of the new technology through the populace. When it came to Cleo Cooper-Smith's death, Mr. Brentworth had both motive and, perhaps, opportunity.

As did Silas Griggson. During the ball, he'd disappeared for a time; he might have rigged the wiring then. As for motive, I didn't believe he would ever have become engaged to Cleo. Her aversion to him had been plain to see. Moreover, he had demonstrated his temper and his bullying tendencies when he threatened me in my own home because I refused to let him have his way. It didn't take much to imagine such a man seeking revenge on Cleo for rejecting him.

Then there were the army officers, Dorian Norris and Sam Caldwell. Though, in truth, their links to Cleo were far more tenuous. If it weren't for the coincidence of Oliver Kipp's death and what I'd overheard at Fort Adams, I'd have dismissed them from all suspicion. But even if they had been somehow complicit in Oliver's death, why kill Cleo as well? Had the pair known something that made them a liability?

Mrs. Kipp's own words served to throw suspicion on her. She wished Cleo had died sooner, so that her son might still be alive. She could never have her wish, but did she have her revenge instead?

That left Camille, who for all appearances had stolen a valuable necklace from her mistress, and who might, according to the maid, Nora Taylor, have argued with Cleo on the morning of the ball.

My suspicions circled like the gulls searching for snacks out over the waves. I didn't linger in the spray kicked up by the rocky promontory for long. After obliging Barney with a quick brushing down, I hitched Maestro to my carriage and set off for The Breakers.

Chapter 10

❧

When I arrived at The Breakers shortly after ten o'clock, I left my carriage on the service driveway, near the children's playhouse, and walked up to the house. When Theodore Mason, the butler long in the employ of Cornelius and Alice Vanderbilt, admitted me, voices rumbled from somewhere beyond the Great Hall. One of them sounded like the youngest Vanderbilt brother, Reggie. I hoped the other belonged to Max Brentworth of the Newport Gas Light Company. I questioned Mason about whether my aunt and uncle, Alice and Cornelius Vanderbilt, had arrived from New York.

"It's not clear yet whether Mr. and Mrs. Vanderbilt will be coming up this year, miss."

"Oh, dear." My relatives loved this house, and no wonder. Built in the style of an Italian palazzo, it boasted ornate yet airy rooms and glorious views of the Atlantic Ocean. The Breakers had been designed to impress, to awe, perhaps even to intimidate, yet for those who knew its secrets, this was also a comfortable, cool, welcoming haven from the bustling world of New York and beyond. Cornelius and Alice would not stay away without very good reason. "Is Uncle Cornelius doing as badly as that?"

I expected him to summarily reassure me. He did not. "Mr. Vanderbilt is fighting his hardest to come back from his illness. He needs our prayers."

"He has them. And every week I remind the congregation at St. Paul's to keep him in theirs." I gestured to the Great Hall. "Who is here, then? I believe I hear Reggie's voice."

Mason rolled his eyes a bit. "Yes, that's Mr. Reginald. He and Mr. Brentworth of the gas company seem to be having a difference of opinion. The trouble is I believe Mr. Reginald's opinions differ from his parents' as well. Would you like me to announce you?"

"No, if it's all right, I'll just go on in. I'll see if I can help settle their differences."

As I climbed the carpeted steps from the vestibule into the Great Hall, I heard Mason murmur, "Good luck."

I followed the voices across the Great Hall. The doors onto the loggia stood wide open, emitting ocean breezes that swept through the hall and were cooled by the marble floors and walls. The gentle bubbling of the indoor fountain, a delightful surprise beneath the main staircase, lent to the illusion created by the painted ceiling three stories high of this being an outdoor courtyard. I passed the fountain and entered the billiard room, where I found my younger cousin, Reggie, and Mr. Brentworth in what seemed a lively debate.

"It's archaic and no longer needed," Reggie was saying. He held a billiard cue in his hands, and in emphasis of his statement he loudly sent the cue ball skidding into a cluster of balls. No ball rolled into a pocket, and Reggie lined up his next shot. Clearly, this was not a friendly game between the two men, for Mr. Brentworth held no cue stick and watched my cousin with a perplexed look.

"Mr. Vanderbilt, your parents wanted both electricity and

gas lighting for this house. You mother was explicit about it. While she appreciates the convenience of electricity, it is her opinion that people look their best by gas lighting and that is what she wishes for the affairs held here each summer."

Reggie propelled the cue ball once again. It ricocheted off a bumper and went wide, missing the other balls. Reggie swore and straightened. "Yes, well, Mother won't be holding her usual affairs here anymore, at least not in the near future, if ever. Don't you know my father is laid up—"

"Reggie." I stepped into the room, surprising both men. Reggie beamed at me.

"Hello, Em. It's good to see you." He hurried over to kiss my cheek, and when I removed my hat he took it from me and tossed it rather haphazardly onto a nearby sofa.

"I thought I'd stop by and see who had come up from the city. Is it only you?" Reggie nodded and I turned to the other man, extending a gloved hand. "You must be Mr. Brentworth, of the Newport Gas Light Company. I'm Emma Cross, Reggie's cousin."

I could see by his expression that being Reggie's cousin didn't do much to recommend me to him. "Very nice to meet you, Miss Cross. I believe, that is, don't you own Gull Manor that used to belong to Miss Sadie Allan? I believe we installed the gas system originally, and have done maintenance on the place."

I smiled my most brilliant smile. "Indeed, you are right. The lines are clear and working properly, thank you."

Reggie returned to the billiard table and leaned to strike another ball. The force of his shot sent it bouncing off the cloth surface. With a clunk it landed, rolling, to strike another cluster. Two balls dropped into a corner pocket. "When are you going to electrify that old pile of stones you live in, Em?"

I didn't miss the tightening of Mr. Brentworth's mouth. So I hadn't misunderstood as I'd entered the room, and neither had Mason been wrong when he said Reggie and Mr. Brentworth were experiencing a difference of opinion. But what was Reggie up to?

"Oh, I don't know." I smiled at Mr. Brentworth. "I'm not one for fixing what isn't broken. Gas suits me perfectly fine."

"If it's the expense you're worried about, I'm sure my parents would—"

I stopped Reggie right there with a "No, thank you." Though my Vanderbilt relatives had shown me boundless generosity over the years, I remained careful of what I accepted from them. Their gardeners tended my property every so often, and they had equipped Gull Manor with a telephone. Living so far out of town, the device could potentially save a life, should one of us fall ill or have an accident. But I valued my independence, and though Aunt Alice and Uncle Cornelius wanted only the best for me, their definition of what was best didn't always agree with mine.

"I'm fine with the way things are, Reggie," I said.

"Suit yourself." To Mr. Brentworth, he said, "You can schedule your blasted inspection if you want, but it'll be a waste of time."

"Really, Mr. Vanderbilt . . ."

"Reggie," I interrupted, "are you actually proposing ripping out the gas system? Have you spoken to your parents about this?"

"I've taken charge of the house in their absence. Neily can't, since Father won't let him set foot on any of the properties, and Alfred is too busy running the New York Central. And now that Gertrude is married, she could care less about the place."

I doubted that, but I was beginning to understand what fueled my cousin's high-handedness when it came to managing the house in his parents' absence. His eldest brother,

Neily, had been the heir apparent until he angered his parents by marrying Grace Wilson. Before that, he had been entrusted with important family and business matters. Next in age, Alfred had taken Neily's place, and following his father's apoplexy two years ago, had stepped in as head of the New York Central Railroad, along with his uncles William and Frederick.

What, then, for young Reggie, who was no longer a child yet not quite an adult? His parents had never set high expectations for him. Perhaps, being the youngest son, he had been seen as a spare rather than an heir. They loved him, perhaps too much, and had allowed him more freedom than he knew how to use productively.

He tapped several more balls with varying results, and now positioned his cue for another shot. I circled the table to him and took the stick from his hands. "Reggie, you're going against your mother's wishes. If I were you, I'd let Mr. Brentworth do his job and stay out of it. You'll be building your own house one of these days, and then you may do as you like."

He made a face. I placed the cue back in his hands and turned aside, but not before catching a whiff of spirits. It didn't surprise me. Reggie had been indulging in alcohol these past few years, beginning at far too young an age. I'd mentioned it to Neily once, but he had shrugged it off. Reggie was merely doing what many young men did, he told me. It would pass, nothing to worry about.

But worry about my young cousin, I did.

"Fine," Reggie said at length. "Go talk to Mason about it." With that he dismissed the hapless Mr. Brentworth, who hesitated a few feet beyond the billiard table with his hat in his hands.

I smiled at him again. "There then, Mr. Brentworth. You may schedule your inspections and any repairs and maintenance you deem necessary. I'm sure Mr. and Mrs. Vanderbilt are grateful for the personal attention you give to the safety of all who dwell beneath this roof."

"I take my business seriously, Miss Cross." He gave a little bow. Though I didn't entirely doubt his word, I might have pointed out that he had never personally called on me at Gull Manor to schedule maintenance of any kind. In fact, it was up to me to make sure my own gas lighting system was kept in good order. But then, I was merely a cousin several times removed from the present Vanderbilt family.

Mr. Brentworth excused himself. Reggie gave him no acknowledgment, but as soon as the man disappeared into the Great Hall, he made another face and shook his head. "Desperate to keep us all dependent on his outmoded system."

"Reggie, your mother *did* specify that she wanted both. I remember her saying so during the planning of the house."

"Senseless. Why, do you know the Berwinds will have *only* electricity? Theirs will be the first house to do so. No stinking gas in *their* new cottage."

"It doesn't stink."

"It does. What's more, it turns the walls and ceilings black."

"Not if it's properly maintained, which is why Mr. Brentworth is here. I see no reason why you should be bullying the poor man." I shook my head but smiled at the same time. "You're growing more incorrigible by the minute, Reg. What you need is—"

"A motorcar," he supplied with a bounce on his toes.

"I was going to say employment," I corrected him, feeling a bit like a scolding, elderly aunt.

He scowled good-naturedly. "*Pshaw* on that idea. Have you heard about motorized carriages, Em? They're coming soon, any day now, and I intend to be one of the first to have one. Just picture it, me racing around this island . . ."

"You'll probably kill yourself and everyone in your path."
I spoke with laughter. Reggie could be contrary, stubborn,
imperious, and downright rude, but somehow he always retained a boyish enthusiasm that endeared him to those
around him—most of us, at any rate. I wished I could remain
stern with him, help him find a useful path in life. But he'd
only laugh and tease me, and make me laugh in turn.

Though I would have liked to follow Mr. Brentworth and
attempt to strike up a conversation with him as he made his
notes for the maintenance to be scheduled, Reggie insisted I
play a round of billiards with him. I hadn't the talent for it,
and though I managed to sink a few balls into the pockets, he
beat me easily. He offered me some of the same libation he
was enjoying, but I declined. I had little taste for whiskey or
brandy, unless it was a few drops in a strong cup of tea.

While we played, I decided to take advantage of an opportunity and ask him some questions. "Did you know Oliver
Kipp?"

He glanced up from aligning his next shot. "Ollie? Sure.
We were at St. Paul's together in Concord." I nodded as he
said this. All the Vanderbilt boys were educated at St. Paul's
Academy in New Hampshire, and from there went on to
Yale. Neily and Alfred had excelled in their studies at St.
Paul's. Reggie's performance had been rather less spectacu-
lar. "We ran in different circles, though. He's a couple of
years older than me."

"Was," I corrected him.

"Oh, right." He straightened and leaned his cue stick
against the table. "Poor Ollie. I heard what happened. Poor
devil just couldn't handle the pressure, I guess." He wrinkled his nose. "Didn't seem like him, to freeze up like that."

"No? What was he like?"

"Steady. Logical. He was bookish, you know. Wanted to
be a military lawyer."

"Oftentimes bookish men don't have the stamina for battle."

"Like you would know?" He laughed as I conceded his point, then sobered. "You're right, though, from what I've heard. But Ollie wasn't the nervous type. There was nothing reckless about him. I don't think he ever made a move without thinking it through first. Like I said, he was steady. The kind of man who would make a good officer and attorney."

I grew more and more puzzled as Reggie contradicted what I'd learned about Oliver Kipp. "In your opinion, was he the kind of man whose broken heart would induce him to drop out of West Point and rush off to war?"

"Em, haven't you been listening to me? Ollie thought about things, weighed the pros and cons, the benefits and disadvantages. He never rushed into anything."

Oliver Kipp, a budding lawyer and officer who approached life with careful consideration, versus a West Point dropout who enlisted in the army to forget the woman who broke his heart. Which one had been real? If the former, what events set him on a collision course with fate, and why?

More than ever, the link between Cleo and Oliver, both alive and in death, seemed key in discovering who had murdered her—or perhaps both of them, whether directly or indirectly.

Reggie and I played another few rounds. Finally, Mr. Brentworth came to take his leave, informing Reggie that he and Mr. Mason had settled on a date for the work to be done. I placed my billiard cue into the rack on the wall and retrieved my hat.

"Mr. Brentworth, I walked here," I lied, seizing yet another opportunity. "I wonder if you would mind giving me a ride into town?"

Before he could answer, Reggie said, "I'll order one of our carriages to take you, Em."

"That's all right, Reggie. No need to bother. If Mr. Brentworth is agreeable, I'll arrange for a ride home later."

"But that doesn't make sense," Reggie murmured.

Mr. Brentworth bobbed his head to me. "I'd be happy to oblige, Miss Cross."

"Lovely. Along the way perhaps you could advise me on how often I should have my gas lines inspected."

Minutes later, as I settled onto the carriage seat, I slid closer to Mr. Brentworth by a couple of inches that might or might not have given a certain impression. If Mr. Brentworth believed me to be subtly flirting with him, all the better, though I didn't sit so close as to confirm his suspicions. We chatted about the lovely summer weather, my uncle Cornelius, the grand house we had just left. This gave me an opportunity to bring up another sumptuous mansion, Ochre Court.

"I saw that you attended Mrs. Goelet's ball the other night," I said sadly.

"Yes, that's right. You were covering the event for your newspaper, weren't you? Which one is it?"

"The New York *Herald*. Never did I suspect I'd be reporting on such a tragic event."

"No, indeed." He guided us along Bellevue Avenue, each of us nodding at the acquaintances we passed.

When he didn't seem about to add anything to the subject, I ventured an opinion. "Electricity is perhaps too new to be trusted. Would you say so, Mr. Brentworth?"

"Electricity is nothing new, Miss Cross. Its current uses are new, and therein, perhaps, lies the problem."

"Then you believe more work is needed."

"As with any innovation."

He was being rather evasive. I tried to trigger more of a reaction. "You're not against it, then?"

"Why should I be?"

"You *are* the owner of a gas company."

"Gas isn't going anywhere anytime soon."

He had just echoed my own thoughts. Was he truly this confident in his business prospects? "But not everyone feels the same, sir. Yesterday, I witnessed men protesting outside the Newport Illuminating Company. And I heard that just this morning at The Elms—"

Mr. Brentworth tugged the reins and brought the carriage to a jarring halt. My hand flew to my breastbone as I lurched forward, then flopped backward against the back of the seat. Mr. Brentworth turned angry features toward me. "I'll thank you to leave this carriage at once, Miss Cross."

"What?"

"You heard me. Down from my carriage." Within his glowering gaze and the tightness of his fists around the reins, I sensed a growing fury that made me fear for my safety. "I'll not move another inch until I am rid of you. So unless you wish to sit here indefinitely, you'll go."

"But . . . what did I say?"

"Now, Miss Cross." The order came through clenched jaws, convincing me to step down. I had no sooner done so than Mr. Brentworth set the horse to a brisk trot that raised a dusty draft around my hems.

What had I done? I thought back over the last few statements I had made. I'd spoken of Cleo Cooper-Smith's death at Ochre Court, and then the Newport Illuminating Company. Yes, and his demeanor had instantly changed. Yet, that wasn't entirely true. During the whole conversation, he had been reticent, agreeing or disagreeing with me in brief snippets that revealed little of his true thoughts.

But talk of the protest outside Newport's electrical company had sent him into a kettle of rage. Presumably, the protesters, or most of them, had been Mr. Brentworth's own workers, and the same could surely be said about this morning's ruckus at The Elms, where gas workers opposed the building of a house powered solely by electricity.

Had Max Brentworth sent them? Or instigated their unrest with threats that they would all soon lose their jobs?

Perhaps he, or one of his workers, had somehow rigged the tableau and caused Cleo's death. Mr. Brentworth's behavior today certainly didn't clear him of suspicion. Yet, from the grave, Oliver Kipp whispered to me that if Max Brentworth had a hand in Cleo's death, it had nothing to do with emerging technologies.

Mr. Brentworth might have ordered me from his carriage, but he hadn't left me stranded in the middle of nowhere. I stood on Bellevue Avenue several streets up from Ochre Point. A short walk would bring me back to my carriage at The Breakers. I retreated along the way, but turned in sooner than I might have and raised the heavy knocker at Ochre Court. The time had come for me to have a talk with Ilsa Cooper-Smith. I could no longer avoid it, though her sister had died only two days ago.

A heavy stillness continued to pervade the house. Swaths of black crepe covered mirrors and draped the mantels, while closed doors sealed the entrance to the drawing room. The butler informed me Mrs. Goelet was not receiving, but nonetheless showed me onto the rear terrace, where I found Grace and Mrs. Goelet's sister-in-law, Mrs. Robert Goelet. Of Ilsa Cooper-Smith, I saw no sign.

They occupied a garden table beneath the shade of the arched loggia, with their respective children, baby Corneil and the beautiful little Beatrice. The child seemed unaffected by the trauma of Cleo's death, was just then playing with the abundance of lilacs spilling over the wide rim of a bronze urn. She turned around, a spray in her hand, no doubt hoping for her mother's appreciation, and spotted me coming out from the Great Hall.

"Mama, who's that?"

Grace, cooing and teasing Corneil's rosebud lips with a fingertip, looked up. "Emma, how lovely. Do come sit with us. Harriette, have you met Miss Emma Cross? She's Neily's cousin."

Harriette Goelet was as blond as her daughter, and possessed a similar ethereal beauty, as if she had just stepped out from a Renaissance painting. The expression she showed me, however, was less than angelic. Clearly, she shared the opinion of most of her peers, that someone of my station had no business intruding on her lovely summer day. For Grace's sake, I pretended not to notice and took a seat at the table with them.

Grace immediately transferred Corneil into my arms. "Here you are. What do you think of my son?"

"Oh, Grace, he's lovely." A pain stabbed deeply and sharply at my heart, and as I instinctively cradled the baby close to my bosom and lowered my face to inhale his lovely baby scent, Grace exclaimed at what a natural mother I'd make.

"It's as if you had experience." Her hand flew quickly to her lips. "Oh, I'd forgotten. I'm sorry, Emma."

"No, it's quite all right, don't worry."

"How is Robbie? Do you hear much news of him?"

She spoke of the newborn we had sheltered at Gull Manor during the summer of ninety-six. How instantly the child had burrowed into our hearts, mine and Nanny's and Katie's. He had left us too quickly, gone as if he had never arrived, leaving us with empty arms and a too, too quiet house. Corneil reminded me of that time, and of how I had realized then how very much I might be giving up if I decided never to marry.

My mouth curved in a small, bittersweet smile. "You did

this on purpose, didn't you, Grace?" I accused her without rancor. Grace had made it abundantly clear she would like to see me married to Derrick.

She had been raised on the notion that every woman should marry, that every woman should *wish* to. My indecision baffled her, for to her it seemed a clear choice, as it would have been to Nellie Bly. *Marry a rich man.* Derrick Andrews was certainly that. Yet I had known women who chose not to marry, or at least put marriage off until they felt confident it was the right decision. My own aunt Sadie had remained single her entire life, choosing independence and self-sufficiency over the security of having a man see to her needs. And last summer, I had seen with my own eyes the spirited determination of Senator George Wetmore's two adult daughters, each of whom had turned down numerous suitors because they would not marry without love, or allow themselves to be valued for their inheritances alone.

I therefore stood in good company with my unwomanly stubbornness, as many would term it, but as with all of life's decisions, there were compromises to be made and sacrifices to suffer.

The baby whimpered and I jostled him gently. When his dimpled little hand closed around my hat ribbon, I let him tug the bow loose. I regarded Grace and Harriette. "How is Mrs. Goelet? And Ilsa?"

"Still understandably upset, as are we all." Harriette's manner remained stiff, though not rude. "That is why we're here, to be on hand should my sister-in-law need us."

I regarded her daughter, busily collecting lilac blossoms. She ran to her mother and deposited her little handfuls of purple petals into Harriette's lap. I nodded at the child as she once more toddled to the balustrade. "And Beatrice?"

"She hasn't mentioned a word about what happened," Harriette replied. "Other than that she wished she could have her red rosebud back."

"Her rosebud?" Grace lightly frowned in question.

"Yes. Do you remember the posy she handed to Cleo during the tableau? The flowers were supposed to have all been white. Beatrice had slipped in a single red rosebud. I don't even know where she came by it." Harriette's gaze scanned our surroundings, as if she were searching for the rosebush. There were numerous varieties growing on the property, and probably on her own property next door.

"Perhaps during a walk with her nurse," I suggested.

"Yes, I suppose."

"I'm glad to see you, Emma, but what brings you here today?" Grace asked.

"I'm hoping to speak with Miss Ilsa," I replied, deciding for now not to mention that I also hoped to speak with Mrs. Hendricks, the housekeeper.

Harriette looked perplexed. "Why would you need to speak with Ilsa?"

"I have a couple of questions concerning her sister's passing."

"Such as what? What business—"

Grace reached over and pressed a hand to Harriette's wrist. "It's all right. Emma has experience with such things. She can help find the answers to what happened to Cleo."

Harriette searched Grace's gaze for a long moment before she nodded and turned her attention back to her daughter. I followed her line of sight, and saw, beyond the terrace, a young woman with a parasol strolling on the lawn. She stepped up to the raised gardens and approached a stone railing, where she stopped to look out over the Cliff Walk and the ocean beyond.

"Is that Miss Goelet?" I asked.

"Yes, that's May," Grace replied. "She's been unsettled by all that's happened, too."

"I'd think she would be more than unsettled, and yet I remember you telling me, Grace, that she and Miss Cooper-

Smith weren't especially good friends, for all they were close in age."

Grace and Harriette exchanged glances, and Grace said, "They got on well enough, but their interests were rather different."

How different could the interests of two debutantes be? I rose from the table. "If it's all right, I'd like to have a word with her."

I didn't wait for permission, but neither Grace nor Harriette protested as I started down the terrace steps. Behind me, little Beatrice cried out, "May I go, too, Mama?"

Harriette obviously demurred, for I heard no footsteps pattering to catch up with me. I purposely walked with an audible stride so as not to startle Miss Goelet with my approach. She turned as I reached her, her expression becoming puzzled, and perhaps a bit wary.

"You're Miss Cross, the reporter. I remember you from the tea party and the ball."

"That's right." I smiled, hoping to put her at ease. "I wondered if I might ask you some questions about Miss Cooper-Smith. You see, I'm assisting the police in discovering what happened to her."

"Why you?" She sounded merely curious.

"It's something I do from time to time. My occupation puts me in a position to be useful."

"I see." She played with the bow on the handle of her parasol. "Well, I don't know anything about what happened to Cleo."

"No, I didn't suppose you did, but you knew her."

"Not well, I'm afraid." She frowned. "That is to say, I'd known her for many years, but I cannot say we were good friends. Not as our mothers were."

"Then she didn't tend to confide in you?"

"Rarely." She folded her parasol and leaned it against the

railing, then turned to peer out over the ocean again. "This has been dreadful on my mother. First my father a year ago, now this." She placed a hand on the stone rail and smoothed it back and forth where two sections met to form a wide angle. "Do you see how this balustrade is shaped? It's like the bow of a ship. Mama has always loved to set sail. She loves traveling overseas, but often Papa would have preferred to stay here. So he had this upper garden shaped like the bow of a ship so she could stand here and pretend. He thought, perhaps that way, she might be more willing to stay home." She laughed sadly. "It didn't work, and we sailed to England last year. That's where Papa died, you know."

"Yes, and I'm terribly sorry for your loss."

"Thank you." She bowed her head, hiding for a moment beneath her hat brim. When she reemerged, the wary look had returned. "I don't mind you asking me questions, Miss Cross, but please leave my mother be. She's taking this very hard."

"I can understand."

"Can you? You see, she blames herself for my father's passing. She regrets having gone to England last summer, and thinks perhaps if we had stayed home Father would still be alive." She shook her head sadly. "I don't believe so, and I've tried to dissuade her of the notion. And now, she blames herself for Cleo. She thinks if only she hadn't thought of installing the Edison bulbs, Cleo might still be alive."

"I sincerely hope in time your mother will come to feel differently." I didn't add that this, too, made me determined to find the truth. No one should have to bear the unnecessary guilt of another person's death.

"Thank you, Miss Cross. But you didn't wish to ask me about such things. You want to know about Cleo."

"Yes. Miss Goelet, were you aware of who her beaux were?"

The question startled her. She compressed her lips before replying. "I believe she had many hopefuls. Many of them attended the ball. Cleo had a way of attracting male attention."

I didn't doubt that. "Was Oliver Kipp among them?"

"Oliver?" She shrugged, unperturbed by the name. "I suppose for a time. At least I'd seen them together last spring. But more recently she had her eye on someone else." I heard a faint derision in her voice. She tapped her fingers against the railing, perhaps unconsciously. Finally, she murmured, "Robert."

"Your brother? But he's—"

"Younger than Cleo was, yes. But he is also going to be a very wealthy man someday rather soon. And I think . . ." She turned to face me again, careful not to brush her skirts against the stone balustrade. "I doubt very much Cleo loved Robert, but I believe she saw our family as a haven where she could be safe."

"Safe from what?"

"I'm not sure exactly. But lately, she seemed nervous, jittery. Oh, it might have been because of the ball. Every girl has an attack of nerves before her coming-out. But I did notice her paying much more attention to Robert these past several days than ever before."

"Do you think he returned her regard?"

"Miss Cross, you know how boys are." She sighed. "He was flattered and followed her about like a pup when he thought no one was looking, especially Mama. He left her alone at the ball, of course."

I found this especially interesting. "You mother would not have approved of them marrying?"

Miss Goelet shrugged. "Heaven only knows. I doubt very much Mama was aware of Cleo setting her cap for Robert, if indeed that is what she had done. She might only have been trifling with him while waiting to see who would offer for her."

I decided to subtly change tack. "The tableau was the most elaborate I'd ever seen or heard of. Was your coming-out similar?" I knew very well that Miss Goelet's coming-out had been a much more dignified affair. Did Miss Goelet feel any jealousy toward Cleo, that perhaps her mother had done more for a friend's daughter than her own?

"Good gracious, no." A chuckle accompanied this assertion. "Oh, my parents spared no expense for me. It was wonderful and sumptuous and I felt like a princess. But I didn't feel any need to dress the part of an ancient queen and put on such a display."

I perceived no prevarication in her answer. I believed her sincere. "Then why do you think your mother planned such extravagance for Miss Cleo?"

"She didn't. The *tableau vivant* was Cleo's idea. And Mama went along with it because she promised Cleo's mother she'd do her best by the sisters." Her lips pursed regretfully. "For Cleo, at any rate. There wasn't a coming-out for Ilsa, for obvious reasons. It would only have served to emphasize her lack of prospects."

Yes, poor Ilsa. But Cleo's insistence on a Cleopatra-themed *tableau vivant* seemed to confirm my theory that the Cooper-Smiths had been intent on hiding their penury until Cleo had secured an engagement. Yet she had issued a direct cut to Silas Griggson's attentions, a man who could have made her richer than many wives of the Four Hundred. Which in turn led me back to my theory that the Cooper-Smiths, and perhaps Cleo personally, had something to fear from Silas Griggson.

When I returned to the terrace, Grace handed Corneil to a maid who in turn tucked him into a wicker pram, thickly padded and lined in satin. Grace stood. "Come with me. We'll see if Ilsa is feeling up to speaking with you." Once we reentered the house, she grasped my forearm and spoke quietly. "I asked my sister about Cleo's gowns, and yes, she most certainly did pay for them. She seemed reluctant to discuss it further so I didn't press her. But it's safe to assume the Cooper-Smiths have found themselves in reduced circumstances."

"Thank you, Grace."

When we reached Ilsa's door on the second floor, Grace knocked softly, then retreated down the corridor. Ilsa seemed surprised to see me, but invited me inside. I expressed my sympathies and inquired after her health, and asked if there was anything I could do for her. Her replies were gracious and subdued. She looked pale and drained, as though she hadn't slept in days, which, understandably, she might not have. She offered me a seat and refreshment. I accepted the former, declined the latter.

"I've been asking questions concerning your sister's passing because I care very much about the truth of what happened," I said as we made ourselves comfortable in the sitting area of her bedroom. "Some of the answers have led me back here, to you."

"What kind of questions have you been asking, Miss Cross?" Though she had seemed calm enough at first, now her hands worked convulsively, clutching one moment, fidgeting with her skirts the next, only to then grip the arms of her chair. "I don't understand. I know you are a reporter, but . . ."

I leaned toward her, speaking quietly. "Ilsa, I know the man, the electrician, who has been blamed for your sister's death." She compressed her lips, frowning, and I hastened to reassure her. "I wish to see your sister laid to rest with no lingering questions about how she died. As I was saying, I know Dale Hanson quite well. I've been acquainted with him my whole life. He is not an irresponsible person, or a heavy drinker, or inept at his profession. I do not believe he is responsible."

"Then . . . who?" Again, her hands fluttered and fussed. "And how can I help you? I have no idea what happened. How could I?"

I responded diplomatically, not wishing to unduly distress her. "Perhaps you know more than you think. I would like to help you remember everything you might have observed before and since the night of the ball."

"Oh . . . all right." Her fingers twisted together.

"When you and I first met, you were in the ballroom. What were you doing there?"

"I told you at the time. I was making sure everything would be perfect for Cleo."

I nodded as if I had merely been refreshing my memory. "And while you were in the drawing room and ballroom, did anyone else come in? Besides me, of course."

"No one. I was alone the entire time."

"Did you go up onto the dais?"

"I did. I wanted to be sure the Edison bulbs were placed just so, to show off Cleo to her best advantage. And the flowers, of course. I wanted to make sure they were fresh."

"How afterward, you left the ball somewhat early, before the tableau. Where did you go?"

Her mouth turned down as she no doubt remembered Mrs. Russell's unkind words, and how her sister failed to come to her rescue. She murmured, "I went up to my room for a bit."

"And when you came back down . . . ?"

"It was time for the tableau. I went into the drawing room along with everyone else." She sighed. "You see, Miss Cross—"

"Emma, please."

"You see, *Emma,* I never saw anything out of the ordinary. I don't think I can help you at all."

She stood up, her uneven gait taking her to the window. Looking out, she fiddled with the edge of the curtain. I spoke to her back. "Ilsa, can you tell me if your sister had ever shown an interest in Lieutenant Dorian Norris? You know who he is, don't you?"

She spun about as quickly as her infirmity would allow. "Of course I know Lieutenant Norris. He and Oliver went to war together. And before that, his family attended many of the same events as my family. What do you mean, did Cleo ever show an interest? As in wishing to marry him?"

I nodded even though that hadn't been my exact meaning. I watched the effect this notion had on her. She seemed utterly taken aback. Had Mr. Griggson been lying in his claim about a dalliance between Dorian and Cleo? Or had Dorian's illicit attempts to meet with Camille confused Mr. Griggson into believing he'd been trysting with Cleo? Ilsa's next words seemed to suggest so.

"Cleo never paid him any special attention that I noticed."

"Before he went off to the war, Oliver and your sister broke off their liaison."

Ilsa sighed again, this time deeper, laden with regret. "Yes, they did."

"Are you sure it had nothing to do with the lieutenant?"

"She never mentioned him. Never met him anywhere on her own. I'd have known, Emma. She and I were close. She wouldn't have kept something like that from me."

"Wouldn't she? Even if she felt guilty for rejecting one man in favor of another?"

Ilsa adamantly shook her head. "She wouldn't have had any opportunity to sneak off and meet anyone without my knowing." She limped back to her chair and sank heavily into it. A pang of guilt struck me. These questions were draining what little stores of stamina she possessed. But for Cleo's sake, and for Dale's, I had no choice but to persist.

"Were you angry with her for anything?" I alluded, of course, to those unkind words of Cleo's, and also to how so much attention centered on Cleo, with few if any expectations raised on Ilsa's behalf. Why wouldn't she have resented her sister? It was a risky question, and I braced for her to lash out and protest her innocence in her sister's death. Her reply astonished me.

"Yes, I was angry with her. More than that. I was *incensed* with her."

Chapter 11

"She never should have broken it off with Oliver," Ilsa continued. I let go the breath I'd been holding, having been almost certain I'd been about to hear a confession. "Cleo did him an ill turn, Emma, and he didn't deserve it. Perhaps he'd be alive now if only Cleo hadn't spurned his affections."

Hearing her echo Mrs. Kipp's sentiments, it took me a moment to recover from my astonishment and find my voice. "Surely there must have been a good reason for her actions. Perhaps they argued, or they merely didn't suit."

"Oliver would never have argued with my sister. He was a gentleman, always."

"Could he have been the one to break it off?" I asked, remembering what Dorian Norris had said about the matter.

"Oliver? Never. He loved my sister, I know he did. And believe me, they suited better than Cleo and that awful Mr. Griggson."

On that I couldn't have agreed more. But if Oliver hadn't broken it off, as Dorian claimed, there had to be some logical reason for Cleo's actions. Oliver was a gentleman in the social sense, an officer—or would have been if he hadn't dropped out of West Point—and though his family fortune came nowhere close to that of my relatives or the Goelets, he was wealthy enough. A young woman like Cleo Cooper-Smith, with a limited dowry, wouldn't squander a marriage opportunity like that without good cause. I simply couldn't shake the notion of her affections having strayed from Oliver to someone else.

"Ilsa, could Robert Goelet have won your sister's affections?"

"Robert?" She let out a laugh. "Oh, Robert is nice enough and will be wildly wealthy when he comes of age, but no. First of all, he was too young for my sister. Secondly, he barely noticed Cleo, or me for that matter."

"Are you sure?" I didn't want to betray Miss Goelet's confidence, so I didn't allude to where I'd gotten the notion.

"Completely. Cleo certainly never mentioned him, not in that way."

Miss Goelet must have been mistaken, or perhaps had allowed her imagination to run away with her. I didn't doubt, given that she hadn't held Cleo in the highest regard, that she might have been overprotective of her brother's interests.

If not Robert or Dorian Norris, then who . . . ?

Patrick Floyd, the family friend? Jesse had suggested perhaps both sisters were in love with him, had fought over him. Mr. Floyd might have led them both on. Meanwhile, his own wife might have committed suicide after discovering her husband's unfaithfulness.

I put the question to Ilsa.

"Patrick?" Her breath caught in her throat and her complexion burned hotter than a candle flame. She pushed unsteadily to her feet and stumbled, prompting me to jump up from my seat and offer my hand to her. She found her balance without my help and limped again to the window. "No, indeed not. Cleo and Patrick? What a silly notion."

I followed her to the window, where she stood with one hand pressed to the mullioned panes, the other clutching the neckline of her dress. At the ball, I had seen her adoring looks at Patrick, the depth of feeling in her eyes. At the time I had believed that affection to be all on her side, with Patrick feeling for her only the regard of a brother. Her reaction to my question now brought on a new theory and I placed a hand on her misaligned shoulder. "Ilsa, I do believe one of the Cooper-Smith sisters has been involved with Mr. Floyd, but I no longer think it was Cleo."

She said nothing for a long moment, but I felt her trembling beneath my hand. And then she turned and was suddenly in my arms, sobbing wildly.

"Oh, Miss Cross. Oh, Emma. I've been wicked, so *very* wicked. I never meant to harm Matilda. Never meant for her to . . ."

Harm her how? Jesse had also wondered if Ilsa had been at the Floyd home the night Matilda died—the night the gas line had been left open with no flame. Could Ilsa have done such a thing to rid herself of her rival for Patrick's heart?

Her tears flowed unhindered, and with her in such a state I could do nothing but stroke her back and murmur soothing phrases. But good heavens, she had had an affair with a married man? Even though I had guessed as much, hearing her admit it shocked me to my core. When her distress began to subside, I led her back to our chairs, pulling mine closer so I could hold her hand.

"How long?"

She sniffed and wiped the backs of her hands across her eyes. "Since about two months before Matilda . . . before she . . ."

"Died," I said gently.

"Yes, but we never did anything You must believe me. I mean, we went for walks, we read books together, we held hands . . . nothing more."

I wished to believe her. I found nothing worldly or fallen in her manner, nothing but an innocent woman-child who was desperate to be loved and valued. She proved that with her next words.

"No one before Patrick had ever cared for me. And he does, Emma. He still does, though since Matilda's passing he has kept a distance, out of respect. He didn't wish ill on her either. It's just that they married young and had nothing in common. He tried but he could not make her happy. She had become erratic and melancholy."

"Did he make you promises back then, while his wife still lived?"

"No, not then. But more recently. Someday soon, he and I will be together."

I wagered he had promised her that, and more. I wondered what game he played at. The fact that he hadn't yet taken Ilsa's virtue did little to endear him to me. In my opinion, turning his affections to one woman while married to another made a mockery of both of them.

Had he used Ilsa to be rid of a wife who had grown burdensome? Perhaps, but even that despicable action suggested no reason why he would have murdered Cleo. I only wished I could say the same about Ilsa.

Once more composed, she went into the bathroom to wash her face. I used the opportunity to ring for tea. It arrived quickly, almost as if it had been ready and waiting—had Grace predicted the necessity for it? Meanwhile, I considered everything she had said so far, and compared it to what I remembered from her sister's ball. A thing or two puzzled me. I waited until Ilsa had drunk about half of her cup of tea, speaking of light matters until I deemed her restored enough to continue with my questions. If the previous ones had been difficult for her, these promised to leave her distraught.

But they had to be asked.

"Ilsa," I ventured slowly, "I couldn't help but notice, during the ball, that your sister wasn't always kind to you."

She looked up at me in surprise. "What do you mean?"

Was she deliberately playing the innocent, hoping to disconcert me? "I'm thinking specifically of the incident with Mrs. Russell."

"Mrs. Russell?" Her chin tilted, but then righted as she took on a look of comprehension. "*She* was not very kind to me."

"I certainly agree with you. She was most unkind. But your sister, forgive me for saying, did not exactly come to your defense."

"Well . . ." I watched closely as she groped for a response. She crossed her feet, then quickly uncrossed them and set them flat on the floor. "Sisters often argue. Do you have a sister, Emma?"

"No, only a brother."

"But surely you know that when siblings argue, nothing very serious is meant by it."

"True, in most cases. But . . ." I chose my words carefully. "You and Cleo weren't arguing that I saw. Mrs. Russell's thoughtlessness hurt you, and your sister compounded the offense by making light of the situation."

I braced, expecting a fresh round of tears. However, Ilsa merely stared down at her lap. "My sister was right. I should not allow the words of others, however hurtful, to daunt me."

"But you *were* daunted." I thought back to the incident, and made a realization. "You didn't walk off in tears because of what Mrs. Russell said. It was what your sister said that sent you from the ballroom."

She had begun shaking her head before I'd quite finished the comment. "No, it had nothing to do with Cleo. It was Mrs. Russell."

"Ilsa, had you and Cleo argued that day? Had she been unkind to you earlier?"

"No, never. She was always so good to me."

"Was she? Or did she apportion her kindness out of obligation, as one does to a relative for whom one feels little true affinity?"

"What a terrible thing to say." She placed her cup and saucer on the table beside us and pushed to her feet.

Knowing she was about to demand I leave, I hurried to make my point. "Someone argued with your sister that morning, loud enough to be overheard through the walls."

"Who says we argued? Was it Camille? Cleo yelled at her that morning. I heard them."

"Never mind about your lady's maid. Did you and your sister argue?"

"Are you accusing me . . ." She trailed off and gulped, and sank back into her chair. Her head drooped, and then moved up and down several times. "We did, Emma. We argued frightfully that morning. It was because I was feeling so drained, and I told her I might not be able to be present through all the festivities ahead of us." She looked up at me, her eyes once more awash. "You can't understand how exhausting it is, having my condition. Simply standing, holding myself as straight as I can, is as taxing as a hard day's labor."

I nodded my sympathy, if not my understanding, for she

was correct. Having always enjoyed robust health, I could not fully appreciate her plight.

"She told me I was being selfish, that I should wear my brace as my physician recommended. That I was just making excuses. Oh, but Emma, the brace hurts. It makes things worse. Cleo said I was being difficult and called me a martyr that morning, and when she said it again that night . . ."

I reached over and patted her hand. "Ilsa, tell me again what you were doing in the drawing room that afternoon, when Mrs. Goelet gave specific orders that no one be allowed into the room."

"I told you." Her gaze wandered from mine. "I wanted to make certain everything was ready."

"Is that really all?"

Her breathing became more rapid, and she shrank down into her chair. "I . . ." Her brow creased. "Oh, all right. Perhaps it was petty of me, but I wanted to know what it would be like."

"Being up on the dais that evening," I guessed.

She nodded. "Having all the attention, feeling like a queen. Like Cleopatra. But I'm no queen, am I? Just as Cleo's name suggests ancient Egyptian royalty, mine suggests exactly what I am. Ilsa—ill. How apt, as if my parents had glimpsed the future and seen what I would become."

Was I finally learning the truth about the sisters' relationship? "No, Ilsa. Your name is lovely. You mustn't think that. But it upset you, didn't it, Cleo always having all the attention?"

"It wasn't just the attention." She sounded like a plaintive child. "It was all the expectations that went along with it. Everyone predicted a glorious future for her. Mother asked Mrs. Goelet to see to Cleo's marriage, but she made no such request for me. 'Poor Ilsa, she'll need to be taken care of for the rest of her life.' First Father, then Cleo. Yes, it was expected that I'd spend my life in some corner of Cleo's home like a poor, maidenly aunt. Only, Cleo's not here anymore to take me in, is she?"

"It angered you to be seen that way, didn't it?" I asked quietly, and with as much sympathy as I could muster. And I *was* sympathetic. But I was also very nearly holding my breath again as I waited to discover just how angry Ilsa had been with her sister.

She didn't hold back. "Yes, I was angry. At times, furious. Before *this* happened to me"—she indicated her torso with a brusque flourish of her hand—"I was the prettier child. The more charming child. Everyone said so. I *had* the attention, Emma."

"I was struck by your beauty the first time we met," I told her truthfully. She blinked and darted her glance away again. "What did you do before I found you in the ballroom?"

She shrugged. "I walked up onto the dais, sat on Cleo's throne, pretended"—she swallowed—"pretended I was her, gazing out on a room full of admirers."

"Did you touch anything?"

"I couldn't help touching a thing or two. The throne, the flowers." Her gaze caught mine sharply. "What are you implying? That I . . . ? That's absurd. I wouldn't have the first notion of how to rig the wires. None whatsoever."

While on the surface that seemed true, how could I know how much of the electrical work Ilsa might have witnessed? Had the drawing room been kept locked at all times during the preparations? Surely the doors must have been open—from the hall, from the terrace—to allow the equipment and decorations to be brought in. No, I guessed it wasn't until all had been made ready that Mrs. Goelet had sealed off the rooms to preserve them in their perfect state for the evening's entertainments.

And then I realized she hadn't denied the possibility based on her love for her sister, but rather on her lack of technical knowledge needed to devise such a murder. I took my leave of her soon after, resolving to stop at the hospital as soon as possible and check in on Dale. Perhaps, if he was awake and able to speak, he could tell me who passed in and out of the drawing room before the ball. If not, I would have to track down his assistants.

Before leaving, I said good-bye to Grace and went below-stairs to seek out the housekeeper, Mrs. Hendricks, and ask her if she had any news about Camille. She invited me into her parlor and closed the door to ensure our privacy.

"I've kept a close watch on her, Miss Cross. So much so, she's taken to giving me quelling looks and trying to dodge me at every turn." The woman crossed her arms over her black worsted bodice. "Little good it does her. There's not a soul in this house that I don't know where he or she is."

"But the necklace, Mrs. Hendricks. Is it still where we found it?"

"It is. I still think the police should be informed. I do not suffer a thief in my house, Miss Cross, and if Mrs. Goelet found out—well, I shudder to think."

This gave me pause. "I don't want you to get into any trouble over this. Perhaps I should speak with Mrs. Goelet and—"

"Don't you dare disturb the mistress. She's been through enough, losing her dear friend's daughter and feeling partly responsible."

"Yes, and I'm sorry to hear she feels culpable. I'll leave it be for now, but if you do run into difficulty because of me, I'll take the blame."

She didn't reply, but I detected a glint of relief in her eyes.

* * *

After collecting Maestro and my carriage, I headed back into town. Along the way I reviewed everything I had learned at The Breakers and Ochre Court that morning. Max Brentworth must be feeling threatened by this new onslaught of electricity, or why would my questions have prompted him to order me from his carriage? I entertained little doubt that he was behind this new rash of protests involving his workers from the Newport Gas Light Company. I didn't believe he would go so far as to murder a young woman intentionally, but perhaps he only meant to deliver a shock, thus frightening the Four Hundred away from electrical power.

I could much more easily envision Mr. Brentworth at the root of Cleo's death than Ilsa. Today I believed I had seen the real Ilsa, rather than the one she wished to project to the world. Not the sweet-tempered, proper young woman who was content to live in the shadow of her beloved sister, but the Ilsa who had suffered both injury and insult at the hands of others—including her sister—and who understandably harbored bitter resentment at the unfairness of her situation. She admitted to arguing with Cleo that morning, and suffered yet another offense from her sister that evening. Had her resentment pushed her too far?

Finally, I considered what Camille intended doing with the broken diamond necklace. Presumably, she would sell it. She and Dorian Norris were forced to keep their courtship a secret because his family would never approve. They would probably cut him off, leaving him next to destitute. But if the couple found their own source of money, they would be free to marry. Did Camille act alone in stealing the necklace, or had Dorian encouraged her? Camille might be waiting to leave Newport before attempting to sell the piece, especially if Cleo had discovered the theft before she died and threatened to have her arrested. If all this proved true, the question remained whether Camille or Dorian, or both, arranged for Cleo to die.

These revelations didn't rule out other suspects, such as Silas Griggson, a man with much to conceal. I couldn't shake the notion that perhaps Cleo discovered something to incriminate Mr. Griggson in the New York tenement collapse. Then again, Lorraine Kipp blamed Cleo for her son's death, and might have seized the opportunity at Ochre Court to take her revenge.

While I planned to visit the hospital and speak to Dale Hanson, I nonetheless turned my carriage onto Spring Street and came to a stop outside a two-story clapboard building that housed several small businesses downstairs and apartments upstairs. I walked to the corner and opened the door beneath the sign that read THE NEWPORT *MESSENGER*.

Unlike the *Observer*'s offices, this small establishment boasted no anteroom. A clerk occupied a desk at one side of the rectangular room, facing the window onto the street. In the other corner, sat Derrick Andrews.

He came to his feet after glancing up and seeing it was me. "Emma! What brings you here?"

"I'm honestly not sure," I replied, feeling foolish. What *had* prompted me to take this detour?

"Whatever the reason, it's good to see you." The clerk cast a quizzical glance at us, and Derrick made the introductions. "Jimmy Hawkins, this is Miss Emmaline Cross." I winced slightly at his use of my full name, which I considered altogether too fussy for a sensible woman like myself.

Mr. Hawkins, a man of perhaps my own age if not a year or two younger, came over to shake my hand.

Derrick explained, "Jimmy worked for my father for a

while but came down from Providence to be my clerk here. He's been quite a godsend. Nobody's better organized."

"It's a pleasure, Mr. Hawkins."

The telephone rang, summoning the young man back to his desk. Derrick gestured toward a closed door through which the muffled sounds of the workday could be heard. "Would you like to see the place? We've done quite a lot since you were here last summer. I've added a new press."

Derrick's pride in showing off his presses and his newsroom staff of three was infectious, and I couldn't help envisioning being the proprietress of a similar operation. However, any thought I might have had of Derrick selling me the *Messenger* were dashed by his enthusiasm. I had been correct in assuming, a year ago, that being disinherited by his father and cast out of the family newspaper business, the Providence *Sun,* would only rouse his creativity and ambition to make a success on his own. True, beside the *Sun,* the *Messenger* paled in terms of scope and subscriptions, but I didn't doubt that in time, the two businesses would rival each other.

He led me back through to the front office and to the street door. "I thought you might wish to talk," he said as he ushered me outside. "We'll have more privacy than in the office."

As we set off along the sun-drenched sidewalk, I told him about my morning and what I had learned since our sojourn to Fort Adams, including Miss Goelet's claim that Cleo might have wished to marry her brother. "I tend to discount that as particularly important," I told him. "Robert is only eighteen, and I believe Miss Goelet might have been speaking out of resentment of Cleo's hold on her mother."

"You're probably right about that," he said. "Even if it's true, it's hardly a reason for anyone to commit murder. My money is on Griggson. It sounds most feasible that Miss

Cooper-Smith learned something about him she shouldn't have and he needed her out of the way."

"You think it's linked to the tenement collapse?"

His hand went to the small of my back to guide me past a deliveryman and his handcart. "I'd wager the collapse is likely one of many instances of shoddy and dangerous construction. And of skimming funds off such projects."

"I think so, too. What do you know of Silas Griggson? He seems to me to have sprung up from almost nowhere, a wealthy, powerful man with little or no background."

Derrick chuckled. "Oh, he has a background, you can be sure of that."

"Yes, but nothing that suggested he would become a leader in the construction industry, with buildings in almost every New York neighborhood. I couldn't trace the source of the money that allowed him to buy his way in."

"That alone tells us he's a dangerous man." Derrick's voice took on an ominous note. "And that his position was ill gained."

"Griggson is the obvious choice in Cleo's death, assuming she learned something she shouldn't have. What about the others?"

We came to Trinity Church and entered the churchyard, strolling beneath the trees and the shadow of the soaring steeple.

"Such as the sister?" he asked.

"Or Mrs. Kipp, for instance. And Max Brentworth."

Derrick shook his head. "Possible, but doubtful. Consider what each had to gain from Cleo's death."

"Revenge. Satisfaction based on jealousy. A return to gas lighting in new homes." I ticked them off on my fingers.

"Revenge wouldn't bring back Mrs. Kipp's son. Nor would satisfaction restore Ilsa's health. And you say she believes herself to be in love, with marriage prospects."

"Does a murderer always think in logical terms?" I challenged.

He leaned with his hands against the rounded edge of tombstone marked from the previous century and stared at the backs of the buildings blocking our view of the harbor. "Sometimes they do. A strange, twisted sort of logic. Something tells me this matter is more twisted than most."

"In that case, we certainly can't rule out Max Brentworth, for twisted logic might have convinced him sacrificing a young woman would benefit his business." I stood beside him, breathing in the scents of grass and loam and the faint brine carried from the bay. The sensations steadied me, as they always did. "I can't rule out anyone until I learn more. I need to speak with Dale Hanson," I said, remembering my initial reason for coming to town. "If someone had observed his work in the drawing room, he or she might have gained enough understanding to wrap stripped wire around the throne's metal legs. Even an infirm young woman."

"You're right," he conceded with a nod.

"Not that I wish to believe it of her. I truly don't." I gave a soft laugh. "I liked her immediately. She captured my sympathy, but more than that, she charmed me. Ilsa is childlike and ingenuous, but she's no fool. And her feelings run deep." I remembered I had something else to tell him. "Silas Griggson offered to buy Gull Manor."

He straightened abruptly. "You're joking. What did you say?"

"I told him no, of course. He persisted, even vaguely threatened me. Finally, I ordered him out." I frowned as I relayed more of the conversation. A shiver rippled across my shoulders. "Do you think he'll be back?"

He reached for my hands, turning me to face him and all but wrapping me in his palpable concern. "Have you mentioned this to Jesse?"

I shook my head as apprehension churned inside me. For the most part, I had put the incident behind me, but Derrick raised new fears of a powerful man intent on having his way.

"I think you should," he said, emphatic. "I don't like this. I don't like that he insisted, and that he said your relatives wouldn't be able to help you. Talk to the police, Emma. If you don't, I will."

Chapter 12

Derrick offered to accompany me to the hospital, but I preferred to go alone. The solitude would help me think. Need I fear reprisals from Silas Griggson? His threats hadn't been made in public. No, his attempt to bully me had been private and quiet, and that suggested he had very much meant his words. Suddenly, even knowing I would have the support of a United States senator brought me little comfort. George Wetmore might wield political power, but men like Silas Griggson bought and sold government favors as though they were commodities on the stock market. And I wondered if even someone of George Wetmore's stature and unblemished character would emerge unscathed from a run-in with the likes of Mr. Griggson.

Still, I would never sell Gull Manor, not at any price. That being the case, I had no choice but to dig in and face whatever schemes Silas Griggson sent my way.

At the hospital, I was overjoyed to find Jesse dressed and downstairs, preparing to leave. His doctor was handing him a list of instructions to follow at home. Jesse grinned at my approach.

"Emma, I don't suppose you came to see me?"

I loathed watching his hopeful expression fade, but I couldn't lie. "I came to see if Dale is awake and up to answering a few questions. But I'm delighted to see you looking so well." I placed my hand in his offered one, and to my great satisfaction he gave it a warm, if still slightly tremulous, squeeze. "You're getting your strength back."

"I am." His grin returned. "Slowly but surely. I think . . . that is, the doctor believes I'll regain the full function of my hands, or nearly so. Enough, Emma, to be able to stay on the force." Though he said this last quietly, I felt the power of the emotion behind the words.

"I'm so glad, Jesse. I've been so worried."

Together we walked away from the front desk, into the waiting area. Seeing it was empty, Jesse asked, "So what is this about wanting to question Dale?"

I explained as I had to Derrick, except for now I left out the part about Silas Griggson. I'd take Derrick's advice and let Jesse know, but later. Jesse listened carefully to what I had to say, nodding. When I'd finished, he said, "With you around, maybe the force *doesn't* need me."

"Don't be silly."

"I'm glad you're here, because I wanted to tell you something. I mentioned your theory about a left-handed culprit to Chief Rogers, and after talking to the officers who took statements at Ochre Court, he rejected the idea. Not one of them remembered anyone signing an affidavit with a left hand."

"Are they sure they can remember everyone with complete accuracy?"

"Left-handedness is rare so it stands out, and it's the type of thing we're trained to notice."

I nodded and reluctantly gave up on the only clue I had

managed to find on the scene. After all, I'd been discreetly looking for my left-handed culprit with each person I questioned, to no avail. "Do you know if Dale is up to talking? How is he?"

"He's not well yet, but he's awake. I know he'll be eager to answer any questions you might have. He feels responsible for my injuries. Keeps apologizing, though I've assured him numerous times it wasn't his fault. He couldn't have known the circuits hadn't been turned off, but I should have known better than to attempt to grasp someone who was being electrocuted."

"You wished to save him, and you might have done just that. If not for you, who knows what might have happened . . . ?"

Jesse turned pink at the praise, and changed the subject. "Why don't you and I go up together?"

"I can hardly think of anyone who *wasn't* in the drawing room at some point while we were installing the lights." Dale lay back against the pillow, his face nearly as white as the linen. His hands rested on top of the thin blanket that covered him to midchest, the one that had received the shock wrapped in bandages. Hannah had told me the skin had blackened and would eventually peel—painfully. The doctors still hadn't determined how much damage would be left in the nerves.

I occupied a chair while Jesse stood at the end of the bed. Dale began naming those who had been in the drawing room before the day of the ball. "Both Cooper-Smith sisters, Mrs. Goelet and her daughter, her sister-in-law, and her little girl, the housekeeper, footmen . . ." He paused to draw a breath. "It wasn't until the morning of the ball, after we made the final adjustments, that Mrs. Goelet ordered the doors locked. She didn't want the guests coming for the afternoon tea to spoil the surprise for later."

"Beatrice," I mused aloud, thinking about Harriette Goelet's lovely little daughter. "The child witnessed everything, yet has no idea what happened, thank goodness."

"She admired the flowers very much, especially the red ones," Dale said with a smile. "She kept reaching for them, but her mother told her she mustn't touch."

"Well, she somehow got her hands on one of them. She gave it to Cleo in the posy she handed her on the dais that night."

"Children have their ways," Jesse said with a slight smile. "So with everyone staying at Ochre Court having been in that drawing room sometime during the installation of the lighting, there is no telling who might have observed enough to understand the wiring."

I frowned in thought. "The wire wrapped around the legs of the throne was thicker than the wires used for the Edison bulbs."

"I'd forgotten about that," Jesse replied. "Dale, that means a strong current, yes?"

Dale nodded. "The thicker the wiring, the stronger the current."

"So the person responsible understood wiring and currents. Not to mention knowing where to obtain thicker wiring." I regarded each man in turn. "That suggests someone with a sure knowledge of construction, does it not? And not merely someone who had been casually observing the preparations."

"You're thinking we can rule out Ilsa," Jesse said evenly.

"Miss Ilsa Cooper-Smith?" Dale glanced at us both in astonishment. "You suspect that kind lady?"

I nodded, somewhat ashamedly.

"She arranged for refreshments to be brought to my two workers and me," he told us with no small measure of indignation.

MURDER AT OCHRE COURT   189

"We had reason to suspect her, Dale." Jesse circled the space until he stood opposite me across the bed. "But Emma's conclusion makes sense. It's highly doubtful Ilsa would have had the knowledge to commit the act. Or Mrs. Kipp, for that matter," he added, glancing at me for agreement.

"No, nor a lady's maid or an army officer who hails from the Four Hundred. But a construction mogul and the owner of a gas company surely might." I stood up from my chair. "I believe we have narrowed down our suspects."

Jesse and I said our good-byes to Dale and prepared to leave, when footsteps alerted us to a new arrival on the ward. We expected a doctor to enter, and were surprised when Patrick Floyd appeared in the doorway. He stopped short, looking as surprised as we were. Recovering quickly, he continued until he stood beside Dale's bed.

Dale gazed up at him without a trace of recognition, but an expression filled with apprehension. "Yes? Have you come to see me, sir?"

Realizing Dale must believe Mr. Floyd to be an official representing the law, I hastened to reassure him. "Dale, this is Mr. Patrick Floyd. He's a friend of the Cooper-Smith family."

My efforts fell flat, as Dale's wariness only intensified. "I want you to know, sir, how very sorry I am—"

"That's not why I've come," Mr. Floyd interrupted, but not unkindly. "I see the detective is here. Has he been asking you questions? Are you in need of a lawyer?"

"Our questions were general ones," Jesse said, "and not intended to incriminate anyone."

Mr. Floyd's scrutiny descended on me. "You're that reporter from the *Herald*. Are you intending to drag this man's good name through the mud?"

"Most assuredly not." My chin came up. "Dale is an old friend, as is his sister. I'm here to help him, not hurt him."

Mr. Floyd nodded, some of the hostility fading from his handsome features. "I'm glad to hear that. And I'm here, Mr. Hanson, to offer assistance with your case. I've asked a few questions of my own around this city, and I have come to believe you are blameless in Miss Cleo's death. If you need funds for proper legal counsel, I would be happy to provide them."

Part of me wished to rejoice at this boon. Only a couple of short hours ago I felt ill-disposed toward Patrick Floyd for having treated his wife and Ilsa wrongly, for leading on an innocent young woman while being married to another. But this act of generosity toward Dale certainly restored him in my estimate, for the most part. And yet . . .

Another part of me, where suspicions lurked, found this sudden good fortune rather questionable. Patrick Floyd claimed he had asked questions on Dale's behalf. Why? What did he know or care about Dale or any Newporter? Why this altruism on his part?

Had he something to gain by it?

"There is no case against Dale, Mr. Floyd," Jesse pointed out. "No charges have been filed. At least not yet."

Patrick Floyd assessed Jesse from down the length of his slightly aquiline nose. "I'm sorry, but I've come to speak with the patient and offer him my assistance. It's inappropriate for a member of the police force to be here while we discuss the legalities he might be facing. Likewise, a reporter. If you both wouldn't mind."

I silently questioned Dale with a look. He nodded. "I'd very much like to hear what Mr. Floyd has to say. I'm very grateful to him."

Minutes later, Jesse and I exited the hospital. I offered him a ride to his home on the Point, but he insisted on going directly to the police station. Along the way, I told him about

Silas Griggson's determination to purchase and destroy Gull Manor.

I made one more stop before heading for home. I had considered putting off this next encounter, but my conscience dictated otherwise. Maneuvering onto Bellevue Avenue in town, I stopped across the street from the Casino, at Stone Villa. A pair of masonry owls, the familiar symbol of the New York *Herald*, eyed me sternly as I passed through the gateposts at the end of the short driveway.

My feet dragged a bit as I approached the three-story Greek revival mansion, and I took my time climbing the steps to the columned veranda that stretched the length of the main portion of the house. I half hoped James Bennett would not be at home, or that he would be otherwise occupied and unable to see me on such short notice.

But no, the butler showed me into the receiving room and went to announce me to his master. Unlike the last time I visited this house, Mr. Bennett did not come down to the Spartan receiving room to speak with me in these rather uncomfortable surroundings. The butler escorted me up the stairs to a study that faced the street and afforded a view of the Casino's facade and entrance. Mr. Bennett, a man with a long straight nose, a stern profile, and a piercing gaze, awaited me on his feet and stretched out a hand in greeting.

"It's good to see you, Miss Cross. I assume you're here to discuss the Ochre Court incident."

I nearly winced at his bluntness, but held my reaction in check. Calmly, I shook his hand. "No, sir. I'll have that story for you shortly—"

"Yes, we'll want to run it as soon as possible, but we want all the facts, don't we? This turned out to be no ordinary society affair, didn't it?" He gave a laugh I found most inappropriate for the circumstances and gestured for me to take a seat. He took his own in a great wingback chair opposite me. "By George, you've got your hard news story after all. I won't stop you from pestering everyone involved, but be warned. If something unfortunate should befall you in the course of events, I'll have to deny ever giving you permission to report on anything other than frocks and decorations."

I suddenly wanted to rise from my seat and slam the door on my way out. Instead I breathed myself back into a state of calm. "Mr. Bennett, did the New York *World* shy away from allowing Nellie Bly to investigate an insane asylum? Or travel around the world unaccompanied? Do you think they said, 'If anything happens to you, Miss Bly, we'll have to disavow all prior knowledge of your endeavors'?"

Mr. Bennett didn't attempt an answer, but mutely regarded me as if I'd taken leave of my senses.

"No," I replied to my own question. "They did not. They celebrated her achievements in the most public way."

"I'm sorry, Miss Cross, but what *is* your point?"

"My point, sir, is that Nellie Bly—and others, including Elizabeth Bisland—set a precedent for female journalists. I don't see why I must scratch a path that has already been well worn."

He waved a dismissive hand. "Bly, Bisland—that was nothing but sensationalism. And anyway, neither is as young as you, Miss Cross. Your desire to report on hard news is not only dangerous, but improper."

"When you hired me, Mr. Bennett, you led me to believe that was exactly what you wished from me."

"I'm sorry if I ever gave you that impression. The truth is, and I believe you already know this, I hired you because of your associations with the members of the Four Hundred."

He leaned forward, lips curling in a smile that oozed conde-
scension and set my pulse pounding with ire. "And hasn't it
paid off? Your columns are very popular. You should be
proud of your work."

"I am ashamed of my work for the *Herald,* Mr. Bennett."
He pulled back, looking stricken. I plowed on. "I will complete this final article, but immediately following that I will
be resigning from the *Herald* news staff."

"You don't mean it."

I stood to assure him that yes, I most certainly did. "I
thank you, Mr. Bennett, for the opportunity you've afforded
me. It would seem our objectives are no longer compatible. I
wish you all the best."

"Miss Cross . . ."

With my heart pounding in my ears and my face flaming,
I half-blindly made my way downstairs and out to my carriage. I didn't take a full breath until I'd gone quite a ways
down Bellevue Avenue, past Marble House at least. There
was no turning back now. I had burned a bridge and now I
must live with the consequences. At Stone Villa, I had talked
of having to forge an already well-worn path. But now I
must create an entirely new path for my future, and travel it
for good or ill.

"Jesse, I think it's time to question Randall Cooper-Smith
again," I said on the telephone the next morning.

I had once more gone over everything I had learned, this
time with Nanny. We had discussed and considered and the-
orized until the mantel clock struck the half hour after midnight. One man stood at the center of everything—Cleo's
death, the tenement collapse in New York, Cleo and Oliver
Kipp parting ways, and now, threats to my own way of life.
Determined to hold him responsible for his misdeeds, I had

followed him to Newport, and would have done so independently of Cleo's coming-out ball.

"I pried precious little out of him when we last spoke," I said, "but I believe Mr. Cooper-Smith has vital information about Silas Griggson."

"And you're convinced Silas Griggson murdered Miss Cooper-Smith."

"I'm almost positive of it. Or, if not him personally, someone in his hire. But Mr. Cooper-Smith seems to have little respect for women, and none at all for society reporters. I fear he'll shirk my questions. It would be better if we go together."

Jesse's ironic response took me aback. "I'm doing well, thank you for asking."

I placed my hand on the wall beside the telephone and leaned my forehead against the call box. "I'm sorry. I should have asked. I'm just so . . ." I trailed off, unsure exactly what it was I felt. A desire to see justice for Cleo, yes. But frustration, too. I had formally resigned from the *Herald* yesterday and as soon I completed this last article, I would be without employment. Uncertainty about the future had kept me tossing last night as much as my questions about Cleo's death.

But neither consideration gave me a reason to barrel along at full speed with my plans while ignoring my friend's health. "How are you doing this morning, Jesse?"

"I'm all right, but still a bit shaky. I'm beginning to fear . . ." He cleared his throat. "To fear that I won't be able to handle a weapon with any degree of accuracy."

"You mustn't think that. You only want for the proper time to heal, you'll see."

"I'm sure you're right." He paused, his silence transmitting his lack of certainty across the wire. "Now, about Cooper-Smith. I agree it's time to question him more fully."

"He's staying at the Casino."

"Odd he's not with his daughter now."

"I think so, too. They're both grieving. One would think they would need each other."

"You don't think the problem is Mrs. Goelet, do you? That for some reason she won't allow him to stay at Ochre Court?"

The notion took me by surprise. "I hadn't considered that."

"Perhaps we should."

Jesse and I met outside the Casino an hour later. It being only midmorning, we believed our chances of finding Mr. Cooper-Smith in were good, and we were correct. But he wasn't alone.

I waited by the desk clerk's station while Jesse went and knocked at Mr. Cooper-Smith's door. The clerk, a bespectacled youth sporting slicked-back hair and a waxed but fledgling mustache, had glared daggers at Jesse's refusal to allow him to announce us to Mr. Cooper-Smith. It was most indecorous, he had protested. But Jesse had wished to catch Mr. Cooper-Smith off guard. What better way than to have a police detective pound on his door?

The clerk continued to eye me with disapproval. The presence of a woman on the Casino's second floor obviously made him ill at ease. I ignored him, hoping Jesse would return soon enough with Randall Cooper-Smith in tow.

But it was two voices, not one, that emanated from the guest room as the door opened. I recognized the visitor's voice at once. It belonged to Silas Griggson. I wondered what Jesse would do. Under normal circumstances, it might have been fortuitous to be able to question them at the same time, but these circumstances were anything but normal and I feared

Mr. Griggson's presence would stifle any degree of honesty Mr. Cooper-Smith might have been inclined to show us.

Mr. Griggson himself solved the dilemma by striding from the room, forcing Jesse to step out of his way. "We'll conclude our business at another time, Randall," he said as he traversed the hallway. When he came upon me he stopped short. He didn't bother to hide his sneer. "Well, if it isn't Miss Cross. Have you given my offer any further consideration?"

Did my legs tremble slightly as he glared his disregard at me? Yes, they did a bit, but thank goodness for the skirts and petticoats that hid the evidence of it. "No, Mr. Griggson, I have not. In fact, I had quite put it out of my mind."

"*Humph.*" His mouth twitched. "We'll see, won't we?"

He walked off and didn't look back.

"What was that all about?" the clerk asked. He pushed his glasses higher on his nose. "I don't like the looks of him and I can't have any trouble here. Mr. Bennett and the board of directors will not abide trouble."

I shook my head. "It was nothing. Nothing at all." But my legs were still trembling.

We further dismayed the desk clerk with Jesse's request— put more as a demand, really—that we be allowed to use one of the card rooms, empty at this time of day. The clerk once more scrutinized me. "Her, too?"

Jesse didn't dignify the question with a reply, refraining from pointing out that if he hadn't wished me to be present for the discussion, he and Mr. Cooper-Smith might have talked in Mr. Cooper-Smith's room. He merely gestured for the clerk to unlock the door to the nearest card room. Randall Cooper-Smith stood by shuffling his feet and looking none too pleased, especially with me. I seemed to be incurring the wrath of numerous men this morning.

Jesse and I had discussed our line of questioning before entering the building, and I had informed him of Silas Griggson's accusation concerning Randall Cooper-Smith and the tenement collapse. I placed my notebook on the baize-covered card table and readied my pencil. As we had agreed, I let Jesse begin the interview. "I know this is a very difficult time for you, Mr. Cooper-Smith, and I'll make this as easy as possible. Now, please explain the nature of your business with Silas Griggson."

Mr. Cooper-Smith started, clearly unnerved by the question. I didn't doubt that Mr. Griggson's visit had left him unsettled. "What has that got to do with my daughter? And why is *she* here?" He jerked his chin in my direction.

"Miss Cross is assisting me," Jesse said calmly. "She'll be taking notes. Perhaps you hadn't realized, but I was injured during the initial investigation at Ochre Court."

The man's obvious displeasure didn't fade, but neither did he react with anything approaching guilt at what Jesse told him. "Yes, but why her specifically?"

"Because there is no reason to expend more manpower from the police force for a simple questioning. And because, as a reporter, Miss Cross is a skilled note taker."

I suppressed a chuckle and sat at attention, my pencil poised above my notebook.

"And as for how this relates to your daughter, sir," Jesse continued, "all background information about those who knew her is relevant. Now then, Mr. Cooper-Smith, please tell me about your business with Mr. Griggson."

"I'm an architect," he said defensively. He raised his hands, palms up. "Griggson is a developer."

Jesse nodded as I jotted down this unhelpful information. "And do you work with other developers?"

"Of course I do. Griggson is merely one of many."

"It's my understanding that you and Mr. Griggson share more than a business relationship. That you are also friends." Jesse's gaze met Mr. Cooper-Smith's.

The man blinked and broke eye contact. "We've a good working association. Is there something wrong with that?"

"Mr. Cooper-Smith, are you aware that one of Silas Griggson's projects failed recently, resulting in the collapse of a building? Several residents died and numerous others were injured."

"Of course I'm aware of it."

"Did you design that building?"

Mr. Cooper-Smith sputtered and pulled back in his chair. "I . . . yes, I did. But my design was sound. It's already been established that the foreman was skimming funds from the project. He purchased shoddy materials and pocketed the difference."

"Did you find it at all suspicious that only hours after the man was bailed out of jail—by Silas Griggson—he was found floating in the East River?"

"What? Why you . . ." The blood drained from Mr. Cooper-Smith's face. He pushed to his feet. "I don't have to be subjected to this. It has nothing to do with my daughter."

"Sit down, sir," Jesse ordered, though his voice remained calm. "If you'll bear with me, you'll soon see that this very much relates to your daughter. Now then. Did you find this at all suspicious?"

The man hovered for another few seconds, his posture stiff, his face as white as the whitest marble. Then, slowly, he sank back into his chair. "It seemed . . . irregular. Yes. But suspicious? I don't know. Perhaps the guilt got to him."

"Or perhaps someone put him in the river." Jesse raised an eyebrow. Mr. Cooper-Smith's hands fisted on the tabletop. He looked frightened, unnerved. I scribbled away in my notebook for appearance's sake, but none of this was important, was nothing new—not even the man's reaction to Jesse's implication that Silas Griggson was responsible for the foreman's death. Jesse was leading him down a carefully planned path. He suddenly changed tacks. "How well did Mr. Griggson know your daughter?"

"What?" Clearly thrown off balance again, Mr. Cooper-Smith procured a handkerchief from his coat pocket and dabbed at his brow. "Not well. They, that is . . . they were as acquainted as any of my business associates with my daughters. He had been to the house for dinner upon occasion. Afterward he and I would retire to my study to consult on mutual projects."

"Is it not true that Mr. Griggson wished to marry your daughter?"

Mr. Cooper-Smith shot me a reproachful glance. "No, it is not."

"Hmm." Jesse frowned as if puzzled. "Surely that is contrary to how Mr. Griggson felt."

"You've been listening to *her*." He thrust a finger in my direction. I merely kept writing. My pencil scratched its way across the paper, causing Mr. Cooper-Smith to wince.

"Mr. Cooper-Smith," Jesse said gently, "if Miss Cross heard it from Silas Griggson's own mouth that he intended marrying your daughter, surely others were privy to the same information. I have no doubt I could find several other witnesses to corroborate Miss Cross's claim."

"Why are you doing this?" Mr. Cooper-Smith raked a hand through his hair, revealing a balding spot he had, until now, kept carefully concealed. "Cannot my daughter be laid to rest peacefully?"

"No, sir, for she didn't die peacefully." I set down my pencil and folded my hands across my notebook. Jesse gave me a slight nod. "I believe you're afraid to acknowledge the link between Mr. Griggson and your daughter. Has he threatened you? Is that what he came here to do this morning?"

"Griggson? Don't be absurd." His protest filled the quiet room, echoing off the walls.

"I know he is quite capable of threats, Mr. Cooper-Smith." I tilted my head and smiled slightly. "He has threatened me."

"Why would he threaten you? What could a foolish girl like you possibly have that a man like Silas Griggson would want?" As he fumed, I compressed my lips. Our gazes locked, his filled with the realization he had all but admitted that, under the right circumstances, Silas Griggson would indeed resort to threats. Before I could respond, he went on. "Never mind. There are times I'd like to threaten you myself."

"Now see here, sir." Jesse's voice became a growl. I held up a hand.

"That's quite all right. I understand Mr. Cooper-Smith's frustrations. Dealing with a man like Mr. Griggson would wear on the most patient of souls. Well, here is something else to try your patience, sir." I paused, straightening my shoulders for dramatic impact. "He has accused you of causing the building's collapse."

He shoved away from the table, his chair scraping back several inches. "Me? That's impossible. Why would he implicate me?"

"Because he's trying to cast blame everywhere but on himself, I would imagine." I assumed a sympathetic air, not entirely feigned. "Should he take his claim to the authorities, you will come under scrutiny."

"My designs will speak for themselves."

"Unless they've been tampered with," I pointed out.

I would not have believed anyone could grow paler still, but Mr. Cooper-Smith did.

"This is why it would be advisable for you to cooperate with us," Jesse said. "Did Silas Griggson threaten you or your daughter? And is it possible she knew something about him, perhaps about the role he played in the collapse of the building, that put her in danger?"

His mouth opened and closed more than once as he clearly debated his options. He might continue to deny it, but Jesse and I had the answer to the first question. Unfortunately, the second answer, which could prove key in bringing Cleo's murderer to justice, remained elusive.

He drew in a slow breath, refusing to meet either Jesse's or my gaze. "There is nothing I can tell you. If what you're suggesting is true, I have no knowledge of it." He came to his feet. "That is all I have to say. May I go?"

Had it been up to me, I'd have seen if a day or two in a jail cell might loosen his tongue. Luckily for him, Jesse took a more lenient approach. He admonished him not to leave town, and we left.

Out on the sidewalk, we once more consulted. "He's lying," I said, not bothering to lower my voice despite the pedestrians shuffling by. Attracted by the costly goods arranged in the Casino's shop windows, none of them paid us any attention.

"Of course he's lying. Griggson obviously got to him before we arrived."

"Then why didn't you press him?"

"We put the fear of God in him, and for now, that's enough. He's afraid of Griggson, and that's putting it mildly. I think we have the answer to why he's not staying at Ochre Court with Ilsa."

"I don't understand."

Jesse walked with me to my carriage. "He's putting distance between himself and his remaining daughter. I'd stake my reputation on it."

"Keeping her safe," I said, and Jesse nodded.

"Safer than if they were residing under the same roof, at any rate. In the meantime, Ochre Court provides her with a relatively secure haven. The place is nearly a fortress. What happened to her sister was possible only because so many people were in and out of the house for the festivities. That's not likely to happen again in the near future, especially if he's not there to tempt the killer into returning."

"And the housekeeper always knows who is coming and going," I told him. "She told me as much."

Jesse handed me up onto the leather seat. "There's nothing more reliable than a good housekeeper. Still, Cooper-Smith is taking no chances and is staying away."

"So if he's protecting Ilsa," I reasoned aloud, "it must be because he believes Griggson is responsible for Cleo's death. But then *why* won't he help put Griggson away?"

"Assuming we're correct in our assumptions, the answer is obvious." Jesse shook his head and shrugged. "He has no confidence in the workings of the law. He's afraid Griggson will use his political power to have the charges dropped, and then he and his daughter will be in more danger than ever."

"Do you think Griggson's political influence is that extensive?"

"A New York real estate developer? I'd be surprised if it wasn't."

"Detective! Detective!"

A boy I recognized from the Newport *Observer,* one of the newsies who sold papers on street corners all around town, came running along the sidewalk. "I've got a message for you, sir." When he reached us he whisked his cap off his head and doubled over. "From Officer Binsford," he panted, straightening slowly. "Sorry, I ran all the way from Marlborough Street. He says he's heading to The Elms with some of the other officers. Wants you to join him there."

"Did he say why?"

The boy shook his head. "Only that there's trouble."

Jesse handed him a coin, and the boy ran off. Our gazes met. "I'll take my buggy and meet you out there," he said to me.

Chapter 13

✦

Jesse and I left our buggies on Bellevue Court, a side street off the main avenue beside The Elms' property. Before we'd gone very far the unrest here became apparent. Men were shouting and foul language permeated the air. Several other reporters had arrived before us. I recognized one young man Derrick had introduced me to at the *Messenger*. And Ed Billings, my onetime fellow reporter at the *Observer*, stood safely beneath the shelter of a weeping elm. He saw me and nodded in what seemed more of a challenging gesture than a friendly one. Ed and I had locked horns frequently when I worked for the *Observer*. I'd discovered early on he would rather read over my shoulder than track down the facts of a story for himself, but it was almost always his articles that ran because Mr. Millford didn't believe people wished to read serious news written by a woman. The unseemliness of it offended the sensibilities of the populace, or so he told me on numerous occasions.

I ignored Ed and focused on my longtime acquaintance on the police force, Scotty Binsford, pushing his way through a throng of workers converged beside the massive, rectangular cavity that would be the basement and cellars of the completed house. Several other policemen were attempting to restore order, but their demands and pleas went unheeded.

Jesse flashed me an incredulous look along with a terse order to venture no closer to the ruckus before he himself charged in, badge in his outthrust hand. I immediately saw the wisdom of remaining where I was, especially as tensions intensified and a roar went up. I clamped my teeth in worry for Jesse and the other officers and craned my neck to follow their actions.

Soon, two sets of men began to take shape in my sights: ones in woolen flat caps, shirtsleeves, and corduroy trousers, versus others in shabby street clothes wearing dented derbies and battered straw boaters. It didn't take me long to understand that the construction crew, and specifically the electrical workers, were warding off a confrontation by disgruntled gas workers from town.

The chaos seemed to expand and I backed away, putting more distance between me and the mounting anger. I lost track of my fellow reporters, Ed included, as more than a few fists waved in the air, some making contact with jaws or shoulders or chests. Were there enough policemen present to quell the unrest? I was beginning to think not, to think perhaps I should rush over the nearest property and beg the use of a telephone to call Chief Rogers at the police station. Then a familiar face and baritone caught my attention.

Max Brentworth, taller and broader than the more wiry workmen, moved through the unruly tangle. I watched as he grabbed shirtfronts, suspenders, and coat lapels, and roughly shoved men aside. I couldn't distinguish his exact words, but his scowls conveyed his growing anger. Had he instigated this?

I whisked out my pencil and notepad and began making

notes. If anyone was seriously injured, I wanted to keep an accurate record. Suddenly, two scuffling men went tumbling over the flimsy fence erected around the gaping chasm and plummeted some twenty feet down.

The shoving and fighting ceased, but a new outcry went up. With the fate of the two workers now my foremost concern, I circumvented the activity and hurried along to the front of the property, where I could get closer to the fenced-off perimeter. Below me sprawled the bowels of what would be Newport's next great house. Gazing down at the web of pipes, ductwork, and cables made me dizzy. Ladders descended at intervals from ground level. They swarmed now with men hurrying down and converging on the two prone workers. Not far from them stood the great coal furnaces that, I'd been told, would burn day and night to generate electricity for the house.

A pair of stretchers appeared—I assumed they were kept on hand for just such emergencies—and were lowered into the pit. The injured men were carefully rolled onto them, and then ropes were attached for the arduous task of raising the stretchers back to ground level. The reality of two hurt individuals, their fate still unknown to those above, had done what the police could not: restore a modicum of order. At any rate, the anger seemed to have diminished as all of the men peered down at the rescue efforts. Perhaps they were remembering that they were all Newporters. Max Brentworth continued circulating through the crowd, but he, too, seemed far more composed than previously.

The immediate danger over for now, I made my way back over to the others. When I got there, I chose a man at random, and was gratified to realize he and I were acquainted, fellow longtime residents of the Point. He was not one of the Elms crew, I realized at once, for his clothing matched that of the men who had come here from town.

"George, what happened?"

"Emma, is that you?" He was large and brawny, with unruly dark hair and a wide nose. We hadn't seen each other in a good long time, but I knew he didn't mean the question literally, for he recognized me as surely as I did him. Still, I nodded, and he went on. "Honestly, I don't know why I'm here. I work for Brentworth, and I've been hearing a lot of talk lately about how we're all going to lose our jobs. So, when the others decided to come out here, I tagged along."

"Could have gotten yourself hurt," I admonished him. "And then where would Louise and the children be?"

He belatedly whisked off his derby and ducked his head. "You're right. I shouldn't be here." He glanced about warily.

"Why don't you go," I whispered, "before the police start making arrests?"

His face filled with alarm. "Do you suppose they will?"

"I don't know, but if I were you I wouldn't wait to find out."

With another cautious look about him, George Riley slipped away. One of the stretchers had been raised to ground level, and was now being maneuvered onto solid ground by several men. It seemed everyone involved had decided to put their differences aside and work together. One of the men being rescued raised a hand in the air to signal that he was conscious and, I hoped, not in terrible pain. I breathed a sigh of relief for him.

"Making trouble, Miss Cross?"

My sigh became a gasp. Max Brentworth stood at my shoulder, and as I turned to gaze up at him, his scowl forced me back a step. "What do you mean?"

"I mean, Miss Cross, that your being here reeks of foul play. How dare you?"

"How dare I what?" From the corner of my eye I searched for Jesse or Scotty but saw no sign of either of them.

"How dare you stir up trouble to sell newspapers."

"Oh? One might accuse you of the same thing, Mr. Brentworth, except that rather than selling newspapers, you're trying to save your business."

His eyes narrowed. "Do you think no one realizes how reporters like you manipulate events and orchestrate trouble to create stories where none would have existed otherwise? It's no coincidence your reappearance in this city coincided with the rising of tensions."

"You've greatly overestimated my influence if you think I'm capable of orchestrating this." I wanted to laugh, except that I found nothing funny about being in such close proximity to a man of his size and apparent strength. I very much supposed he began his career like much of his workforce, as a laborer, and through constant toil, sharp wits, and yes, perhaps a bit of intimidation here and there, worked his way to the position he currently held.

I refused to let him intimidate me, or at least, let him *see* that he intimidated me. "If anything, it would be you inciting your workers to protest the use of electricity in the new houses being built. Admit it. You feel threatened by it, don't you, Mr. Brentworth?"

"I'll have you know I've invested in the development of electricity. I might own a gas company, but I'm neither stupid nor blind to the future."

"Oh," I said rather lamely. This unexpected turn robbed me of much of my bravado.

"Besides, do you think I would put men's lives and livelihood at risk in pointless displays of civil disobedience?" He moved closer to me, his bulk blocking out all else. A ripple of fear went through me, yet I could not believe he would harm me in so public a setting. "Are you that foolish, Miss Cross?"

"Are *you*? Do you think *I* would put lives at risk to sell a story? I grew up here. I know many of these men. If I wished to oppose the use of electricity over gas, I could certainly think of many safer yet more efficient means of doing so. At the same time, when I see a story unfolding, yes, it is my job to report on it. Not to create it, Mr. Brentworth, but merely to relay the facts."

We stared each other down for several seconds. Then, almost imperceptibly, his stance relaxed. The knot in my stomach eased.

"It seems we've reached an impasse, Mr. Brentworth."

"Perhaps we have," he said, begrudgingly. He took my measure, as I took his. Could I have been wrong about him?

"Why *are* you here?" I asked in perhaps too demanding a voice.

He took my tone in stride. "To keep my men out of jail by persuading them to maintain some semblance of order. You can go around and ask them if you like."

"Well, then . . . I'm here to cover an ongoing story, one that seemed to begin with Cleo Cooper-Smith's death. And no other reason." I emphasized that last, still indignant at being accused of manipulating events to my own advantage. Then I relented. "Perhaps I misjudged you, Mr. Brentworth."

"Perhaps I misjudged *you,* Miss Cross." He didn't look at all happy about this admission. I supposed Max Brentworth did not like being proven wrong.

I frowned, but no longer in anger. "So then, this is why you ordered me out of your carriage. Because you thought I was trying instigate unrest among your workers."

"Well . . ." He lifted his chin and sniffed. "Yes."

"Your doing so only made me suspect you all the more."

His scowl returned. "Of murdering Miss Cooper-Smith?"

It was a question I didn't care to answer, so I said, "Can you vouch for your men, that one of them wasn't involved?"

"I believe I can." His mouth slanted ruefully. "I apologize for ordering you out of my carriage."

"I apologize for suspecting you of murder." We stood in

momentary, awkward silence. I compressed my lips. He shuffled his feet. Finally, I said, "If you learn of anything that might be significant about the night of the ball, will you please tell Detective Whyte?"

"I will." His brusque manner persisted, but his hostility was gone.

Jesse insisted I go home following the incident at The Elms. "Have Nanny make you some of her potent tea, and for a little while at least don't worry about any of this. I'm back to work now. Let me handle things."

Standing beneath the trees lining Bellevue Court, I regarded the concern on his earnest features, his half-Irish complexion lightly freckled by the summer sun. My instinct was to protest, to tell him he was the one who should go home. He had left the hospital only yesterday. He needed more rest, more time for his hands to heal.

But he wouldn't wish to hear it. And he certainly wouldn't be willing to accept the notion of my putting myself in danger while he went home and put his feet up. His next words proved me correct.

"You shouldn't have come with me to The Elms. You so easily could have been hurt among all those enraged men. Things are getting out of control, Emma, and it's got me worried. Not just as relates to this case or even this particular occurrence. But when I see Newporter against Newporter, I know something is terribly wrong."

I plucked a fallen leaf from the brim of my hat. "Times are changing."

"They've always *been* changing, and I've seen festering resentments before, but somehow this is different. Sometimes I'm afraid Newport doesn't belong to us anymore—to those of us who were born here and live every day of our lives here. This city's become the property of . . ." He stopped short with a sheepish look.

"Of people like my relatives."

He nodded. "People like the Vanderbilts do a lot of good. Progress, charities, universities. But those are general things. They seem blind when it comes to the daily lives of ordinary people. They came sweeping into Newport twenty years ago and began reshaping it to suit their desires, and I don't see that we're any the better for it."

I touched his forearm. "I don't think we can blame my relatives and their friends for today's events. Can they be faulted for wanting what is new and innovative?"

"The best money can buy," Jesse said with a touch of bitterness. It wasn't like him, this blanket condemnation of an entire group of people. He knew as well as I that money or no, there were good people and bad people and every type of character in between. He was tired, I reasoned. Tired and still worried about his physical recovery.

I could not help him with that, but I *could* prevent him from worrying about me; that much I could and would do for him. "I'll go home. You're right. I could use some of Nanny's strong tea. Would you like to join me?"

"I have work to do." He gestured to where the uniformed policemen were gathering up those protesters who had resorted to violence. I nodded, having already known he wouldn't be sipping tea with me at Gull Manor. Keeping busy at his profession would be the best medicine for him. "We'll be letting most of them go," he assured me. "But a few hours at the station house might persuade them to mind their manners next time."

When Mrs. Hendricks telephoned, I considered alerting Jesse at the police station and letting him handle this new matter. I even told Nanny that that was my intention. She chuckled, and coaxed me to finish my tea before I returned to Ochre Court.

"I just said I'd let Jesse see to the matter," I pointed out with an indignant huff.

"I know you all too well, Emma. When a call comes, you answer it."

I pushed my teacup aside on the kitchen table, where we often had tea in the afternoons, rather than bring our light repast to the front rooms of the house. It was easier, and in our informal household, there was no one to raise an eyebrow at our lack of decorum. "You're right, Nanny. Mrs. Hendricks said Camille has left the house and the necklace is gone. I need to go."

She pushed my cup and saucer back toward me. "But not before you drink up and finish your sandwich." Nanny had made her delicious chicken salad with the leftovers from last night's roast.

"Perhaps I should go with you, Miss Emma." Katie drained her own cup and stood to bring her dishes to the kitchen sink. Patch, lying on the mat by the garden door, stirred and lifted his head, no doubt hoping for a falling crumb or two.

"You know, Emma, that might not be a bad idea." Nanny refilled her cup from the old earthenware teapot—the one guests never saw. "Maybe what this Camille won't admit to you, she'll say to Katie."

Katie turned around from the sink, a dripping washrag suspended in one hand. "Or do you suppose a lady's maid would turn up her nose at a maid-of-all-work?"

"Camille might balk at talking to me, but I can guarantee you Mrs. Hendricks will know the truth before too long. Camille left the house, and the necklace she stashed under her mattress is gone—the necklace that matches the broken section Grace and I found in Cleo's bedroom. There can only be so many explanations for this, and it shouldn't be too difficult to figure out which of them is the truth."

"Poor Camille." Katie sighed and took the cup and saucer I handed her.

Nanny scoffed. "Poor Camille? That's not what you said the other day. You said someone should remind her of her place."

"And so they should." Katie added more washing soda to the dishwater. "Still, I can't help feeling sorry for her. Stealin' from her employer like that? She'll likely go to jail, won't she?" Katie shuddered. "It'll be awful for her, and maybe she did it for her family. Maybe someone's sick like, and they're needin' the money."

I hadn't the heart to contradict my kindhearted maid. Camille might indeed need money, but it was to facilitate her marriage to Dorian Norris, and not out of any desire to help anyone else. Perhaps she would go to prison for her crime. I only hoped that crime didn't include murder.

A short time later, I drove up Ochre Court's service drive and was discreetly admitted by the housekeeper. She hadn't told me much on the telephone, and I didn't quite know what to expect. What if Camille had taken the diamond necklace and left the island? Had it been a foolish decision on my part not to confront her immediately?

Mrs. Hendricks's satisfied expression piqued my curiosity further as she led me to her private parlor and closed the door. In a high-backed, uncomfortable-looking wooden chair, Camille sat stiffly upright, her eyes glittering shards of anger. A young footman stood at attention a few feet from her.

"The moment I realized she'd left the premises, I sent Edgar after her. He followed her into town and intercepted her outside Herrmann's Jewelers on Thames Street."

"I know the place." I regarded Camille's defiant expression. "What *can* you have been thinking?"

"I can tell you that." Mrs. Hendricks spoke with the brisk efficiency of someone who was no one's fool. "She intended selling the piece and boarding the first ship, skiff, or wherry to the mainland."

"That's not true," Camille snapped.

"Didn't you realize the jeweler would question where you got the necklace?" My incredulity quelled any outrage I might have expressed. Her actions left me truly baffled. "You wouldn't have made it to Jamestown before he sent the police after you."

"I wasn't trying to steal anything," the young woman insisted. Her obstinacy also puzzled me. I would have thought she'd show an ounce of contrition to win our sympathies.

Mrs. Hendricks addressed Edgar. "Tell us exactly what happened."

He took a step forward, almost like a child's tin soldier put into play. "It didn't take me long to catch up to her, although I stayed far enough back that she never noticed me. She went straight to Herrmann's. No detours. Walked like she had a purpose."

"Of course I had a *purpose,*" Camille interrupted, nearly spitting the last word.

Mrs. Hendricks made a slashing gesture at the air. "Go on, Edgar."

"When she reached the shop she just stood staring through the window, not like she was admiring the trinkets on display, but like she was steeling herself to do something. Then she nodded, like she made a decision, and went inside. I went in right after her. I told Mr. Herrmann what she was up to and what my errand was, and I told Miss Tate if she didn't come back to Ochre Court with me she'd be having a visit to the police station instead. Mr. Herrmann offered to telephone the station, but I told him no, we would handle it here."

"Thank you, Edgar." Mrs. Hendricks lifted her eyebrows as if all questions had been answered and Camille found guilty as charged. Yet, I wondered . . . "That will be all, Edgar. You may go."

The young man frowned, clearly wishing to remain and see how matters progressed. I suspected theft at Ochre Court rarely if ever happened, especially under the sharp watch of Mrs. Hendricks. Other than the horrendous occurrence the night of the ball, this incident had probably constituted the single most exciting day of Edgar's career. With no choice but to resume his regular duties, he dragged his feet as he crossed the room.

As soon as the door closed behind him, Camille leaped up from her chair and rushed to where I stood. "This is all a misunderstanding. I would never steal from Miss Ilsa. I was only trying to make things right before she found out . . ."

"Be silent, girl, and sit back down. No one told you to get up." The housekeeper said more calmly to me, "I had her brought back here only because of your request, Miss Cross. But I believe it's time we called in the police."

I thought Camille might speak up against that idea, but she merely dragged herself back to her chair, plunked herself down into it, crossed her arms, and assumed an insolent slouch. I had no argument for the housekeeper's suggestion either. Despite Camille's protests, she had been caught in the act, both of having stolen merchandise hidden beneath her bed, and of attempting to dispose of it. If the theft also connected Camille to Cleo's murder, the police needed to know. But would a few more minutes make a difference?

"May I ask her a few questions first, Mrs. Hendricks?"

"I suppose it couldn't hurt. She's certainly not going anywhere now."

"Where is the necklace?" I asked. The housekeeper retrieved the familiar velvet bag from her desk and handed it to me. I opened the drawstrings and poured the strand of diamonds into my palm. They glittered innocently in the glare of the room's electric lamps, as though I held a handful of stars.

Perhaps it had not been fair of me to forgo questioning Camille when we first discovered the necklace in her possession. My thinking had been to watch her, to find out what her next move would be, and whether she would somehow implicate herself in Cleo's death. But assuming she had nothing to do with the murder, had I allowed her to further incriminate herself by falling prey to temptation?

I had known desperate women before, aplenty. They had performed desperate, and some would say immoral acts, but through understanding their plight I had declined to judge them and had found ways to help them. Instead of approaching Camille's situation with understanding, however, I had assumed the worst of her from the start. Perhaps I had done so because of the aggrieved way she had spoken of being in service, or had it been because of her secret courtship with Dorian Norris? *Had* I judged her because of it?

Perhaps I had allowed society's unfairness to color my own thinking, so that I had, without quite realizing it, found fault with the notion of a maid marrying a member of the Four Hundred. I cringed to consider it and became determined to help her if I could. I didn't know if I could protect Camille from the law, but perhaps I could help her explain her actions to the police, and thereby help her face the coming ordeal.

I brought a side chair closer to her and sat. She pulled away as though trying to distance herself from me. Pretending not to notice, I spoke kindly but firmly. "Camille, tell us why you took the necklace. Was it an act of revenge against what you perceived to be unfair treatment by Miss Cleo? Or did you steal it as a means of being able to marry Dorian Norris? You must tell us exactly what happened if we are to help you."

In any other circumstances I would have expected a humble, beseeching reply. Not from Camille. Instead, she once more vacated her seat and swept by me, going to the far wall to peer up through the high-set window. She stood there for several seconds, her chest heaving, her breath as audible as if she had just finished an arduous race. The housekeeper and I traded mystified looks. When Camille whirled to face us, it was not with meekness or shame, but with brazen hostility.

"I did no such thing, but at least someone has finally asked me what happened. I'll thank you for that, Miss Cross, if not for your suspicions. I never stole that necklace. It was given to me."

"By whom?" Mrs. Hendricks demanded.

"By Miss Cleo. *She's* the one who stole it, from Miss Ilsa."

Chapter 14

Camille took in our astonished expressions. "That's right,"
she said, "Miss Cleo stole it from Miss Ilsa's room the day
before the ball. It had belonged to their mother, the most
valuable thing she had owned, passed down to her from her
grandmother. Being the elder sister, Miss Ilsa inherited it
when their mother died."

The moment she paused for a breath I stole my chance to
question her claim. "Assuming Miss Cleo did steal this from
her sister, why would she then give it to you? That makes no
sense."

"Oh, it does. You see, Miss Cleo broke the necklace. I
don't know how, I wasn't there at the time. But that morning, she called me into her room to help her dress, and she
brought out the necklace. She said she was going to wear it
later at the ball, and told me to put it on her so she could see
how it looked. When I did, it simply fell apart in my hands."
Camille's hands fisted and went to her hips in a show of outrage. "She tried to blame me, said I pulled the setting apart. I
never did, it was a lie, and I knew she had already broken it
but wanted someone to blame."

"You argued with her that morning," I said, remembering what the housemaid, Nora, had told me.

Camille was nodding. "You're right, we argued. I didn't like being accused of something I didn't do. It wasn't fair. But Miss Cleo said it would be my word against hers, and her father would send me packing. She made me take the necklace and ordered me to take it to town and have it fixed on the sly. It couldn't have been ready in time for the ball, but as soon as it *was* ready, I suppose Miss Cleo would have slipped it back into Miss Ilsa's room."

"Didn't she worry that Miss Ilsa would wish to wear the necklace to the ball?" I asked.

Camille shook her head. "Miss Ilsa never wore the necklace. She said it brought too much attention to her, and she didn't like that. She treasures it, though, because it was her mother's. She said she planned to give it to her sister's daughter someday, if she ever had one. You know, because she can't have children of her own."

"And you were taking the necklace to be repaired when Edgar found you at Herrmann's."

"That's right, Miss Cross. Just trying to right a wrong without Miss Ilsa finding out. I . . ." She glanced down at her feet, then back up at me with fierce expression. "I didn't like to hurt Miss Ilsa with the knowledge her sister stole from her. She didn't have to ever know that, did she? She deserves to properly mourn Miss Cleo without bad feelings."

"If any of this is true, you were taking an awful chance," Mrs. Hendricks said sternly. "It certainly looks as though you stole this necklace."

"Then why on earth would I bring it to a jewelry store here in Newport? Why wouldn't I hide it until we all left the island and try to sell it somewhere in New York? Then if Miss Ilsa discovered the piece missing, I could have denied everything. She might have thought it was lost during her travels."

"Except that we found the necklace beneath your mattress."

Camille started, her gaze locking with Mrs. Hendrick's imperious one. I watched as a realization dawned on her. "You went through my room?"

"That's right." The housekeeper's chin lifted higher. "There is no privacy in this house for anyone suspected of stealing."

"But . . . why?" She was genuinely taken aback. "How could you have known about the necklace at all?"

I opened my handbag and drew out the small strand of diamonds I'd found in Cleo's bedroom. "Because of this. I found it in Miss Cleo's bedroom the day after she died. And then when I was told about an argument coming from Miss Cleo's room the morning of the ball, I deduced this broken necklace could have had something to do with it."

"I don't understand." Camille assumed a puzzled frown. "Why wouldn't Miss Cleo have given me all the pieces to have fixed?"

That was a very good question. I stared down at the gems in my palm, and an unsavory truth dawned. I thought of Cleo's fine dresses but lack of jewelry and accessories. "I wonder if Cleo never meant to wear this necklace at the ball, and purposely broke it in order to keep a fistful of diamonds for herself."

Camille's mouth dropped open. The housekeeper nodded sagely. "You may be right about that, Miss Cross." She turned to address Camille. "Would Miss Cleo have needed money?"

When Camille hesitated, I raised my suspicions concerning the family's finances. "I noticed the fine gowns among Cleo's possessions, but an utter lack of anything else of value. That's unusual for a young woman coming out. I'm going to guess that this necklace is the only piece of costly jewelry the family owns these days."

"There was more jewelry," Camille admitted, and then hastily added, "I don't know what happened to the rest." Her chin came up defensively. "But little by little the sisters stopped wearing the other jewelry they inherited from their mother. None of it was as fine as that necklace, but nothing to sneer at either."

Perhaps Cleo hoped to obtain enough money from the diamonds she kept to allow her to put off marriage for a while. To escape Silas Griggson. Perhaps she planned to steal off somewhere and live quietly until a more favorable option presented itself. We would never know for sure, but it seemed the most likely answer. For now, I wanted to believe Camille's story. Despite her haughtiness, or perhaps because of it, she had gained my sympathy. "I'm afraid there is little choice but to see if Miss Ilsa will corroborate any of Camille's story."

"I'm afraid you're right, Miss Cross." Mrs. Hendricks released a regretful sigh. "And it's going to be a sad moment either for Miss Ilsa, realizing her sister stole from her . . ." Her gaze shifted to Camille and narrowed. "Or for this one here, if we find out she's lying and call the police and have her hauled away."

"If you'll excuse us," I said to the housekeeper, "I'm going to take Camille upstairs."

The woman frowned. "Without me?"

"Mrs. Hendricks, this matter is now between Miss Ilsa, Camille, and I, and I am acting on behalf of Detective Whyte." That was *almost* true, and I hoped the housekeeper didn't challenge me on it. I firmly believed this next round of questioning would be easier on Ilsa with fewer people in the room, not to mention the woman's stern expressions wouldn't help either. "Since Camille doesn't work for you and Ilsa isn't a permanent member of this household, I simply don't see any reason for you to accompany us, although I do thank you for your assistance in the matter thus far."

"Oh, but . . ." Her shoulders sagged as she apparently perceived the logic in my argument. "Very well. But please do not disturb Mrs. Goelet or disrupt the servants' duties."

I assured her we would do neither, and, velvet bag in hand, rode the elevator with Camille up to the second floor. I didn't relish the ride any more than the first one I'd taken. As the conveyance lurched upward, I felt as though my stomach dropped to my feet.

Outside Ilsa's door I knocked softly, but received no answer. I knocked again. From behind me, Camille reached to open the door. I almost stopped her, but she was, after all, still Ilsa's lady's maid. She pushed the door open to reveal an empty room.

It was then voices drifted to us from down the corridor and around the corner, from the main gallery that overlooked the Great Hall below. We followed the sound, our footsteps muffled by the woven runner with its rich colors, and entered the open square gallery supported by columns and arches fashioned from deeply carved teak. A rainbow of light from the massive stained glass windows at the half landing of the Grand Staircase bathed that end of the gallery. We proceed in the opposite direction until we reached a sitting room. The door stood open.

I was surprised to see Ilsa not only smiling but giggling softly, but perhaps I should not have been. Beside her sat handsome Patrick Floyd, and unlike his somber demeanor at the ball, or his authoritative air when he visited Dale at the hospital, today he seemed relaxed; he seemed to be enjoying himself in his present company.

"Ah, so we meet again, Miss Cross," he said in his pleasingly deep voice.

"Thank you again for what you offered to do for Dale. He's a good man." As when I saw him at the hospital, however, I found myself assaulted by conflicting emotions. He had stood by Ilsa at the ball, even refused to dance with someone else when she suggested he do so. He had appeared at the hospital in his guise of guardian angel to offer Dale the legal help he might need, but would be unable to afford on his own.

Yet Mr. Floyd had also encouraged Ilsa while still married to another woman, and this raised in me a wariness of even his most altruistic acts. A whisper inside me, no greater than the stirring of a breeze, suggested that perhaps Patrick had something to do with his wife's death—something rather more direct than straying from his marriage vows. No official suspicion had fallen upon him, however, for he had been away at the time. I tried to reassure myself that, if he had arranged for the gas duct to be left open, the police would have discovered his guilt.

Camille remained behind me in the doorway. Ilsa smiled up at us, her happiness evident. "Miss Cross, have you discovered something about my sister's death?" Her gaze shifted over my shoulder. "Camille, thank you for bringing Miss Cross up. That will be all for now."

I felt rather than saw Camille's hesitancy. "We need Camille to remain," I said. "But if Mr. Floyd would excuse us, there is a matter we need to discuss."

"Oh, I . . ." I had clearly taken Ilsa aback. "Patrick, would you mind terribly? I can't imagine what this could be about, but I'm sure it won't take very long."

"I'll be right downstairs." As he stood, he held on to Ilsa's hand, and bent to kiss it. He relinquished his grasp in a lingering sort of way and left the room.

Ilsa looked up at me in question. "Come in, Miss Cross, and tell me what this is all about."

I sat beside her on the silk-upholstered sofa and opened the velvet bag. "Do you recognize this?" With a gentle shake of the bag, I deposited the diamond necklace in Ilsa's lap.

"This was my mother's. Of course I recognize it. How did you come to possess it?" Her expression gradually changed from one of puzzlement to one of misgiving. Her gaze shifted. "Oh, Camille, you didn't."

Camille made a disgusted noise in her throat, but I held up a hand to forestall her protests. "Is the necklace yours?" I asked Ilsa.

"Yes, it's mine. I inherited it when my mother passed away."

"I told you so," Camille murmured.

"Did you know it was broken?" I pulled out the second piece and showed her. Her face registered dismay.

"Oh, no! Mama's beautiful necklace. Camille, how could you?"

A wave of scarlet engulfed Camille from neck to hairline. I spoke up again to forestall her explosion of temper. "I don't know that Camille did anything wrong. You see, I found the smaller broken section in . . . well . . . in your sister's room." Camille and I had agreed not to mention my suspicion that Cleo meant to sell some of the diamonds. "Is it possible your sister borrowed the necklace and accidentally broke it? Camille says Cleo asked her to take it to a jeweler in town to have it fixed."

As I spoke, Ilsa stared straight ahead, her expression unreadable. She reached with one hand to the end table beside her, graced by a vase of white flowers surrounding one red rosebud, reminding me of Cleo's posy during the *tableau vivant*. Her fingertips brushed the petals absently.

When I'd finished my tale, she shook her head and whispered, "She did it again."

"Did what again?"

"Borrowed—as you politely called it—my necklace."

"You mean she had done it before?"

She nodded and with what I perceived to be fragile calm, turned her attention to Camille. "Did she tell you why she stole it?"

"She said she planned to wear it to the ball, miss."

"And how did it break?"

"That I don't know, Miss Ilsa. Miss Cleo asked me to put it on her, and when I tried, it fell apart in my hands."

Ilsa let out a long-suffering breath. "She knew I'd never say anything at the ball, not in front of so many people. She'd have hidden it from me until it was too late, and I'd have stood by and pretended nothing was wrong. Why didn't she just ask me? I'd have let her wear it."

"Yes, why didn't she?" I pretended to agree, but this again helped confirm my suspicion that Cleo had been less intent on wearing the necklace than selling part of it. "So you believe Camille's account of what happened?"

She nodded, obviously deep in thought. Then she gave herself a shake. "Yes, I believe Camille's story. I know my sister, Miss Cross. I loved her very much, but she was not without her faults." She ended on a dismal note that tugged at my heartstrings. Camille had wished to spare her mistress this last revelation of her sister's duplicity. I wished now that I had allowed Ilsa to continue in ignorance; I almost wished I had never come upon the necklace at all. But at least it had found its way back to its rightful owner.

Leaving Ilsa and Camille to make their apologies to each other—Ilsa for believing Camille had stolen from her, and Camille for not informing Ilsa of the theft immediately—I once again braved the elevator down to the kitchen level. Upon exiting, I found a slender figure dressed in a maid's uniform waiting for me.

"Nora, you startled me," I said after a gasp.

"Is that Camille in trouble?" she asked bluntly.

"If she were, it really wouldn't be your concern, Nora. But no, she isn't."

Her expression fell, her disappointment evident. "Well, perhaps she should be. I don't trust her, Miss Cross. She's had visitors—at night. Male visitors. Or maybe just the one, but certainly a man and that's not allowed. She meets him in the service yard."

"This sounds like a matter for Mrs. Hendricks. Have you mentioned it to her?"

"No, not yet."

"Then why tell me?" I asked, genuinely puzzled.

"I just thought you should know, Miss Cross, since you've been helping the police."

I scrutinized her features, really very lovely despite the severe lines of her coif and linen cap. "You think this could have something to do with Miss Cooper-Smith's death?"

Her vivid green eyes became large. Uncertainty mingled with her suspicions. "I don't know. Maybe not. But there's something strange about that Camille. She's not like other girls in service. She's too full of herself, thinks she's better than the rest of us. She doesn't know her place."

Yes, I didn't doubt Camille gave that impression to the other servants, and they resented her for it. Katie had reached the same conclusion, that Camille didn't know her place. Did Nora, who knew Camille personally, have good reason to mistrust the lady's maid, or was she, like Katie, merely upholding the servants' strict code of conduct?

"Why do you say that, Nora? What has she done? I mean besides meeting a gentleman caller outside at night."

"Isn't that enough?"

"No, I'm afraid it isn't, at least not where I'm concerned."

She fidgeted with her cap. "It's just a feelin' I get when I look at her. It's not a good feelin'. There's something in her eyes, especially after she meets with that man. I think she's schemin' something with him. My gran could always know a person just by lookin' at 'em, and so can I."

"I'm sorry, Nora, but that isn't enough to accuse a person of wrongdoing. Perhaps Camille isn't suited to service, but we shouldn't hold that against her."

Was it a crime to think of oneself as better than one's circumstances, to feel frustrations at the limits life had arbitrarily placed on one? I didn't think so. I had seen Camille's brand of determination before, in women like my aunt Alva, who chafed against the role of mere society hostess. Alva's ambitions and, yes, her intelligence, prompted her to lash out at society in the form of fierce competition to rule over the Four Hundred as the wealthiest, grandest matron of all. I believed that was why she coerced her daughter, Consuelo, to marry the Duke of Marlborough. Poor Consuelo might abhor "Sunny," but Alva could now boast being the mother of a duchess.

If Aunt Alva were free to choose the course of her life, what might she achieve?

Camille would never be a duchess, but if she stayed her course, she might just become the wife of a Knickerbocker. Her gentleman caller could be none other than Dorian Norris; hence the reason for the nighttime secrecy. Still, Nora had been correct about overhearing the argument coming from Cleo's bedroom. Cleo had been accusing Camille of breaking the necklace, and Camille had been defending herself. Nora had been right to tell me about that argument. I shouldn't disregard what she was telling me now.

She smoothed the front of her apron. "I'm sorry for wastin' your time, Miss Cross."

"You haven't, Nora," I hastened to assure her. "Please continue to keep watch, and if something specific does happen, please let me know. You remember I live at Gull Manor?"

"Yes, miss." She bobbed a curtsy, looking slightly mollified.

I had no sooner arrived back home, dozens of thoughts and theories swimming in my brain, when the telephone summoned me to the alcove beneath the staircase.

"Emma, it's Grace. Darling, you promised to dine with Neily and I, and I fear if I don't pin you down we'll never see you."

I laughed softly at Grace's typical tendency to exaggerate. "You do understand I've been busy?"

"I do, and that is precisely the problem. You are always busy, always taking on the problems of the world."

Another exaggeration. "Hardly that. But where I see I might be useful, I do tend to step in."

"Yes, well, you have earned a reward, haven't you." A statement, not a question. "Dinner with your favorite cousin and your dearest friend. I *am* your dearest friend, aren't I?"

She was certainly one of them, despite the significant differences in our personalities and circumstances. "I would love to come for dinner. You have merely to tell me when."

"Good. We'll expect you at eight."

"Tonight?" I glanced at the locket watch pinned to my bodice. "Grace, I've been running about town all day, and there is hardly time for me to—"

"Ah, here come your excuses. I'm not having it, Emma, I am truly not. We'll be as frightfully casual as you please. My mother-in-law would shudder to see it. And it *will* just be us. Rest up a bit, smooth your hair, and toss on a fresh frock. I'll send our carriage 'round to your place by seven forty-five. Will that suit?"

I couldn't help laughing again. "I see you're determined to bully me into coming."

"I am indeed."

It had been a long day, and I longed to put my feet up and sink into the oblivion of a good book. I suppressed a sigh. "You needn't send your carriage. I can—"

"My dear, do stop arguing. I'm sending the carriage. Be ready when it arrives." With that, she ended the connection.

That evening, Neily and Grace's brougham brought me to Beaulieu House, built in the solid, monumental style that had become popular a decade or so before the War Between the States. Upon first glance it always rather reminded me of Chateau sur Mer, with a steep, almost mansard French roof that crowned a stucco facade, dominated by a square turret with wings to either side.

As the carriage approached the house, I couldn't help craning my neck to catch a glimpse of Marble House next door. Only the darkness of an empty hull met my gaze. Aunt Alva no longer used the house. Since her marriage to Oliver Belmont three years ago, they had summered in his cottage, Belcourt, a short distance along Bellevue to the south. I thought it a great waste and held out the hope she would have a change of heart, or lease the property. Aunt Alva had had Marble House built as a statement confirming her perch at the top of society's heap. The result had been a jewel of a house, not extensively large, but a showcase of exquisite workmanship. And now it went unused, unappreciated. Such was the wanton excess of the Four Hundred.

The carriage stopped and a footman came down the steps of the wide veranda that wrapped three sides of the house. After he helped me down, I entered a long great hall tiled in black and white marble, and found Neily and Grace there to greet me. Grace, in a pale pink gown embroidered with roses and vines, hugged me and told me I looked beautiful. Her pledge to be casual hadn't fooled me a bit, and I'd worn champagne-colored silk with a tiered lace skirt, a hand-me-down from Neily's sister, Gertrude.

"I'm glad you could come, Emmaline." Neily embraced me warmly. "We haven't had a proper visit in too long a time, and with everything that's happened, Grace and I thought you could use a respite."

"I'm grateful for it, thank you."

There was a light in his eyes I hadn't seen in some time—since he and Grace had married, actually. Theirs had been a troubled courtship, for his parents had objected so strongly he and his father had nearly come to blows over it. His mother, my aunt Alice, even blamed Neily for her husband's stroke of apoplexy. Through it all, he and Grace had persisted in their plans to marry.

Yet soon after they had, I'd noticed a difference in Neily. A pensiveness, almost a sadness. He had seemed older, floundering, his confidence shaken. I wanted to believe his disinheritance had caused the change, that being cast out of the family and the family business had upended his world. But in my heart, I knew Neily was stronger than that. His response had been to continue his studies at Yale with an eye on obtaining his master's degree in engineering. He returned to the family business, not as the owner's son and heir, but as a mechanical engineer on an ordinary salary. If he couldn't inherit, then he would *earn.*

I feared that, just as Grace and I were two very different people, so too were Grace and Neily, and that marriage had driven that point bluntly, perhaps painfully, home. Where Grace was vivacious and derived her energy from being around people and exciting events, Neily preferred his studies and quiet evenings at home. She kept him on a rigorous schedule of travels and social occasions that can only have left him drained. But tonight, oh, tonight, Neily's smiles reminded me of the old days, when my cousins and I were young and responsibilities hadn't yet set themselves upon our shoulders. Was it fatherhood restoring his youth, or perhaps merely being here in calm, comfortable surroundings, that made the difference?

"It's such a beautiful night, we thought we'd enjoy aperitifs on the veranda before dinner." Grace linked her arm through mine. Her smile seemed cunning to me, and raised my curiosity, even a wariness. We walked through a charming octagonal parlor and out through the open doors onto the spacious rear veranda. Before us, beyond the glowing lanterns above our heads, spread the expanse of lawn and gardens, bordered by the sharp edge of the Cliff Walk and an endless, heaving blackness studded with glinting light.

The freshness of the ocean breeze made me grin as I raised my face to it. But an instant later a voice startled me.

"Good evening, Emma."

My grin became a gasp of surprise. "Derrick."

He moved from shadow into lantern light, the smile of apology on his lips telling me he had been in on Grace's little secret. I had been bamboozled, kept in the dark in case I'd decided to decline the invitation. Though why Grace would think I might, eluded me. I had no aversion to spending time in Derrick's company. I did, however, object to unasked for matchmaking. In this, Grace was no better than my aunt Alice, forever on the hunt for a suitable husband for me.

Still, I couldn't find it within myself to be angry or even annoyed with her, and certainly not with Derrick. I smiled and placed my hand in his offered one. He raised it to his lips for a warm kiss. For all he had worn only a dark suit of clothes, he might have donned his best formalwear, so well did they fit him to his best advantage. His appearance made me glad I'd chosen Gertrude's champagne gown rather than something plainer. Then I wondered what, if anything, it meant that I wished to look my best for Derrick. Perhaps only that this would be an enjoyable evening.

A footman offered each of us a cordial glass from a silver tray. They contained rich, nutty-flavored sherry, intended to stimulate the appetite. With a tiny sip I welcomed the warmth, the richness, and allowed it to spread a sense of well-being through me. Derrick watched me closely, and at the first opportunity, while Grace turned toward the garden to point something out to Neily, he drew me a short distance along the veranda.

"I knew what Grace was up to but I went along with it," he said. "I wanted to talk with you, and heaven knows when else I'd have a chance." He said this with noticeable wryness, prompting me to take the defensive.

"If you wished to speak, you might have telephoned. I'm not so completely preoccupied that I won't take a few moments for a friend."

"That's not what I meant." His eyes gleamed with amusement. "Or not quite," he admitted. Then his humor faded. "I've heard from my father. He wishes to see me."

"Derrick, that's wonderful. I knew he'd relent eventually."

"It's been an entire year."

"Does it matter? He's ready to reconcile."

He went to the railing. I noticed Neily glancing over at us, and then Grace tapping his shoulder and recapturing his attention, in essence giving Derrick and me our moment alone. "I'm not sure I want to reconcile."

"Don't be silly. Of course you do." I searched his features, smoothed and gilded by the lanterns. "This past year hasn't been easy for you. Don't pretend otherwise."

"Of course it hasn't been easy. But it's also been . . . exhilarating. I'm not ready to give up what I've accomplished."

At those words, a thrill of comprehension filled me, an elation on his behalf. "I understand." Of course I did. Isn't that kind of independence, even with its associated risk, exactly what I strived for every day of my life? "Why would you have to give up your accomplishments? You're growing the *Messenger* into a thriving, vital newspaper. Why can't it be part of your family's empire?"

"I don't know that I want it to be."

I watched his profile as he stared out into the night. "I understand that, too. But you can't turn your back on your family, your father."

"He turned his back on me." He didn't say this resentfully, merely stated it as a fact.

"Temporarily," I reminded him.

He nodded and sighed. "Yes, you're right. You always are." His humor returned. "That's why I wished to speak with you. I knew you'd help me see things as they are, without the veil of my anger."

"So what will you do?" A knot formed in my stomach. Reuniting with his father, returning to his rightful place as heir to the family newspaper business, would also take Derrick away from Newport. At the completion of that thought the knot hardened into a churning ball of panic. I didn't want him to go. Good *heavens,* I didn't.

"I'll be heading up to Providence. Soon."

The veranda seemed to tip beneath my feet. I wanted to cry out that he mustn't leave.

And yet, I had left. I had gone to New York to pursue my dream of being a reporter—a real one. I returned to Newport because that dream hadn't materialized as I wished it to, and because I'd missed my home terribly much.

Had that been all? Had nothing else compelled my return to my island home? Or had I been tugged back by feelings I hadn't known existed—or hadn't wished to admit to?

"There is something I wish to ask of you," he said.

I blinked and tried to appear natural, as if my world wasn't violently shaking beneath my feet. "Of course. Anything."

"Not so fast," he cautioned good-naturedly, obviously unaware of my turmoil. *Good,* I thought. "We've discussed this before, and at the time, you weren't particularly keen on the idea." He turned, taking my hand. "I want you to take over the *Messenger.* Now please, before you refuse, think about it. I'll grant you complete autonomy in the day-to-day running of the place. I mean it. I won't interfere."

"Derrick . . ."

His free hand went up to stop me; his other hand tightened around mine as if I'd slip away. "Don't give me an answer now. I understand you aren't ready for any kind of personal commitments. That isn't what this is about, I swear it. But I need someone I can trust to keep the *Messenger* going while I'm away."

I took a moment to compose myself, so that I'd be able to give him a reasonable reply. Meanwhile both my mind and my heart raced, not so much because of what he asked of me, but because of this unexpected revelation that I cared so much more than I'd believed, so much more than I wished to. I'd been lying to myself, and to Derrick and to Jesse, these past several years. Yes, I could run Derrick's *Messenger* for him, I could even believe that he had no ulterior motive than that he trusted in my abilities.

What *I* didn't trust, was that I wouldn't agree to the arrangement simply because I knew it would connect us permanently. I needed time to come to terms with that, and with this part of myself I'd denied for so long, and made excuses for, and barely knew at all.

"Yes, please give me a day or so to think about it," I said more calmly than I would have believed possible. At that moment, I heard a small commotion from Neily and Grace.

"Did she just say yes?" Grace whispered.

Neily shushed her. "It's none of our business."

"It most certainly is," Grace shot back. She silently clapped her hands. "Oh, I knew it was only a matter of time."

Oh, dear. It seemed she had the entirely wrong idea.

Chapter 15

No matter how hard I tried, I could not dissuade Grace of the notion that Derrick had proposed to me. I told her quite plainly that he had only requested that I take over for him at the *Messenger*, and she had nodded with an expression of joy.

"Don't take too long with your answer," she counseled me. "Only enough time to make him understand that you are not desperate. But men don't like to be kept hanging. You don't want him to become discouraged and run off."

"Grace, for the fourth time, it wasn't a proposal. He has to return to Providence. His father is ready to make amends."

"Which is wonderful. A wedding should be a family affair. Ill feelings should be set aside."

I sighed and gave up. We had dinner, several courses fit for a celebration, which was exactly what Grace considered this. When she and I left the men to their smoking and brandy and entered the drawing room arm in arm, I made a request I knew she couldn't refuse.

"You mustn't go making any announcements, Grace. Think

of how my relatives would react, to hear rumors about me from outside sources, especially if they aren't true."

"Darling, I promise my lips are sealed. But as soon as you give Derrick your answer, you must inform Alice and Cornelius of this lovely development. And then we'll begin planning."

We sat together, our hands clasped. "I do wish you'd believe me. Derrick did not propose tonight. At least, not in the way you hope. It was strictly business, that is all."

She nodded, grinning, her eyes sparkling. "If you insist." And later, when it came time to leave, she wrapped her scheming little clutches around Derrick's arm and with perfect innocence asked him, "Would you be a dear and drive Emma home?"

He readily agreed, and soon the two of us were proceeding down Bellevue Avenue in his cabriolet. "I'm sorry about Grace," I said. "Once she's taken hold of an idea, there's no prying it loose."

"Neily took a rather more pragmatic approach. He said it would be a splendid idea, whenever you and I are ready."

I smiled. "That sounds like Neily. He seemed happy tonight. Leastwise, happier than I've seen in since . . ." I trailed off, not liking to voice my reservations about his and Grace's marriage.

I didn't have to. Derrick nodded. "They're very different, he and Grace. I think he's sometimes a little overwhelmed by her." When I didn't comment, he said, "It's interesting how a similar upbringing, fortune, and connections are no assurance that two people will be suited to each other."

I heard the implication in his words, that two people can hail from completely *different* circumstances and still suit perfectly. His and my very dissimilar backgrounds had always given me pause. How would I ever fit in with people of

Derrick's ilk, with his family? Never mind that his mother abhorred me; Derrick's peers would always see me as an outsider and an upstart. Oh, I could make my way through a ballroom well enough, or join a dinner party at the home of my relatives without blundering horribly. I knew the correct words, the manners, the protocol. But knowing and being willing to live it, every day for the rest of my life, were two different matters.

The horse's steady gait had helped settle my nerves, my emotions. When Derrick had spoken of leaving Newport, I had panicked as surely as if I'd stood upon the deck of a quickly sinking ship. In that moment I had known what I wanted with a clarity I'd never experienced before. But now, with the stars slowly passing above our heads and the night noises softly blending with the distant waves—and yes, with the gentle nudging of his serge-clad shoulder against mine— the urgency receded. I breathed in salt-tinged air, sweetened by the blossoms of Bellevue Avenue's many gardens, and believed that somehow I would find my way. If Derrick and I were meant to be together, we would be, his family and social conventions notwithstanding.

"I think they'll be all right," I said after Derrick turned the carriage onto Ocean Avenue. "The birth of Corneil has surely brought them closer, and Neily has his studies and his work to keep him occupied while Grace seeks out her social amusements. I know of successful marriages with shakier beginnings than theirs."

"Mmm" was all he said. He had fallen quiet. Was he contemplating our own circumstances? Thinking about his request to me, or perhaps wishing to take it further, to bring truth to Grace's suspicions? The notion gave me a tiny thrill, but then I noticed Derrick wasn't preoccupied at all. With a furrowed brow he peered into the darkness beyond the carriage lanterns, his face slightly raised.

Just as I was about to inquire what had so caught his attention, my nose itched and a sense of alarm went through me. "Fire."

He nodded, straining to see into the distance. Suddenly, his hand went up, his finger pointing. "Is that smoke in the distance? Just there."

It was. The coastline along Ocean Avenue twisted and turned. One moment we could see a thin, swirling grayness against the sky, and the next it vanished around trees and hills and rocky peninsulas. "Derrick, hurry."

I hadn't needed to tell him; even as I spoke, he made an urgent clucking sound that sped his horse's steps. With each bend we rounded, my fears grew. I knew every turn and bump in this roadway. Every property. Every house. The farther we went, the more certain I became.

"Gull Manor." Dread nearly choked me. "Nanny. Katie. Oh, Derrick . . ."

He prompted his horse to a near gallop, jarring and jostling us every step of the way. I didn't care. I practically stood up on the footboard in my effort to see up ahead. Smoke continued to curl against the sky. Not a great deal, but enough to firmly lodge my heart in my throat.

Finally, the carriage tilted sharply around the last bend and onto the front drive. My greatest fears were realized. Flames danced behind the window of my little-used dining room, devouring the curtains. Beyond that, I couldn't see, didn't know how much of my house might be burning. Outside, Nanny, in a housecoat and her hair in rags, stooped with her hand around Patch's collar. He yelped and barked and strained to bolt free. Her arm quivered from the pull of his weight but she held on fast. They both seemed unharmed, but where was Katie?

I cried out for Derrick to stop the carriage. The vehicle

was still rolling when I leaped down off the seat and, skidding, ran the remainder of the way. Nanny turned, saw me, and called out my name. At my approach, Patch managed to tug loose from her fist and bounded to me. Nanny followed with a vigor I'd not seen in her in years.

Our arms were around each other in an instant. "I'm sorry, Emma, so sorry. I don't know what happened, I don't . . ."

"Where is Katie?" I yelled. From the corner of my vision I saw Derrick running toward the house. "Is Katie inside?"

Nanny was shaking her head. "We all got out. Katie ran to the Edwards's place to use their telephone. She's calling the fire department."

"Were any of you hurt?"

"No, we're all right."

My knees went weak with relief, but only momentarily. Derrick had disappeared inside the house, and through the window I could see the flapping shadow of his coat as he beat at the flames. I dared not wait for the steam engine to come all the way from Wellington and Lower Thames. "Stay here," I commanded Nanny. "And hold on to Patch."

"Emma, don't," she shouted, but I was already to the front door and ducking inside. Wearing no carriage jacket and my wrap being too light to battle a fire, I detoured into the parlor and grabbed up the lap rug I always kept on hand for chilly days. I barely registered my immense relief that the fire didn't seem to have spread to any other part of the house.

Yet.

In the dining room, Derrick beat at the cushion of the chair at the head of the table, nearest the window. The curtains smoldered, but the dancing flames had been subdued. In a corner of my mind I noted that most of the fire was already out. It could not have been burning long before Derrick and I arrived home. Still, I thumped the lap rug against glowing spots on the curtains and the area rug, lest the flames leap back to life. In the past I had seen how fast fires could spread and how quickly they became uncontrollable. Derrick came up behind me, nudging me out of the way.

"Go. I'll finish here."

My breath heaving, I shook my head. "It's my house, if anyone should risk their life, it's me."

He swore and touched his fingertips to the window frame, quickly, then again, testing, I realized, for heat. Assured he would not be singed, he shut the window.

"To stop the breeze from fanning the flames," he said unnecessarily. I nodded and hurried around the table to close the side windows as well.

At a run I left the room, heading to the kitchen. Grabbing a bucket from the pantry, I filled it at the sink and ran back along the hall to the front of the house. I doused every smoking surface. Suddenly Derrick was before me, wrenching the bucket out of my hands. He tipped it toward me and water sloshed onto me, soaking the front of my skirts.

Steam rose from the sodden fabric. My fear spiked in retrospect as the singed edge of my petticoat peeked out from my hem. I hadn't realized . . . I might have burned to death. Derrick's arms went around me. He pulled me tight against him and swore again. His ragged breathing buffeted me for several seconds and rendered me breathless as well. Then he released me.

From the road came the clanking of the fire wagon. Derrick seized my hand and we hurried back outside. I shivered as cool ocean air hit my wet skirts. Pulled by four horses, the steam and hose wagon clattered up the drive and stopped close to the house. Several firemen hopped down and began unwinding the hose. The steam engine hissed, its pistons

242   *Alyssa Maxwell*

turning and pumping, ready to send the water coursing in a forceful spray.

"I think we've got it out," Derrick said to the firemen, "but please make sure."

Katie had returned by then, and I joined her and Nanny in a tangled hug, with Patch pressing his warm, trembling body against my legs. Derrick spoke to a fireman while the rest of the men scrambled into the house. I heard the tramp of feet on the stairs. The fire had been confined to the dining room, but I didn't mind their caution. We waited out on the drive until they declared the house safe. Then they left my property with a promise to return with the fire marshal in the morning.

After securing the windows at the front of the house, Nanny, Katie, Derrick, and I sat around the kitchen table, each of us cradling a cup of hot tea between our hands. I had changed my damp evening gown for a sturdy flannel nightgown and robe, which I secured tightly around me. None of us could think of sleeping, not just yet. There were too many unanswered questions about how the fire had started.

"It seems highly coincidental for this to happen on a night I'm away from home," I said. I stared into the steam rising from my cup and once again said a quick prayer of thanks the fire hadn't been worse, that no one I cared about had been injured.

Derrick studied me before replying. "As if to suggest that, while you were away, Katie and Mrs. O'Neal became careless."

I nodded, but Nanny bristled. "I never lit the lamps in that room tonight. Not even a candle."

"Nor me, Miss Emma," Katie said, the fear still evident on her face. "I hadn't set foot in the dining room since this mornin' when I opened the windows."

"I believe you both. Don't worry." I sipped my tea, welcoming the strength of the brew and its warmth inside me. "Even if there is a problem with one of the gas lines, a fire couldn't have started without a flame." I went very still. Gas lines. Patrick Floyd's wife had died because of an open gas line.... But why would Patrick Floyd attack my home?

"Emma, what is it?" Nanny leaned closer to me, scrutinizing my expression as Derrick had.

I shook my head to clear it. "Just a thought, probably nothing. But we'll want to have the gas lines inspected just in case." I thought also of Reggie's argument with Mr. Brentworth concerning just such inspections, and Mr. Brentworth's hostilities toward me. I had believed our differences resolved. Had I been mistaken?

Derrick guessed the train of my thoughts. "Are you wondering if this was done as a warning?"

"I am. From any number of individuals."

"Silas Griggson," he said, his voice low and threatening.

Yes, that name, too, raised my suspicions. "He wants Gull Manor so he can knock it down. Perhaps he decided to burn it down instead."

He thought a moment, finger tapping on the tabletop. Then he shook his head. "If Silas Griggson wanted to burn the place down, something tells me we wouldn't be sitting in this kitchen right now. But as a warning, yes, I can see him trying to frighten you away."

"Emma, let the police finish the investigation." Nanny's quiet voice bordered on pleading.

"I'm afraid it's already too late for that, Nanny." I smiled to reassure her, but I experienced my own doubts. It was one thing to endanger myself in the name of justice. But endangering Nanny and Katie? They hadn't chosen to become involved in Cleo Cooper-Smith's death. They shouldn't have to suffer for my decisions.

But as I had said, it was too late to turn back. It made me more determined than ever to expose Cleo's murderer—perhaps now an arsonist as well. "We'll have to see what the fire inspector discovers tomorrow. I wonder if someone didn't simply throw a lighted match in through the window. It would have been easy. In the dark, no one would have noticed a person creeping close to the house."

Nanny shuddered. "To think we're no longer safe in our own home, that we have to worry about locking our doors and windows. I never thought I'd see the day. Not here."

At a weight against my knees, I glanced down to see Patch leaning his chin against me. I frowned. "Odd that he didn't bark."

Katie gasped. Her hand flew to her mouth. "He did. Oh, Miss Emma, I didn't realize. He was in the kitchen with me. I was finishin' up the dinner dishes when he started barking, and he crossed my path and nearly tripped me. I told him to hush and go lie down. He whimpered like, but did as I told him. I'll wager that was when . . ." Her face crumpled.

I reached over and placed my hand over hers. "Don't go blaming yourself, Katie. We all know how Patch can forget his manners sometimes and needs a scolding. A bird, a squirrel, anything can set him off. You couldn't have known what was about to happen."

"No, but from now on I'll be payin' him better mind."

The ringing of the telephone echoed from the corridor, startling us all. We flinched, and then I rose to answer it. "I have a good idea who it might be."

I wasn't wrong. I'd barely uttered a greeting when Jesse's voice burst in my ear. "Emma, I just heard. Is everyone all right? What happened?"

"Yes, we're all fine, and I don't know what happened. Derrick and I came home from dinner with my cousin to find the dining room curtains on fire. Most of the room survived just fine, and it didn't spread to the rest of the house."

"I'm coming out there."

"No, Jesse, don't. It's not necessary. As I said, we're fine."

After a lengthy hesitation, he asked, "Is Derrick still there?" I heard a slight strain in his voice.

I longed to say no, that Derrick had left, but I couldn't lie, not to Jesse. Especially not after what occurred at Beaulieu earlier. Derrick's news of returning to Providence had changed something in me, forced me to acknowledge feelings I had been ignoring for too long.

"Derrick is here," I said, finding myself taking a gentle tone. The last thing I wished was to hurt Jesse. I hurried on, anxious to reassure him about our safety. "We've closed and locked the downstairs windows. The doors are shut tight." As if to reiterate that claim, light perspiration dotted my forehead. It was July; we normally welcomed the cooling ocean breezes, especially at night. At least we could feel safe in keeping the upstairs windows open.

Then again, could our perpetrator toss something high enough to reach the second floor? Would he—or she—be so brazen as to come back tonight?

"Is he . . . staying?" Jesse swallowed audibly. "If you won't let me come out there, I'd sleep better knowing he was there. Not that I'll sleep much in either case."

"I . . . no, I think I'll send Derrick home soon. We can take care of ourselves here. Patch will alert us if anything is wrong. It turns out he tried earlier, but Katie thought he was merely being an unruly pup, barking at the night noises. We know better than to ignore him now."

"If there is anything—anything at all that doesn't seem right, you're to call the police station and then call me."

"I will, Jesse."

"Promise me."

I did, and hung up feeling bereft and traitorous. I wished I had not gone to Beaulieu earlier, wished Derrick had never mentioned leaving Newport. Wished I could return to my notions of independence and remaining unmarried—anything rather than having to face making a decision and hurting someone I cared so much about. I feared I would find excuses to put off that decision, to pretend it wasn't hanging over me. But it was. And it would, until I took responsibility and admitted what I wanted.

But for tonight, at least, I needn't do anything. I could put off that moment, for now.

Derrick never did leave that night. He slept on the parlor sofa, cramped and uncomfortable, his head resting on one arm and his feet dangling over the other. By the time I came downstairs he was already up and having a light breakfast with Nanny and Katie. I noticed how he flinched slightly each time he turned his head a certain way. I hoped the kink in his neck would work itself out before very long.

"Thank you for staying," I said to him. "I believe we all slept better for your being here, though I fear you hardly slept at all."

"I offered to make up the guest room," Katie said with a shake of her head.

"It wouldn't have been proper, me sleeping upstairs." He rubbed at his shoulder.

Nanny nodded her agreement, but said nothing. Instead she offered him another blueberry hotcake and another cup of coffee.

Before coming into the morning room I'd peeked into the dining room to survey the damage in the daylight. The acrid odors of smoke and dampness made me cough, while sorrow pressed against my breastbone at the ruination of the curtains and the matching seat cushions Aunt Sadie had made a decade ago. All the fabric in the room would need to be replaced, the area rug as well. The table showed scorch marks that would require a thorough sanding and refinishing. The walls and ceiling would need a new coat of paint, and of course the window frame, blackened and half consumed, would need to be rebuilt.

It could have been so much worse. No one had been injured. And had the fire started in the parlor, the upholstered furnishings, pillows, and books would have provided a good deal more fuel. The flames might have spread faster, reaching the rest of the house before help arrived.

Derrick left soon after breakfast, and I couldn't help being relieved, especially since Jesse had telephoned to say he would be accompanying the fire marshal. After asking Nanny, Katie, and me a few questions, the two men went into the dining room. I could hear them moving furniture and speaking in low voices. I strained to overhear, yet I kept clear of the room to allow them to do their job. When they finally came out, Jesse warned us to keep the doors and windows locked at all times, until they discovered who had set the fire. In a gloved hand he held up a blackened rock wrapped in the remains of charred cloth.

His expression was grim. "We suspect this had been soaked in kerosene." He handed it to the fire inspector, who slid it into a leather case he held.

"It was most certainly arson," the man confirmed. "Unless you're in the habit of wrapping rocks in accelerant-soaked cloth and tossing them about."

"Indeed I am not." Despite my rising anger, I felt real fear, too. Just as I had felt fear when Silas Griggson stood in my parlor and assured me my house would be his. I considered again that the fire had been started in the dining room and not the parlor. The conclusion I reached made me suspect Griggson all the more. "I don't think anyone meant to burn this house down. I think it was a warning."

"I concur," Fire Inspector Filby said. "At least in that whoever did this could have chosen a more efficient means of burning the house down had that been his intention. Even taking into account his hurry to be away, he might have poured kerosene or linseed oil directly onto the curtains and rug and followed that with a lit match. Such a fire would have caught instantly, burned hotter, and spread faster than this one did. Judging by the scorch marks, I believe this fire smoldered on the rug a while before catching hold."

Jesse remained behind when Mr. Filby left, his observations echoing my own thoughts. "Silas Griggson wants you out, one way or another. He might have believed a stunt like this would achieve his goal."

"Little does he know me."

Jesse nodded his agreement.

"I have his card in the parlor. He's staying on Webster Street. I want to go there right now and confront him." Even as I declared my intention, I hesitated at the notion of an arsonist leaving behind his calling card as proof of his interest in possessing the house. Though it seemed ill advised, Silas Griggson might believe himself to be that far above the law. He hadn't been implicated in the New York tenement collapse. He could easily evade charges in a minor house fire where no one had been injured—or so he might believe.

"He's dangerous, Emma."

"Obviously. So ask a couple of officers to meet us there."

"Assuming he's still there." Jesse glanced in the direction of the dining room. "He might have cleared out by now."

"Oh, I have a feeling Silas Griggson isn't going anywhere until he gets what he wants, namely Gull Manor. I believe he's that arrogant and that sure of himself."

Jesse regarded me with part resignation, part admiration. He held out a hand. "All right. Let's go."

Chapter 16

Jesse and I lingered at home long enough for him to telephone the police station and arrange for two officers to meet us at the address indicated on Mr. Griggson's card. Then he and I set out together.

Webster Street intersected Bellevue Avenue and continued east to dead end at the Cliff Walk and the ocean. The street also skirted the northern border of Ochre Court. No wonder Mr. Griggson had chosen to lease a house here. Even on foot, he could be at Ochre Court in minutes. No bachelor's rooms at the Casino for him. I wondered, had he hoped to lure Cleo to this lovely clapboard house, with its arched, mullioned windows, on its tree-shaded property? If she had not wished to go willingly, would he have found a way to coerce her?

While Jesse guided the police buggy onto the short, circular driveway, I glanced down the street toward Ochre Court. I couldn't see the house, not from this angle, but I spotted a familiar figure about fifty yards away. Or the back of a figure, I should say. A man in military uniform hurried along the street, one hand raised to keep his cap on his blond head.

"That looks like Sam Caldwell."

Jesse leaned to see past me. "The captain?"

"Yes. I wonder if he was just visiting Mr. Griggson."

"Do they know each other?" Jesse sounded skeptical, just as I had questioned their acquaintance when I'd seen them speaking at the ball. On the surface it seemed unlikely that a man of Griggson's questionable background would have anything in common with a young officer who hailed from the Four Hundred, but times were changing. However much it galled the old guard, families like the Astors and the Goelets were no longer the untouchable bastion of society. People could now buy their way in. My own relatives had; it had taken several generations, but they had won the right to dance upon the same gleaming parquet floors as those who considered themselves old money, American aristocracy.

Obviously, Silas Griggson had paid his entry fee, or he would not have been a guest at Mrs. Goelet's ball, and she would not have considered him an eligible catch for her friend's daughter.

"I believe they do know each other," I told Jesse. "I don't know how. It could have to do with real estate matters. Perhaps Sam's family is having a house built, or they might own property that's being developed for rental housing."

"Do you wish to ask him something? Should I catch up to him?"

"No, it doesn't matter. Let's go in and have that chat with Mr. Griggson."

Jesse pulled the carriage up by the front door and we alighted. When I would have raised my hand to knock, I discovered the door ajar. Jesse and I traded curious looks, and, frowning, he nudged me behind him.

Slowly, he widened the door and put one foot over the threshold. "Hello? Is anyone home?"

No answer came. I craned to peer over his shoulder, scanning the front hall for signs of a disturbance. Everything looked in order. The ticking of a clock met my ears. The only other sounds were those from outdoors, birds chirping and carriages rumbling along nearby Bellevue Avenue.

"Stay outside," Jesse murmured. Need I say I followed him inside, staying close at his heels, my hand on his shoulder as we tiptoed into the house? We crossed the front hall and entered a wide doorway into the parlor. Here, too, everything appeared tidy. But something felt wrong, something that prickled at my nape. Jesse felt it, too, or he would not have continued to hold out an arm in an attempt to keep me behind him.

We continued through to a dining room, furnished in such dark woods and heavy curtains as to essentially block out the daylight. The shadows seemed to breathe with a palpable presence. Jesse and I lingered in the doorway, framed on each side by floor to ceiling pocket doors that had been slid to a partially closed position. A darker shadow crept out from behind the far end of the long dining table.

"Jesse, there." I pointed, even as I tensed to flee. But then I realized nothing had crawled or moved, it had merely been a trick of the shadows and my own eyes that had yet to adjust to the darkness. Whatever lay beyond the table remained inert, lifeless.

Jesse moved to a window and yanked open the curtains. Sunlight fell in a thick shaft to illuminate the room, the table, and a prone Mr. Griggson.

"Jesse!"

He was already at my side. Mr. Griggson, in his shirtsleeves, vest, and dark trousers, lay on his back. His eyes were closed, his body utterly still. My breath suspended, I raised a shaky finger to point down at him, or, rather, at the odd discoloration that drew my gaze.

"What is that?"

The center of Mr. Griggson's forehead was marked with a kind of blackened, irregular star.

Jesse swore and fell into a crouch beside the prone man. "Emma, go. Please."

"What is it?" But the answer was already dawning on me. That was no star, but jagged flesh and bone, blackened by gunpowder. "A bullet wound."

Jesse stood. "There's nothing we can do for him."

"But . . . who?" My features tightened in disbelief. "Sam Caldwell?"

"We don't know for sure the captain was even here. Come on. We need to go. I need to alert the station house and the coroner."

I nodded vaguely as a sense of unreality took hold of me. I grew cold and shivers racked me. Jesse saw and drew me to him. He ran his hands up and down my arms.

"Let's get you out of here." He started me toward the entryway, when I dug in and stopped.

"The wound. It reminds me of something."

"Tell the coroner."

"No. Let me check." I turned back to the body, but Jesse was quicker and stepped in front of me.

"All right, tell me. What is it?"

"His right wrist. The underside. He has a tattoo, a star. The wound reminded me of it."

His eyebrow tightly knitted, Jesse knelt beside Mr. Griggson's body again and tugged his shirtsleeve up. Yet where the tattoo on his pulse point had been, now there was only a flesh wound, as if—

"It's gone. Not just gone. Removed." I shuddered and squeezed my eyes closed.

"Cut away," Jesse murmured. He lowered Mr. Griggson's arm to the floor and pushed to his feet. He grasped my forearms again. "You said it was a star? Are you quite certain of that?"

"I . . . Fairly certain. I only saw it for a second or two." I thought back to when Silas Griggson stood in my parlor, demanding to buy Gull Manor. When he had thrust his calling card at me, I had believed he was going to strike me. My eyes were riveted on his hand, his arm. His sleeve had ridden up and I had seen the star rendered in black ink. "Yes," I amended. "I'm certain."

Jesse swore again. "Two stars."

I shook my head. "What do you mean?"

"As you said, the wound is like a star, to match the one he had on his wrist."

"But that one is gone."

"Yes. This was no crime of passion, or anything we've ever seen in Newport before, at least not in my lifetime. The wrist, the bullet wound—this contained a message."

My throat ran dry. "What kind of message? And for whom?"

"I don't have the answers to those questions, not yet. But this much I do know. It was an execution. The black star is a symbol of New York's Five Points Gang. Or it was, at any rate, early on, when the gang first formed. They wore it on their wrists as a sign of solidarity and as a warning to rival gangs. At least, the young ones did. The ones who came up through the ranks."

"Came up through the ranks?"

"The ones who started as boys, running messages, committing petty crimes for the gang. They worked their way up to more serious crimes."

"That would explain how a man as wealthy as Griggson seemed to come from nowhere."

Jesse nodded and glanced down at the body. "And now he's nothing once again. He must have crossed them. . . ."

"They'd kill one of their own? A powerful man like Silas Griggson?"

"I can guarantee you there are far more powerful men than Griggson. Men who have their hands in legitimate concerns as well as illegal, and who have influence over Tammany Hall and the New York Police Department. Even the mayor's office."

"Power over Mayor Van Wyck?"

Jesse nodded. Not wasting another moment, he grasped my hand and drew me from the dining room back through to the entry hall. There he hesitated. "There's probably a telephone here somewhere. . . ."

A sense of urgency came over me. "You already told the station to send two men. They should be here any moment. But Jesse, if Sam Caldwell did this, and he's headed to Ochre Court, we have to warn them."

Jesse nodded. "Yes. But not you. If Sam Caldwell did this, I'm not bringing you there. Wait here for my men. I'll go. Stay here, Emma. *Here*." He pointed to the floor where I stood. "Don't go back in the dining room." Without waiting for my response, or perhaps the argument he expected from me, he rushed out the front door. A moment later I heard his carriage hurrying away.

At the sound of a groan, I whirled. My heart thumped wildly. Silas Griggson couldn't be alive. No one could survive a bullet to the head. . . .

A second groan traveled, not from the dining room, but from a room on the other side of the entry hall. I peered through an open doorway into a room lined with bookshelves. A library. A dragging step somewhere inside sent me backing up against the front door. My first thought was to flee, and I wrapped my hand around the door handle.

"Who's there?" a man's voice called weakly. The voice broke into coughing. My fingers tightened, ready to press the latch.

The voice called out again, "Please, help me. . . ."

Recognition washed through me. It was Dorian Norris. I moved to the doorway, seeing nothing but bookshelves, sofas, a table, and chairs. "Lieutenant?"

"Who—who's there?" More dragging footsteps drew my gaze to the far corner of the room, where a figure came into view. He leaned heavily on the frame of a sofa, hunching over, his head hanging. He seemed unable to focus at first, but stared blankly across the room, leaning, struggling to remain upright. Then, his vision narrowed on me. "Miss Cross?"

"Yes, Lieutenant." I rushed into the room. When I reached him I slipped an arm around him and dragged one of his across my shoulders. "Can you walk? You can sit here."

He hesitated before shaking his head. "Please help me out of here."

Once back in the front hall, he swayed precariously. I helped him onto the bottom step. I remained standing, gazing down on him.

"What happened? How did you come to be here?"

After breathing out audibly, he raised his face to me. "Where is Sam Caldwell?"

My pulse lurched. "Was he here? I saw him hurrying toward Ochre Court."

"I followed him here." He lowered his chin again, propping his elbows on his knees and allowing his forehead to fall into his hands. "He's been acting so strangely and . . . this friendship he'd struck up with Griggson. It didn't make sense. Griggson's a dangerous man."

I nodded my understanding. "Then they did know each other?"

He nodded. "Rather too well, I'm afraid."

"So you followed him here today."

"I hoped to help him out of a difficulty. I thought perhaps Sam owed Griggson money or something of that nature."

"What happened when you got here? Was Sam here?"

The lieutenant nodded. "I found the door unlocked, so I came in. As I did, I heard a noise, caught a flashing glimpse of Sam, and then . . ." He shook his head.

"And then *what?*" I pressed him.

"Then I heard someone out here in the hall. It was you."

I stood back a moment, considering. Dorian had said Griggson was a dangerous man, but Griggson was dead. Sam had been here, and apparently he had knocked Dorian unconscious. "Did you hear a gun go off?"

"A gun?" He looked alarmed and shook his head.

With a sigh I sat beside him on the step. "Silas Griggson is dead." With my chin I indicated the doorway into the parlor. "He's through there, in the dining room."

I let this sink in, and then continued. "Lieutenant, have you ever heard of the Five Points Gang?"

"I've heard of them, yes. They've a terrible reputation. Why? Oh, you don't think Griggson—" He broke off, his mouth open. "But then Sam . . . Wait. If Griggson is dead, and Sam was here and . . . and probably knocked me unconscious . . . does that mean Sam . . ." He didn't complete the thought, but I understood and nodded.

"We can't be certain, but it does look that way. The police are on their way now. They'll sort this out."

"Wait a minute." He turned to face me more fully. "Did you say you saw Sam rushing to Ochre Court?"

"It appeared so. He was headed in that direction, and walking fast."

His eyes sparked with fright. Grabbing the newel post beside him, he struggled to his feet, wobbled a moment, then took a couple of steps. "I have to go," he murmured.

"Lieutenant, you're not fit to go anywhere just now. We should wait for the police. Detective Whyte is already on his way to Ochre Court."

He pinned me with a determined, feverish stare. "You don't understand. I must go. Everything I care about is there. Camille." He stumbled his way to the front door and threw it open. I came to my feet, protesting but knowing I would not be able to stop him. Only his physical state had the power to do that now. But with each step his determination shored him up, and by the time he reached the driveway, his stride became firm, fleet. He loved Camille Tate. He needed to protect her.

And then I thought of Grace, of Ilsa, of Mrs. Goelet's daughter, May. Jesse was only one man, and Ochre Court was huge. He would need help, and the police still hadn't arrived. Quickly, I drew out the notepad and pencil I always carried in my handbag. I scribbled directions, tore out the page, folded it, and secured it beneath the door knocker. The policemen would know where to go.

I hurried after Lieutenant Norris.

Chapter 17

When the lieutenant and I reached Ochre Court, I spotted Jesse's buggy on the service driveway. With relief, I followed Dorian to the front door. He pounded on it with his fists, nearly striking the butler when he opened the door. Both men scowled at each other, and then Dorian pushed past him.

"What the . . . ?" The butler turned to pursue the trespasser, but I stepped over the threshold and into his path.

"It's all right. That gentleman is with me, and there's good reason for his haste." I saw that the butler recognized me; his posture relaxed. "I promise you, he means no harm."

"This is highly irregular behavior."

"These are highly irregular circumstances. Can you tell me where Detective Whyte is?"

"Detective Whyte, of the Newport Police?" When I nodded, the man sniffed and his eyebrows went up. "He isn't here, I'm sure."

A feeling of apprehension gathered in the pit of my stomach. "But that's his carriage on the service driveway."

"He hasn't come this way. Perhaps you should check with Mrs. Hendricks."

"Did an army officer come by? A captain? He has blond hair and is about my age, perhaps a couple of years older."

"Miss Cross, are you feeling unwell? There is no one here but the family and their guest, Miss Cooper-Smith. And of course, that rude young man who arrived with you." He stepped aside. "Mrs. Goelet still isn't receiving, but I suppose you had better come in."

I entered the vestibule. Though concern for Jesse made me want to search for him, I reminded myself of his policeman's skills and ability to take care of himself.

He's still recovering from his injury, a small voice inside me murmured. But if danger had come to Ochre Court, my first responsibility was to warn the family and Ilsa.

"I'm going upstairs," I announced, and, without waiting for permission, circled round to the main staircase. Lifting my hems, I ran up, feeling as though the many dolphins and cherubim carved into each stone baluster urged me on.

Something was indeed odd at Ochre Court today. Despite the butler's assurances that no one but the family—and now Dorian—occupied the house, I discovered Ilsa once more ensconced in the upstairs sitting room with Patrick Floyd. This time, however, they were not alone. Miss Goelet sat with them, the three of them seeming to be deep in discussion as I entered the room.

"Miss Cross," Ilsa exclaimed upon seeing me. "What brings you back?" Her expression changed from mildly curious to concerned. "Has something happened?"

I answered with a question of my own. "Have any of you seen Captain Caldwell? He would have arrived only about a half hour ago."

Both Miss Goelet and Ilsa shrugged with mystified expressions. Patrick Floyd scrutinized me, and his even features tightened. "Is there some problem with Captain Caldwell?"

I heard the faintest urgency in his question, as though he struggled to conceal his apprehension. Meeting his gaze, I once again replied with another question. "How did you come to be in the house without the butler knowing about it?"

He visibly bristled. "Is this some kind of accusation, Miss Cross?"

Beside him, Ilsa darted a gaze from Patrick to me and sat up straighter. "I can answer that. Patrick came in through the terrace. I admitted him. The butler was belowstairs—or somewhere—at the time."

"I wasn't accusing," I said truthfully. "What I wished to learn was how someone might be in the house without the staff knowing. Now I know." And the knowledge didn't sit well with me. With a murder having taken place here, it might behoove the residents and the staff to take extra precautions in securing doors and windows, and keeping a sharp eye out for anyone approaching the house from across the property. "Did you lock the terrace doors after coming inside?"

This time Ilsa traded glances with Miss Goelet and replied, "No, I don't believe we did."

Miss Goelet expressed her concurrence. "We're so unused to worrying about such things here, Miss Cross."

"What are you getting at, Miss Cross?" Mr. Floyd came to his feet and gave a firm tug at his coat to straighten it. "Is there some danger?"

"Yes, Mr. Floyd. At least, there might be. I think you should find Miss Goelet's brother and all of you retire to Mrs. Goelet's suite and stay there. You see . . ." I trailed off, loathing to speak what I must. But in order to ensure the safety of Ilsa and the other women, I had to make them understand. "There has been another murder. Silas Griggson is dead, and Sam Caldwell might be involved. The last I saw of him, he was hurrying down Webster Street in this direction."

The two young women gained their feet in an instant.
Their morning dresses swept the floor as they drew together.
"We have to warn Robert and Mama," Miss Goelet cried.

"Yes," I agreed wholeheartedly. Mr. Floyd maintained a
tight silence, his gaze piercing and steady. "Tell them Detective Whyte is here, somewhere, and more policemen should
arrive shortly. But do go to your mother's suite and lock
yourselves in. Mr. Floyd, I think you should accompany
them."

His shoulders seemed to grow wider. "I will, Miss Cross.
And you—"

"I'll be all right," I assured them with more conviction
than I felt. Jesse's failure to materialize worried me no end,
but also instilled in me a greater sense of responsibility to
prevent anyone else from coming to harm. "I need to warn
Camille as well."

"What has Camille to do with any of this?"

"I haven't time to explain now. Please, all of you go." I left
them to do as I had advised and hurried up to the third floor.
A hallway led off the gallery and to several smaller corridors
off which some of the upper servants' quarters were located.
Even had I not known which room Camille occupied, I'd
have followed the voices—two male voices, subdued in volume but filled with anger.

"You murdered Silas," Dorian accused. "I think you're responsible for Cleo, too."

"Liar. I didn't kill anyone and you know it, Dorian."

My breath suspended, I pressed myself to the wall outside
the room. Both men were claiming innocence and accusing
the other. But how can Sam accuse Dorian, when the latter
had been unconscious in Silas Griggson's library? Camille
couldn't know that, I realized, and Sam obviously sought to
deceive her. I edged toward the doorway, peeking in through
the gap between the door hinges and the frame. I searched

both men's hands for weapons and saw none. That didn't mean there weren't any. Camille huddled in a corner of the room, her arms around herself. The arguing escalated, their accusations repeated and denied countless times. Then something changed; the tension in the room thickened, and suddenly Dorian lunged at Sam. He slammed his fist into Sam's jaw. Sam cried out, wobbled, and went down like a felled tree. Dorian swung back a foot in preparation of delivering a kick to Sam's side.

"He's down, Dorian." Camille tugged at his arm. "Stop it. Stop it now. You'll kill him."

He made some reply, but I didn't hear it. I was still thinking about that punch, envisioning it. Dorian had landed that punch . . .

With his left hand.

But no, after Cleo's murder the police had tested everyone, had them sign their names.

And yet, some people, a rare few, possessed equal use of both hands. Could Dorian Norris be one of them?

Had he murdered Cleo? Silas Griggson? Oliver Kipp, in faraway Santiago? My mind whirled as the fragments came hurtling together to form the whole. He had been present at each incident. But why? What induced a young man of good family to turn killer? What link existed between him and Silas Griggson? Surely Dorian Norris couldn't be a member of the Five Points Gang.

"We have to do something for him," Camille pleaded.

"Leave him. Let's get out of here." I heard a yelp as Dorian gripped Camille's hand. "We have to go."

"I don't understand. . . ."

"He killed Cleo, you idiot." Camille seemed not to notice Dorian's insult; she made no comment as he continued. "He came here to kill you as well."

"But why . . . ?"

They would exit the room any moment. I searched my surroundings for a weapon. The bare hallway seemed to mock me. This being servants' quarters, there were no vases, no figurines, nothing to snatch off a table and use to knock a man out.

I slid along the wall with little hope of darting around the corner before Camille and Dorian spotted me. Thank goodness for Camille's stubborn insistence that they couldn't simply leave Sam lying on her bedroom floor. I could still hear her arguing the point. Still, I knew Dorian would win out, would drag Camille along if need be.

"Ah, Miss Cross." Too late. The pair rounded the doorway and stopped short when they saw me. Camille looked frightened and uncertain, and I'd have wagered even she entertained doubts about the man she proclaimed to love. Meanwhile, Dorian attempted to smile at me, an effort that fell short and chilled me. "I've apprehended Sam. He's inside, unconscious. Thank goodness we arrived here in time, or he might have killed Camille. Everything is all right now."

"But why would Sam Caldwell want to kill me?" Camille's disbelief might very well result in her death, I suspected, but not at Captain Caldwell's hands. For her sake, I decided I'd better play along and make a believable show of it.

"Thank goodness, Lieutenant." I feigned vast relief. "Camille, Sam isn't in his right mind. We don't yet know why he murdered Miss Cooper-Smith, or Mr. Griggson, but whatever induced him, he must believe you to have been in your mistress's confidence, that you have information that could incriminate him."

"Let's go, before he wakes up." Dorian started Camille walking, and as they closed the distance between us, I struggled to devise a way to detain him in this house until the police arrived. And then my prayers were answered.

*   *   *

Urgent voices echoed from the vestibule two stories below. I swept along the hallway to the main gallery, supported by low arches rendered in carved, gilded wood, each spandrel column capped by a mythological character gazing down on the Great Hall. When I reached the nearest archway, I hung far over the wide balustrade. When the tops of four heads came into view, three covered by police helmets and one dark-haired, I realized Jesse was not among them. I processed the fact even as I waved my arms wildly. "Up here! Come quickly."

A shove from behind nearly sent me tumbling head over heels. My arms wrapped themselves around the railing, the thickly carved woodwork digging in to my flesh. I shouted down again. Faces turned up to me. Among them I recognized Scotty Binsford and Derrick—the dark-haired one. All four men turned onto the main staircase and raced up.

Hands closed viselike around my upper arms, and I felt my hold on the railing slipping. Dorian was tugging me, attempting to pull me free.

Behind him, Camille protested. "Dorian, what are you doing?"

"I'm attempting to help her, to prevent her from falling."

The lie triggered a protest of my own. "He'll throw me over!"

"Dorian, stop!" Camille came closer, her shout somewhere near my ear. Behind me I felt Dorian's grip wavering as she apparently caught hold of him and tugged. A string of curses flew from his lips and skipped across the biblical mural that stretched across the ceiling.

Dorian released me so abruptly I fell forward, sending my heart to thud wildly in my throat. My chin hit the balustrade, but I instantly swung around and pushed away, attempting to put distance between myself and the open plunge to the

Great Hall. In that moment Dorian's arm swung upward, his fist pummeling into Camille's face. Her head snapped backward but no sound came from her. Her legs buckled and she fell, her back slapping the carpeted floor.

"Damn you, Dorian." Sam Caldwell leaned half a moment in the entrance of the hallway before launching himself unsteadily into the gallery.

Dorian met him halfway with blows that rained down on Sam's face and torso. Sam fought back, but it was obvious he wouldn't last long. The pounding of footsteps echoed from the stairs. The sound became louder, closer, and then Derrick and the policemen burst onto the landing.

With clubs drawn, the officers surrounded the two scuffling men and demanded they cease. Derrick darted past them and came to me. I had fallen to Camille's side, was tapping the back of her hand and calling her name.

Derrick crouched beside me; his own hand descended on mine. "Are you all right?"

I blew out a shaky breath. "You came just in time."

"What was happening here? Why were Caldwell and Norris fighting?"

I looked over to where the policemen were subduing Dorian and Sam, restraining them with handcuffs. Each continued his accusations against the other, and as conflicting charges filled the air, even I became confused. Who was innocent? Who was guilty? I tried to blink away my bewilderment. "I'm not entirely sure. I thought Sam killed Silas Griggson. But it wasn't Sam trying to push me over the railing just now. That was Dorian." I shook my head as I tried in vain to recall each sequence of events. In my mind, the images flashed in disarray.

Camille stirred and opened her eyes. "What happened?" A groan slipped from her swollen lips. Her hand went to cup her cheek, rapidly darkening to a deep purple. "Oh! It hurts!"

"Dorian hit you," I told her without attempting to soften my bluntness. For all I knew, Camille was no innocent in this business either. I helped her to sit up and held on to her while she steadied herself. "What do you know about this?"

"Nothing. I don't understand why they came to blows. Dorian and I were going to leave. That's why he came, to take me away from here. He said he'd grown tired of waiting."

"Just like that?" I shook my head. "So suddenly, he was going to what? Marry you? Without his family's consent and without proper funds?"

"Oh, but it wasn't sudden. We've been planning . . ." She frowned, her brows knitting tightly. "Planning for what seemed ever so long. I don't know what changed, if Dorian came into some money or . . ."

"Or he needed to get away," I suggested.

Scotty had replaced his nightstick on his belt, but the other two officers held theirs up in warning to Sam and Dorian. "Can you clear any of this up, Emma?"

"I'm fairly certain Lieutenant Norris is the man you want." Dorian snorted in protest. I ignored him, and so did the officers. "But honestly, Scotty, I can't say for certain what Sam's role has been."

"If you'll let me explain." Sam started to step forward, only to stop short when one of the officers grabbed him by the arm.

"I followed Sam to Griggson's," Dorian blurted. "He killed him. Shot Griggson straight through the head." Camille winced, as did I.

Sam was already shaking his head, but he remained calm. "*I* followed *Dorian* to Silas Griggson's house. I'd assumed he was going to Ochre Court, to see Camille again. I planned to warn him, because the men of our unit were beginning to talk. Even Colonel Astor had gotten wind of their trysts and was considering informing Dorian's parents. All I wanted to do was keep Dorian from getting himself into trouble. But he didn't come to Ochre Court. He detoured to Silas's house. I waited outside for a while, until I heard a shot, and then I ran in. I found Silas dead and didn't see Dorian anywhere. I assumed he went out the back of the house, and I came here to warn Camille. I found her alone at first." He jerked his chin at Dorian. "Then he showed up."

Silence fell after this explanation. Finally, Scotty said, "Which one do we believe?"

"No one." Derrick helped Camille and me to our feet. "Not yet, at any rate. I suggest you take them both in. Her, too," he added, indicating Camille, who seethed but said nothing.

"He's the guilty one." Dorian thrust a finger at Sam.

Sam glared back at him, but spoke to Scotty. "I'll gladly come with you if it will help."

Before anyone made a move to go, Camille went to Dorian's side. "None of this is true." She spoke with conviction, with her usual bravado, but then her forehead puckered in doubt. "It can't be. Tell them, Dorian. It's all a mistake. A misunderstanding. Please, Dorian..." Her voice rose in question and her eyes pleaded.

Dorian stared at her blankly. If he'd ever had feelings for her, they were certainly not evident now. His eyes were empty, devoid of light or emotion. Dead. I could easily imagine him robbing others of their lives.

What I had yet to understand was why. "This has something to do with Oliver Kipp and Santiago, doesn't it? And the Five Points Gang."

Sam's eyes widened in shock as I spoke Oliver's name. On the other hand, Dorian's eyes narrowed as I spoke of the former, and then flashed when I mentioned the latter. "Did you kill Oliver, Dorian? And then Cleo? Why? What did they do? Or know?"

Derrick's hand made its way to my shoulder and gently squeezed. "Let's let Scotty and the men take them into town. They'll be questioned. Jesse will—"

"Jesse," I exclaimed. "Where is he? Scotty, do you know?"

The large policeman shook his head. "I haven't seen him. Should he be here?"

"We need to search." I went to the railing, as if Jesse would magically appear in the Great Hall below me. "Something has happened to him, or he would be here now."

Scotty started to give orders to the other two men, but Derrick stepped in. "You get these three into town. I'll look for Detective Whyte."

"No, I think one of us should stay behind—"

Derrick cut Scotty off. "Officer Binsford, you're taking two military officers into custody. They're trained fighters. You should have a guard on each of them, plus you need a man to drive the wagon. That'll take all three of you."

Scotty thought a moment, then nodded his agreement.

"Thank you, Derrick." I turned to Camille, who was backing away from the others. "You need to go with the officers. They'll have to question you."

Her swollen face inched upward. "I've done nothing wrong. And I don't know anything."

"You know more than you think you do," I told her quietly. I searched for tears but her eyes were dry, glittering with outrage. Here was no damsel in distress, and something told me that, were she indeed innocent, she would not allow Dorian to drag her down with him. "Please, go with them."

She had yet to be thoroughly convinced. She turned to Dorian. "Is what she's saying true? Did you . . . did you kill . . ."

Dorian's lip curled, his nostrils flared, and he looked

away. Camille's expression hardened. She turned to Scotty. "I'll go with you. But I won't ride next to him."

He gave her a terse nod. "You can ride up front with me. All right, let's go."

Derrick surmised that since the butler hadn't admitted Jesse to the house, he should begin his search belowstairs. Jesse's disappearance baffled me. I had found myself believing Sam's accounts of events. If he spoke the truth, then Dorian murdered Silas Griggson and probably Cleo as well. But at no point since Jesse and I discovered Griggson's body could Dorian have confronted Jesse. I had found Dorian in Silas Griggson's library, and he had not been out of my sight until we parted company in the vestibule of Ochre Court.

Did that mean Sam lied?

I pondered this question as I descended to the second floor and made my way to Mrs. Goelet's bedroom. Along the gallery, my feet slowed. A suspicion took shape in my mind, and I hoped—prayed—I was wrong. Voices again rose from the vestibule, this time that of the butler and a woman. Only a frequent visitor would engage in conversation with the butler. I pricked my ears. Had Grace come to visit? At an exclamation over the butler's description of today's irregular goings-on, I recognized Harriette Goelet's voice. I picked up my pace and hurried along.

After I knocked and identified myself, the lock clicked from inside and Miss Goelet opened the door. Her brother, Robert, stood at her shoulder looking fierce and holding a porcelain candelabra whose raised leaf and floral design looked as if it could do serious damage to a human skull. I hesitated before stepping over the threshold.

From the sitting area, Mrs. Goelet called out, "Robert, put that down. You'll break it."

"Sorry," he murmured. "Can't be too careful. Come in, Miss Cross."

I schooled my features not to show my exasperation that Mrs. Goelet should be more concerned about her candelabra than my head.

"Is everything all right now?" Miss Goelet was eager to know.

I scanned the room's occupants. Mrs. Goelet, dressed in mourning, occupied a sofa upholstered in flowered silk. Ilsa and Patrick Floyd sat nearby. He came to his feet.

"We're most anxious to know what has happened, Miss Cross."

"Captain Caldwell and Lieutenant Norris have been taken in for questioning," I told them.

"What on earth were they doing here?" Mrs. Goelet looked mystified. "What possible reason could either man have for disturbing our peace? They know our household is in mourning."

I couldn't help glancing at Miss Goelet's apricot-hued day gown, or her brother's pinstriped linen coat and trousers. Even Ilsa, though dressed more somberly, had forgone full mourning. It seemed no one's sentiments concerning Cleo's death quite matched Mrs. Goelet's.

"They may have been here to cause mischief, ma'am," I answered her evasively. "We'll know more after the police question them. Until they do, I don't like to speculate."

She seemed satisfied with that answer. "Then we are free to move about the house again? We are quite safe?"

"You are, ma'am."

The woman snapped open the fan she held and waved it in front of her face. "Good heavens, that's a relief."

"Auntie May," called a childish voice from the gallery. Footsteps padded lightly over the runner, and then another voice could be heard.

"Stop running, Beatrice," Harriette Goelet said. "We do not run in the house."

In another moment the golden-haired little girl trotted into the room, with her mother a few paces behind her. "Beatrice, darling, I asked you not to run."

"Auntie May," the child exclaimed again, and ran to Mrs. Goelet. Before she reached her, however, she stopped short in front of Patrick Floyd and beamed up at him. "Did you bring red flowers?"

"Beatrice, mind your manners," her mother scolded. "I'm sorry, Mr. Floyd. She's got a fixation with flowers these days."

"Quite all right." He smiled down at the girl. "I'm sorry, I have no flowers with me."

The child drew up like an army commander in miniature. "But you had a red flower for me in the garden room."

"Oh . . . uh . . . yes." He glanced at the others. "But I haven't any now. I'm terribly sorry. Perhaps next time."

Beatrice shrugged and continued to her aunt. Mrs. Goelet patted her lap and Beatrice clambered up to sit.

Her mother sank into an armchair and sighed. "Beatrice, did you sneak into the conservatory again? You know you're not to walk through the ballroom without a grown-up holding your hand." She shook her head with a rueful grin. "Honestly, this child will get up to all manner of mischief if not watched with an eagle eye."

"I didn't go to the conser . . . conser . . . that room, Mama," Beatrice mumbled, but no one paid her any mind, except for me. I studied her closely, thinking. Out of the mouths of babes . . .

"We'll leave you now that things have returned to normal." Ilsa started to rise. Patrick quickly came to his feet and helped her up.

As they slowly made their way across the room, in deference to Ilsa's difficulties, my mind raced through the past several days. The ball and Cleo's snubbing of Mr. Griggson; his desire to purchase Gull Manor—for a client; events at Fort Adams; the revelation of the courtship between Camille and Dorian Norris; Mr. Griggson's death; Jesse's disappearance. . . .

When Mr. Griggson had demanded I sell Gull Manor to him, and I refused, he said I had no idea who I was dealing with. At the time, I believed he meant himself and hadn't given much thought to who the client might be. At the time it hadn't seemed to matter.

Now, I believed I knew. Beatrice had carried a single red rosebud in her posy for Cleo.

She had gotten the flower in the "garden room."

After allowing Patrick and Ilsa to precede me into the hallway, I couldn't close the bedroom door behind us quickly enough. When I caught up to them, it was to her that I spoke.

"I thought you might wish to know Camille went to the police station for questioning."

Her expression showed alarm. "Has she been arrested?"

"No, and I don't believe she is guilty of anything except perhaps overstepping convention." I ignored Ilsa's puzzled look and continued. "I do believe she can help the police sort out Sam's and Dorian's roles in Silas Griggson's death, and perhaps your sister's as well."

"Poor Cleo." She shuddered. "You know, Miss Cross, I've been resisting the very notion that someone deliberately caused her death. I've wanted to believe it was merely an accident. That's not nearly so terrible. People die of accidents every day; it is part of life. But a murder . . ." Another, more intense shudder went through her, prompting Patrick to move half a step closer to her. "So you think Sam or Dorian killed my sister?"

I avoided Patrick's gaze. "I think Dorian is somehow connected to her death, yes. As for Sam, I think time will prove him innocent."

"I do hope so." Her features tightened. "I don't understand what Camille has to do with any of this."

"Camille had put her hopes on Dorian Norris, through no fault of her own," I explained. "He led her on."

"Oh, how beastly of him." She made a noise of derision. "Patrick, isn't that beastly?"

"It is indeed, my dear." His deep baritone sent shivers up my arms. I took Ilsa's hand and coaxed her to walk again. We were headed toward the sitting room.

"But why would Dorian wish to harm my sister?" she asked, suddenly sounding very young and naïve.

"I believe it has something to do with Oliver Kipp and what happened in Santiago," I replied, "and something that might have occurred in New York."

"In New York? Such as what?"

I chose my words carefully. "Silas Griggson was not an honest man, Ilsa. One of his housing projects collapsed due to slapdash building materials. He allowed a foreman to take the blame, but I think he himself was at fault. Dorian Norris must have been connected to the project somehow. Perhaps only as an investor, but he must have known the truth, and somehow Oliver Kipp learned the truth as well."

Ilsa stopped again, abruptly. "And Oliver confided in Cleo?"

I nodded. "I believe that's very possible. Which means they both knew something that put them in danger."

"Good gracious." Again, she appealed to Patrick. "Can you imagine it, Patrick? My poor sister. Poor Oliver. And here I blamed her for their parting. Why, his sudden departure to the war must have been in an effort to protect her. To pretend there no longer existed a connection between them."

"It's said Oliver died a hero," Patrick said with a sad smile.

"If your speculation is correct, Miss Cross, it seems that was quite true."

"Oh, Oliver. Oh, Cleo." Ilsa's eyes filled with tears. She stumbled a bit as we resumed walking. Even as I helped steady her, Patrick appeared at her other side with a ready hand to help her. As we approached the guest bedroom wing, an idea came to me.

"Ilsa, I can see how distressed you are. You should return to your room and rest awhile."

"I'm not sure I want to be alone right now."

"It would be best," I insisted. "Mr. Floyd and I should leave you alone for a while and allow you time to come to terms with everything. And to rest," I repeated. "It wouldn't do to become fatigued."

As Ilsa looked from me to Patrick, I noticed his gaze upon me, his eyes sharp and assessing. Did he realize what I had realized?

"I've a better idea," he said. "Ilsa, why don't we leave together and go into town to visit your father?"

"My father?"

"Yes. There is . . . there is a matter I wish to discuss with him. With you both." He smiled, the coolness gone, replaced by a warmth of affection. "In fact, can you toss a few things into a bag? I think the best thing for you would be to leave Ochre Court. This is no peaceful haven, is it?"

Ilsa's entire demeanor changed. Her hand went to her bosom and her expression lit with joy. At first her reaction puzzled me, until I realized the implication of Patrick's words. *There is a matter I wish to discuss with him*—*him* referring to Mr. Cooper-Smith. Ilsa believed an engagement with Patrick was imminent.

I could not allow her to leave with him. Nor did I believe for one moment that he intended to make good on his implied promise. Yet again, I would have to play along.

Smiling brightly, I gave her wrist a gentle squeeze. "Go and pack, Ilsa."

Nodding, she turned away and limped into her bedroom. Patrick closed the door behind her, and then wasted no time in wrapping a hand around my throat. "One word, and I snap your neck and then go inside and do the same to Ilsa. Understood?"

I nodded emphatically. His fingers loosened a fraction. "Good. Come along, then."

Chapter 18

With his fingers clamped on the scruff of my neck, Patrick Floyd steered me in the direction of the elevator. I winced in pain but kept moving, while cursing the etiquette that kept the servants away from the family's private rooms during the day unless they were specifically called for. I willed Mrs. Goelet's bedroom door to open and Robert to step out. But no one appeared to intervene. And I very much believed Patrick's threat concerning Ilsa.

"Where is Jesse Whyte?" I demanded after managing to draw sufficient breath to speak.

"That bumbling detective is lying unconscious beneath a patch of hydrangea."

Could I believe him? Could Jesse still be alive? "You didn't kill him?"

"I didn't have to. I came up behind him and he never saw me. I believe in efficiency, Miss Cross, and killing an officer of the law without good reason would have been inefficient. It would have caused an unnecessary to-do."

Relief nearly made me sag to the floor; indeed, I might

have if Patrick hadn't had a firm hold on me. "I was wrong about Dorian killing Oliver and Cleo," I couldn't help observing aloud. At the same time, I began to devise a plan. I needed to incapacitate Patrick and I wouldn't have more than one chance to do it. Of that I was certain. I couldn't risk failing. My life and Ilsa's depended on my success.

Perhaps when we stepped inside the elevator . . . I reviewed some of the defensive maneuvers Derrick had taught me several years ago. I might thrust my heel into Patrick's shin, and then spin around and spear my fingers into his throat, his eyes, shove my palm against his nose . . .

"Actually, you are not wrong, Miss Cross." He spoke like the aristocrat his was, in calm, courteous tones similar to the ones he used with Ilsa. The gentleman, the family friend. The killer. "Dorian did kill Oliver. It was why he joined Astor's Battery. We knew ridding ourselves of a member of the Four Hundred must be done carefully to avoid an investigation. Oliver needed to die. He had learned too much for his own good."

"So Dorian shot him during the battle. On your command?"

"Dorian might not be terribly smart, but he does follow orders."

The idea of a soldier killing one of his own—the betrayal and the brutality of it—sickened me. "The only person to question what happened was his mother."

"And you, Miss Cross." His fingers tightened, digging into my neck and causing my face to throb hotly. "I'd hoped you'd learn to mind your business, especially after I offered to pay your electrician friend's legal expenses."

"Dale."

"Indeed. I foolishly believed you might back off and trust in the legal system. Not that the attorney I hired would have succeeded in having him absolved. Quite the opposite, but you couldn't have known that, not then. You're uncommonly stubborn, Miss Cross. Not even a blazing house would deter you."

I didn't bother to respond to that, for it didn't surprise me. Besides, I was too concerned with drawing each breath. Then his hold eased a bit, and with my next full breath came another realization. "It was you at Fort Adams that day. Talking to Dorian in the tenaille. You were discussing Oliver, reassuring Dorian that Oliver's death was considered an accident. And you were discussing me, too, I believe."

"What?" Surprise gave his voice an edge. I'd clearly startled him. "How could you know that?"

"I was there. I overheard you both talking." Explaining about the listening tunnels didn't seem worth the effort. "And Silas Griggson? Whose idea was it to kill *him*?"

"Griggson had become too sure of himself. He thought he could marry Cleo and control her, keep her from telling anyone what she and Oliver had learned. But he thought wrong. She wanted nothing to do with him. She became a liability, and so did he, once you began sniffing his trail."

"The tenement collapse."

"Yes, indeed. He handled it messily, and it was only a matter of time before some eager reporter decided to take a closer look. I just didn't think it would be a slip of a girl."

"It's been you all long, pulling the strings but letting others do your dirty work." I shook my head in genuine disgust. "I assume you had Dorian rig the electrical wiring that ended Cleo's life. But you were also in that room at some point. You gave Beatrice the rose, didn't you? Was it a bribe so she wouldn't tell anyone she'd seen you?" A cold fear ran through me. Would Patrick feel the need to permanently silence a child?

"I figured out the wiring, and then Dorian did the work.

And yes, the brat caught me. She needs to learn to keep her mouth shut."

I yanked out of his grip, the act wrenching my neck with pain but I didn't care. I spun to face him. "Leave her alone. She's a baby, and no one takes anything she says seriously. You don't have to hurt her."

"We'll see. Now move." When I hesitated, he reached into a trouser pocket and drew out a gleaming length of polished wood that fit snugly in his palm. He gave a flick, and with a flash of light a blade some six inches long sprang forward, its lethal tip pointing directly at me. In the next instant I felt a nudging prick against my abdomen. "Turn around, Miss Cross, and proceed."

My legs could barely hold me for their violent trembling. The elevator door, with its panel of switches beside it, beckoned. I found myself counting the remaining steps as though they might be the final seconds of my life.

I wished to prolong those seconds as long as possible. Would Derrick return and bring Jesse with him?

I remembered what Jesse had said earlier about powerful men with their hands in legitimate concerns as well as illegal, and how they held power over the New York City authorities. With as much bravado as I could muster, I asked, "How long have you been part of the Five Points Gang?"

"Very good, Miss Cross. I'm surprised you figured that out."

He reached around me to push the switch summoning the elevator to the second floor. The cables began their ritual whine as the contraption rose. I prayed someone would be in it, preferably one of Mrs. Goelet's brawny footmen. But, unlike the elevators in New York's office buildings, this one was fully automated, requiring no operator inside to bring it to those awaiting its arrival.

"Exactly how did you reach such a conclusion?" Patrick wished to know.

"Griggson had a star tattooed on his wrist."

"Yes, a stupid tradition from the early years of the gang. Dorian was supposed to have removed it this morning." He sounded peeved.

"He did. But I'd seen it before. When you sent him to bully me into selling my house."

Patrick let go a laugh. "For all your stubbornness, it looks as though I shall have your property after all."

"You'll never have Gull Manor," I snapped. Patrick rewarded me with a sharp jab between my shoulder blades.

The elevator arrived with a clang and a rattle. Patrick's blade jabbed me a second time. "Open it. First the door, then the gate. Slowly, and keep your hands where I can see them or this blade will become intimately acquainted with your right kidney, Miss Cross. Or your left one. It's all the same to me."

I did as he said. The door opened outward like an ordinary door. I then pushed the gate to its folded position. Another jab sent me into the car, a step up since it had stopped a good few inches above the threshold. This lack of accuracy was the reason public elevators were manned by attendants. No such luck for me. Patrick stepped in behind me, grabbed my shoulder, and propelled me in front of him once again.

"Close the door and the gate."

As I did, I asked him, "And Ilsa? Surely you have no intention of marrying her."

"I haven't decided, actually. It could prove useful to marry her. As her sister pointed out, she can be wearisome, but she'd certainly never question me."

I ventured a guess as a renewed sense of queasiness settled in the pit of my stomach. "As your wife questioned you?"

He sniggered meanly. "Matilda should have remembered her place."

"You weren't away the night she died, were you? Or did you send Dorian to open the gas jets in her bedroom?"

"No, that was something I managed on my own, thanks to an old and seldom-used back staircase." With the door and the gate secured in place, Patrick wrapped his hand around the control lever. The car lurched into motion, intensifying my queasiness. The point of his knife continued to tease the small of my back.

"Won't Ilsa be wondering where you are?"

"I'll tell her a telephone call came for me. She won't question it."

"Please, leave her alone. She's lost enough already."

"If I were you, Miss Cross, I'd worry about myself. But if it makes you feel any better, I have no plans at present to hurt Ilsa in any way. As long as she behaves."

Through the gate I saw that we overshot our destination by several feet. Patrick reversed our motion, lowering us inch by jerking inch. Finally, with a jolt that threatened the contents of my stomach, he brought the elevator to rest. Without waiting to be told, I unlatched the gate and pushed it aside.

I opened the main door onto a whitewashed, utilitarian hallway. Not a sound could be heard. Directly across the hall from me were closets whose doors stood open, revealing a diverse assortment of costly-looking clothing in a burst of color that seemed to spill from the interiors. I found this odd. If these closets were used to store the family's extra summer wardrobes, why had the doors been left open?

And did Patrick intend to stuff me into one of them, shut the door, and leave me to molder until someone happened to find me?

"Mr. Floyd, please think this through. With both Sam and Dorian under arrest, and Camille being held for questioning, you'll come under suspicion when I turn up missing. Who else in this house will be blamed?"

"Any number of people. A servant, a worker, a delivery-man. But once I attest to having seen you leave Ochre Court, it will be another good while before anyone realizes you're missing. By then, I'll be on my way back to New York, whereupon I'll board a steamer bound for Europe. With or without our charming young Ilsa," he added with a grin of amusement. "Now, if you please, step out."

With a poke at my back assuring me I had no other choice, I stepped into the corridor. As I did, movement to my right caught my attention. I very nearly turned my head to acknowledge what I'd seen, but some God-given instinct prevented me from doing so.

I moved another couple of paces away from the elevator door. Patrick's step creaked behind me, followed by the airy whir of a rapidly moving object. I heard a clunk, and then the thud of a body collapsing to the floor.

When I turned around to confirm that I'd heard correctly, Nora Taylor lowered the fire extinguisher she held to her side. She panted heavily and stared down at Patrick Floyd's prone form as if not quite sure what she had done. Then she looked up at me, her eyes glazed with shock and urgency. "I heard everything. I was on the third-floor gallery." With her free hand she pressed her stomach, bending over slightly and continuing her effort to catch her breath. "I ran up . . . to be here when the elevator door opened."

"You should really get to the hospital, Whyte. Have a doctor take a look at that head wound. Perhaps Mrs. Goelet will lend you the use of her driver and carriage." Derrick poured coffee into a mug and pushed it toward Jesse. "Drink."

He, Jesse, Nora, and I sat at the table in the servants' hall, going over everything that had happened in the past hour. The police had been telephoned and were on their way back to Ochre Court. After Nora knocked Patrick Floyd out cold, I'd sent her down to the kitchen level to find a pair of footmen. They had restrained Patrick and, upon his awakening, locked him in a storeroom. He, too, would need a doctor to tend the head wound inflicted by Nora's quick thinking with the fire extinguisher. I now understood why the closet doors near the elevator on the fourth floor had stood open. They were mirrored, and Nora had opened them to prevent Patrick from seeing her beside the elevator door, waiting to render him unconscious.

"I'll call for the carriage," she said now and started to rise.

"There's no need for that. Thank you, Miss Taylor." Jesse aimed his next comment at Derrick and spoke with noticeable impatience. "I'm perfectly capable of driving back into town on my own. And I don't need a doctor."

"Stubborn," Derrick murmured, pouring coffee into his own mug.

Jesse winced as he touched his fingers to the back of his head, where bits of dried blood still clung to his auburn hair. Derrick had found him beneath the hydrangeas along the side of the property, unconscious. I'd wanted to throw my arms around him, so great was my relief at seeing him safe and on his feet. Yet I'd restrained myself from giving in to the instinct. Though I'd said nothing to anyone, when faced with the bleak prospect of Derrick returning to Providence, my heart had made its decision.

At least, I believed it had. My reaction to Derrick's news had been swift, unexpected, and, at the risk of sounding overly dramatic, earth-shifting. It had forced me to face a truth. I cared for Jesse deeply. But I could no longer allow him to hope for more, for something I would never quite feel, no matter how much I might try.

As for the severity of the injury Patrick had inflicted, we wouldn't know until and unless we could persuade Jesse to see a doctor. When he and Derrick had come in through the service entrance, Nora had hurried to bring ice, a basin of water, and a cloth, had tended to him as best she could before he finally thanked her but waved her away.

"I'm fine," he insisted now with a scowl that attested to Derrick's one-word summation of his character: *stubborn.*

"You don't look fine," I observed. I reached over and patted his hand, which felt damp beneath my palm. "You're as white as a sheet and as clammy as one left out in the rain."

"Fine. I'll stop by the hospital after I drive back into town." I wasn't convinced, but I let it drop. He took a careful swig from his mug. Then his scowl smoothed away and he returned his attention to Nora. "Miss Taylor, are you sure you're all right? That was an awfully brave but risky thing you did."

I reflected briefly that he had yet to make a similar observation about me – hadn't I been brave as well? But then I noticed a certain glint in his eye that sent my thoughts in a wholly different direction. Meanwhile, a wash of scarlet engulfed Nora's features.

"Me? Oh, I'm as right as rain, Detective. It was quite a dash up those stairs, and for certain some angel musta kept me from trippin' over my own feet, but thank the good Lord I made it before that elevator door opened or . . ."

"Or I might not be here right now," I finished for her. "Thank you, Nora. You saved my life."

She blushed brighter still, her green eyes glittering like gems. She hazarded another glance at Jesse from beneath her lashes. " 'Twas nothing, miss."

"Well, I'm very glad you were there."

I took several fortifying sips of coffee before placing the flats of my hands on the tabletop and pushing resolutely to my feet. "Someone has to explain things to Ilsa, and I suppose that someone should be me." I heaved a breath. "This is going to devastate her. She's lost so much already."

"I could telephone her father," Nora offered and came to her feet. "And ask him to come here."

"Mr. Cooper-Smith is going to have to answer a lot of questions." Jesse frowned at the steam rising from his cup. "I can't believe these men—Griggson, Norris, Caldwell, and now Floyd—were all mixed up with the Five Points gang, and Cooper-Smith knew nothing."

"I think you'll find Sam Caldwell innocent," I said. "And I dearly hope Mr. Cooper-Smith proves innocent as well. They've most likely been threatening him. Jesse, please allow him to come and comfort his daughter. There will be plenty of time later to ask your questions."

He nodded. "Please put that call through, Miss Taylor. Thank you."

Her complexion still rosy, she nodded and stood. She and I left the servants' hall together, parting ways in the corridor, she heading to the housekeeper's parlor to use the telephone, and I to the stairs. I didn't look forward to explaining things to Ilsa. How she must be wondering where Patrick had disappeared to, giving him the benefit of the doubt, certain he would return soon to whisk her away to a life of wedded bliss. Yet I must now reveal him as a monster, destroy Ilsa's happiness, and rob her of her hopes for the future. Reluctantly I placed my foot on the first step, dreading each one that would take me closer to the miserable task ahead of me.

"Emma."

I turned at the sound of Derrick's voice. The step put us at equal height, and I gazed directly into his dark eyes. I saw in them a calm surety that steadied me after the shock and danger of my ordeal with Patrick Floyd, and renewed my conviction of last night. No longer did uncertainty rage within me concerning *this* man, Derrick. The same old barriers between us still existed—his mother's enmity toward me, his family obligations in Providence, our vastly different backgrounds, my own need for independence. Yet I knew—simply knew—we would find a way to overcome them. Somehow. Someday. I smiled at him, my arms at my sides, my heart beating evenly, my mind serene.

"Yes?"

A subtle contraction of his facial muscles altered his expression to one of apology, regret, even sadness. Yet my newfound certainties continued to rest easily within me. "Emma, I wish I could say to hell with it. Turn my back on my father, the *Sun*, all of it. But I can't. It isn't only about my family. There are so many *other* families who depend on us for their livelihood. Their very existence. I can't turn my back on them, and right now there is no one else to take over for my father someday. No one I can trust to continue the *Sun*'s success. For now, I have to return to Providence and make peace with my father." He reached out and took my hand. His next words were a murmur. "I have to go, soon."

I returned the warm pressure of his grasp. "I know."

"Then I'll ask you again. Will you take over at the *Messenger*? Please?"

"Yes."

He blinked, obviously startled. "Really?"

"Yes," I repeated, smiling at his reaction. "Go make amends with your father. I'll take care of your business here."

"You won't have to report back to me. I trust you fully. The *Messenger* is yours to run as you see fit. And no strings attached. I don't expect—"

"Derrick, I understand. And the *Messenger* will be quite safe in my hands, I assure you."

He nodded. For a long moment neither of us said anything, yet a world of sentiment passed between our clasped hands, our locked gazes.

Finally, I broke our contented silence. "I should go and speak with Ilsa."

He released my hand slowly, and we turned away from each other. But the contentment, and my smile, lasted until I reached the second floor and set out upon this last errand at Ochre Court.

Author's Note

Ochre Court is the second largest house in Newport, after The Breakers. Completed in 1892 and owned by the Goelet family until 1947, it was then donated by Robert Goelet (featured as a teenager in this story), to the Sisters of Mercy, who opened Salve Regina College that same year. Originally a women's school, Salve Regina became coed in 1973, and a fully accredited university in 1991. Today, the campus encompasses sixty acres between Bellevue Avenue and the Cliff Walk, includes seven former Gilded Age estates, and over twenty historically significant buildings. Ochre Court serves as the university's administrative building and, unfortunately, is not open for tours except under special, prearranged circumstances. It was an honor and a thrill for me to be able to enjoy a unique, private tour that greatly aided in the writing of this book.

Another tour I enjoyed while in Newport was of Fort Adams, the largest fort of its kind in the United States. The details about the fort were gathered during the tour, including those of the listening tunnels. I have taken some license with the positioning of those tunnels, but the cramped, dark, damp nature described is taken from my own experience.

I also moved the construction of The Elms up a year. Although plans for the house were under way in 1898, building began in 1899 and the house was completed in 1901. Because of owner Edward Berwind's fascination with technology, The Elms was among the first houses in America wired for electricity with no backup source of power. With this in mind, I created the tensions between the electrical and gas workers. It isn't hard to imagine that the prospect of a new technology supplanting an existing one would have led to conflict.

The *tableau vivant,* or "living picture," which in the story features Miss Cleo Cooper-Smith as Cleopatra, had become a popular form of entertainment at Gilded Age social events. Often depicting notable paintings, sculptures, or historic events, the participants dressed in elaborate costumes, took up position, and remained silent and unmoving while their audience sat and inspected each element of the setting.

The New York tenement collapse described in the story is fictional, but newspapers of the time are rife with similar occurrences. Housing for the poor was substandard and dangerous, with such matters as safety, sanitation, and ventilation all but ignored by builders, who routinely cut corners to save project money. It wasn't until the turn of the century that standards began to be established and safety codes enforced.

The Five Points Gang existed in the 1890s and comprised some 1500 members. A gang known for brutal violence, they engaged in robbery, racketeering, and prostitution; used legitimate businesses as fronts for their crimes; illegally influenced elections; and maintained ties to Tammany Hall politics. Al Capone, Lucky Luciano, and other prominent twentieth century gangsters had their start in the Five Points Gang. The star tattoo, however, is my own invention.

Gilded Age journalist Nellie Bly exceeded all expectations for women of her time in becoming an investigative reporter. Two of her most notable achievements were having herself committed to the Blackwell Island, New York, mental institution to report on the appalling conditions there, and traveling around the world, unaccompanied, in seventy-two days, beating the fictional eighty-day record of Jules Verne's character, Phileas Fogg. Despite being an independent and daring young woman, it remained Nellie's goal in life to wed a rich man, and in 1895 she did just that, marrying industrialist Robert Seaman. Seaman was forty years older than Nellie, but by all accounts theirs was a happy marriage based on mutual respect.

A word about Beatrice Goelet. I became aware of her existence after stumbling across her portrait painted by John Singer Sargent when she was about five years old. The real Beatrice, daughter of Robert and Harriette Goelet, would actually have been thirteen in 1898. Sadly, she died of pneumonia only a few years later. I was so captivated by Sargent's expressive portrait of the beautiful little girl, I couldn't help but give her a key role in the story. I decided to make her about three years old, an age at which most children are easily distracted from traumatic events and unlikely to be permanently scarred by them. The painting is among my favorites of Sargent's work.